Dashing forward, Nate grasped her arm. "You broke the trellis, remember? If you put your weight on it again, it might snap."

She shook him off and gave him a cool look. "Only a single board snapped on this side. The far side appears solid."

She was serious! "Don't be daft. Get down from there before you fall to your death."

His stern command failed to frighten sense into her. She gave him a curiously victorious smile. "My goodness, such concern. Are you afraid for me?"

"It would be a better idea to face the men inside—"

"So much for the courage of the legendary White Tiger."

He reached for her, but his fingers only grazed her silken shoulder before she leaped off the railing toward the trellis, her skirts spreading like bird's wings. With as much agility as a monkey, she snagged the crosspiece and clung there. Flexing her arms, she lifted herself until her she found her footing. Her physical strength, her fearless audacity, stunned him.

Amazed, he watched her scramble down, her footing sure, her skirts making only the softest rustle against the vines. He realized that if the trellis hadn't broken earlier, he never would have known she was out there. Never would he have met her.

In seconds, her slipper-adorned feet touched the ground. Lifting her wrinkled skirts high, she dashed into the night. Even after she'd disappeared into the shadows, Nate continued to stare after her, wondering whether all American heiresses were as wild, as unpredictable. And positively unforgettable . . .

Dear Romance Readers,

In July 2000, we launched the Ballad line with four new series, and each month since then we've presented both new and continuing stories set everywhere from medieval England to the American West—the kind of passionate, romantic stories you love best, written by the most gifted authors. At the back of each book, we'll tell you when you can find subsequent books in the series that have captured your heart.

This month, Willa Hix offers the second and last installment in her highly romantic *Golden Door* series. What happens when a British rake forced into the circus business meets a high-wire artist who acts as if *she's* running the show? In **Gone Courting**, you'll find out! Next, the always talented Sylvia McDaniel returns to the sultry heat of New Orleans with **The Price of Moonlight**, the second in her steamy *Cuvier Widows* series. Is the handsome man who happens onto the plantation of a stunned widow the answer to her prayers—or a temptation she can't resist?

The fabulous Tracy Cozzens continues her *American Heiresses* series with **White Tiger's Fancy**, as an impulsive young woman schemes her way into a big game hunt in India—and finds the daring hunter has captured her heart. Finally, reader favorite Suzanne McMinn concludes her sweeping *The Sword and the Ring* series with a tale of childhood love and grown-up decisions in **My Lady Knight**. Enjoy them all!

Kate Duffy
Editorial Director

AMERICAN HEIRESSES

WHITE TIGER'S FANCY

TRACY COZZENS

ZEBRA BOOKS
Kensington Publishing Corp.
http://www.kensingtonbooks.com

ZEBRA BOOKS are published by

Kensington Publishing Corp.
850 Third Avenue
New York, NY 10022

All Kensington titles, imprints and distributed lines are available at special quantity discounts for bulk purchases for sales
promotion, premiums, fund-raising, educational or institu-
tional use.

Special book excerpts or customized printings can also be cre-
ated to fit specific needs. For details, write or phone the office
of the Kensington Special Sales Manager: Kensington Publishing Corp., 850 Third Avenue, New York, NY 10022. Attn.
Special Sales Department. Phone: 1-800-221-2647.

Zebra and the Z logo Reg. U.S. Pat. & TM Off.

First Printing: December 2002
10 9 8 7 6 5 4 3 2 1

Printed in the United States of America

ONE

Mrs. Alexander Drake
Delhi, India
March 2, 1893

Dear Lily,

I hope this letter finds you and your husband well.
I miss you dearly. And now you're a mother! Perhaps
you and your family can return to live here in New
York. I never had an opportunity to become acquainted with your husband before he spirited you
away to live in India. I am pleased that his career is
successful, and that you are happy.

I cannot tell you how thrilled I am that you have
invited Pauline to visit you and enjoy the Season in
Simla. You assured me that the hill station has a wide
variety of social events at which you can show off your
sister. I have been at my wit's end with her. You know
how strong-willed she can be. In the last year, she's
grown even more intractable. She says the most outrageous things, not only to me, but to every proper
gentleman who shows the slightest interest in her!

She refused to go to London for the Season as you
and Hannah did, so I agreed she could come out

into society here in New York. After all, with Hannah's success in becoming a countess, the best families in New York are now extending invitations to my daughters. Believe it or not, even I, with my "regrettable new money," have been in the Astors' precious ballroom.

Yet, now that the door has finally opened to our family, Pauline seems determined to shut it. She does not care about the great boon her two older sisters provided her. (Yes, dear, I completely forgive you for marrying that diplomat of yours instead of the duke. A man with such unnatural proclivities should not marry any woman, and I am grateful your husband rescued you—so to speak.)

But back to the purpose of this letter—Pauline. To my eternal embarrassment, she insulted the Rockefellers' young son when he expressed interest in her. She called him a posturing monkey, right to his face! I am simply appalled. I fear she will ruin your younger sisters' chances to make quality matches among the Four Hundred. Clara and Meryl may still have a chance to marry well if Pauline is—I hate to say it—not about.

Oh, Lily, if only Pauline had been born with a dollop of that gentle femininity you possess. She actually insists she has no interest in marrying! Even worse (and I hate to recount this disturbing tale, but feel I must to give you a full and complete understanding of our predicament), Pauline had been using the trellis by her window as a means of egress. Last week, your father caught her climbing into her bedroom window well past midnight! Heaven knows where she had been or what mischief she had gotten into. She seems impervious to scolding or punishment. (The trellis has since been removed.)

Please, if you can find a man who is willing to take her on, I will be eternally grateful. I don't expect Pauly to land a nobleman as Hannah did. But if he is at least a high-ranking administrator or officer (not merely a subaltern)—oh, there I go, imagining things! I ought not to place requirements on your matchmaking efforts on her behalf. I know you will do your best.

She will be arriving on the Victorious *on April 12. I hope this letter precedes her arrival.*

> *With all my love,*
> *Mother*

Kalka, India

Pauline Carrington felt as if she'd stepped into the middle of a circus. The excitement crackling in the air engulfed her the moment she stepped down from the train onto the station platform.

A dozen dusky-skinned, turbaned men ran past her, shouting and waving. She stepped back barely in time to avoid being knocked off her feet. As if echoing their excitement, the rust red train idling behind her belched steam, and she leaped out of the hot, coal-filled plume.

Tahmeed, her sister's Indian butler, cursed at the exuberant natives in his native Hindi. He was very good at cursing. As *khansamah* to an important family, he saw it as his duty to protect the memsahibs in his care from the riffraff, such as the numerous beggars who had sought handouts from Pauline and Lily at every station stop since Bombay. At first, Pauline tried to give the sorry individuals money, but Tahmeed prevented her, insisting she would be overwhelmed if she opened her purse.

This time, the natives' excitement had nothing to do with the arrival of a wealthy memsahib. Pressing her hand on her straw boater to keep it in place, Pauline leaned over the platform railing. A group of men had gathered on the dusty ground below, talking excitedly in their musical tongue. Pauline heard one phrase over and over. She touched a gloved hand to her sister's arm. "They keep repeating *safed sher.* What does that mean?"

Pauline's married sister, Lily Drake, was too distracted to answer. She was instructing Tahmeed to arrange for hired porters to take them the rest of the way to Simla, in the foothills of the Himalayas. The closer they came to the end of their journey, the more anxious Lily had grown to see her husband, Alexander, and their infant daughter, Cecily, now in the care of their devoted ayah, or nurse.

Once Tahmeed had departed on his errand, Pauline tried again. "Lily? Do you understand what they're saying?"

"*Safed sher?* I only know a little Hindi, but I believe that would be 'white tiger.'"

"A white tiger?" Pauline craned her neck, trying to see through the crowd. Two native men ran past to join the gathering, followed by another, who turned to shout excitedly to the fellows behind him. The crowd had doubled in size, making it harder to see what the fuss was about. "I've never heard of such a creature. Do you think someone has captured one?"

"I'm not sure white tigers even exist," Lily said.

"The Indians are a superstitious people. A white tiger sounds like a story to me."

"Well, I've only seen yellow tigers with black stripes, in the zoo. Don't people hunt them here?"

"Yes, of course. There are so many, and they've been known to terrorize the villages in the jungle. That's why you have to stay in town, or always in the company of armed men."

Armed men? How ridiculous. Pauline knew she could take care of herself if given the chance. She didn't need anybody, and she wasn't weak—even if she'd had the misfortune to be born female. She decided she would learn how to shoot while here in India. She was already excellent at archery. She'd never had the opportunity to use a gun, but if men could shoot, she saw no reason she couldn't master the necessary skills. "So, tigers eat people? How dangerously exciting!"

"I'm sure those who have lost their loved ones wouldn't agree," Lily said with a touch of asperity. "It's a terrible business. A single rogue tiger can kill hundreds of villagers before it's stopped."

"Oh." Pauline chewed her lip, embarrassed that she had so blithely ignored the plight of the victims. "I suppose brave hunters must track down these man-eaters, am I right? I would so love to go on a tiger hunt."

"That would be incredibly dangerous, Pauline. Only the best hunters risk their lives pursuing man-eaters. Besides"—she smiled and tapped Pauline's cheek with her gloved finger—"you didn't travel all this way to hunt game but to hunt a husband. I'm going to make sure our bags are loaded. You stay right here, and don't talk to strangers." With that final piece of advice, she turned and wended her way through the crowd.

Pauline sighed. Already she felt the same constraints that had tightened around her in New York, threatening to suffocate the life out of her. Lily had enthusiastically adopted their mother's role, attempting to convince her of the importance of so-called proper behavior. Pauline already knew she was a lost cause. Every time she drew breath, she managed to break some rule—speaking too plainly, gazing at men too immodestly, slipping away without telling where she was going.

She could scarcely imagine what life would be like without the numbingly complex rules used to imprison young ladies. But how she longed to be free! India had to be different. Unfortunately, for the past four days she had been confined to rail cars shared only by Europeans. The deluxe accommodations had done nothing to acquaint her with the India passing outside her train window. Now that they were disembarking, she prayed the world—in all its vast, confusing glory—would be open to her.

Despite the sweltering heat, she'd become entranced by the exotic country as they traversed the central plains. In fascination, she had stared out the windows at the native men in their loose dress and turbans, at the graceful brown women filling jugs at creekside, at the energetic, smiling children who waved and chased the train. And every hour, the purple mountains rising in the distance grew nearer.

Pauline prayed their stay in Simla would be as exciting as Lily promised. India's British inhabitants retreated to the Himalayan foothills from April to October to escape the heat of the plains. Even the viceroy transferred his offices from Delhi to Simla, making it the most prestigious of the hill stations. Unfortunately, Pauline had little interest in the viceroy or anyone else with a title—an attitude that her mother claimed would drive her to an early grave.

A change in the crowd drew Pauline's attention once more. The cries of *"safed sher"* had transmuted into low, reverent murmurs. The gathering parted, forming an aisle for a small group of Punjabi men in turbans, carrying rifles or packs on their backs.

Three pairs of turbaned men strode to the center of the crowd, then stopped. Then they, too, parted, forcing the crowd to move farther back. Four more bearers stepped forward, carrying a pair of bamboo poles. Trussed between them was the body of a huge cat. A tiger.

Yet the tiger wasn't white at all, but yellow with black stripes. Still the chant of *"safed sher"* continued, the sense of anticipation keen in the air.

Then he stepped through the crowd.

He wasn't Indian at all. He was merely a Brit. Yet this Brit was unlike any man she'd ever seen, either here or back home.

Pauline's heart ceased its steady beat. Or was it her breath that stopped filling her lungs? Not until later could she analyze the odd effect that watching the stranger had on her. He was tall, yes. But not the tallest man she'd ever seen. Brawny, though his arms weren't the thickest a man could have. Yet he had an unusual bearing, carrying himself with an assurance that cried out for respect.

His clothes: that's all it is. He looked like the great white hunter of a child's storybook. Worn khaki shirt and trousers hugged his brawny frame. He wore his shirtsleeves rolled to his elbows, displaying darkly tanned, corded forearms peppered with golden hair. Scarred boots hugged his feet, and a pith helmet shadowed his face. The man had probably just arrived from the jungles outside Kalka. Pauline found herself imagining where he might have been, what he might have seen, what adventures he'd experienced.

Slipping his helmet from his head, he swiped his forehead, further mussing his sweat-darkened blond hair. He spoke a curt order, and instantly one of his servants uncorked a water bottle and passed it to him. He arched his neck back and took a healthy swig. The water trickled down his chin and along his tanned neck. Not satisfied that he'd dampened his shirtfront with his poor manners, he then said something in Hindi and dumped the bottle over his head.

As if a spell had been broken, the men around him cried, "Ahh!" and began elbowing each other, broad smiles lighting up their dark faces.

The stranger also smiled.

That's when Pauline noticed his face. She always prided herself on being above the foolish romantic notions of most girls, those who waxed poetic about the handsome countenances of their beaux. Nor was this fellow exactly handsome. Yet she found herself mesmerized by his features: sharp blue eyes, hawkish nose, square, beard-roughened chin. A scar ran the length of his cheek, from under his left eye to the curve of his jaw. His face spoke of hard living, danger, and power. His smile wasn't the free, easy smile of the idle rich, but the darkly humorous expression of a man not often given to light thoughts. Pauline longed to know what he'd said to make the crowd react with such ebullience.

He looked as if he hadn't lived in civilization for weeks. Or even months. He was hardly a member of polite society. If he dared set foot in any of the hostesses' pristine ballrooms, he would terrify all the ladies present—and most of the men.

She smiled to herself at the image. How she envied him his freedom from society's oh-so-proper constraints! Just then, his eyes flicked up toward where she stood. Then he looked a second time and caught her eye. Pauline froze, shock coursing through her. She felt like a child caught stealing. He knew she'd been staring shamelessly at him. Yet she was far too proud to allow him the satisfaction of seeing her look away, so she stared right back.

After what seemed an eternity, he replaced his helmet on his head and tugged on the brim in the traditional gentleman's greeting to a lady. Then he turned away, never once looking back as the crowd of admirers surrounded him.

Again Pauline heard the phrase *safed sher*. Tahmeed appeared at her side to direct her to the waiting porters. "Tahmeed, why do they keep saying 'white tiger' over and over?" She gestured to the crowd below.

Tahmeed nodded and smiled. "Ah, the mysterious White Tiger has returned from the mountains, having defeated the yellow tiger which hungered for human blood." He pointed toward the man in khakis. "There is he."

Understanding dawned, along with a tingle of excitement. "That's his *name?*"

"That is his legend. He is a *shikari,* a big game tracker. He has rid the villages of man-eating tigers no other man dared stop. For that, he is worshipped by the simple villagers." Tahmeed sniffed at those less educated than himself. "He is a most interesting fellow, but not for one such as you." He waved his finger in her face, then gestured for her to follow him along the platform.

Pauline trailed behind him, irritated anew. Tahmeed clucked over her worse than Lily. She didn't bother to tell him that she certainly had no romantic interest in the fellow.

Even if he was somewhat unforgettable.

Pauline gripped the sides of her rattan *dhoolie* as four *dhoolie wallahs* carried her ever higher into the Simla Hills. Lily had told her they would be rising more than four thousand feet before arriving at the summer capital. More than once, the narrow path wound perilously close to a sharp, heart-stopping precipice.

The *dhoolie* she rode in looked like a small four-poster bed with cotton curtains, which Pauline had tied back so she could view the astounding scenery. In all, a dozen similar chairs snaked up the mountain path. Because of Lily's stature as the wife of a high-ranking government official, Lily and Pauline rode directly behind the district commissioner at the party's head.

After a while, Pauline's nervous excitement subsided and she relaxed in the chair, entranced by the magnificent views appearing around every bend. They passed above deep gorges cut into the hillside, and gentler valleys with terraced fields and villages. Here and there, a graceful temple nestled in the mountains' folds.

As they neared their destination, the ordinary pine around Kalka gave way to rich blue pine interspersed with deodar, the Indian cedar, which took on a silvery cast when its foliage flickered in the breeze. Green parrots chattered and darted overhead, along with yellow-billed blue magpies, their tails streaming behind.

High in the treetops, small brown monkeys screeched and played, swinging from branch to branch above her head. Larger gray langurs hovered in groups under the trees, their black and white faces staring at them curiously.

Pauline stared back, equally curious. Optimism filled her. Here in India, in this wild and beautiful land, perhaps she would discover the life she'd been seeking.

Her *dhoolie* jerked to a stop, throwing her forward. She grasped the front of the box-shaped contraption to steady herself as the entire party stumbled to a halt. Ahead, the commissioner had begun to argue with his *dhoolie wallahs*. From her *dhoolie* ahead, Lily turned to check on Pauline. Despite Lily's reassuring smile, Pauline saw a hint of concern in her sister's creased brow.

Her own *dhoolie wallahs* took advantage of the pause to set down her chair. Pauline began to step out to learn what was happening—until her lead bearer turned around and snapped, "Stay!"

She sank back down, unaccustomed to being ordered about, yet not exactly sure where she'd intended to go. The argument ahead escalated, the men's voices growing louder, their expressions more animated. The commissioner gesticulated wildly. Under his white pith helmet, his gray mustache quivered and his face turned ruddy. Pauline's lead bearer gave another curt order. Suddenly her chair was jerked high into the air, dangerously close to the precipice.

Her heart caught in her throat. She gripped the sides of the *dhoolie* as she saw the jagged rocks hundreds of feet below her. Any moment she could be hurled to her death, her adventure over before it began.

Witnessing her plight, her sister let out a piercing scream, which terrified Pauline more than the *dhoolie wallahs'* threatening actions. Were the natives' threats serious? Would they actually drop her over the edge?

Despite her fear, a part of her thrilled to the sudden rush of blood through her body, to the very real possibility that she could die at any moment. Her attempts to flirt with danger back home now seemed pathetic. In this heart-stopping moment, she felt more alive than in all her previous years as a pampered heiress. Yet she didn't want to die! She had barely tasted life.

A penetrating shout silenced the argument as suddenly as it had begun. Pauline tore her gaze from the pit below her to discover the hunter from the train station striding up the path toward them, followed by a turbaned manservant. The *dhoolie wallahs* spoke in rapid Hindi, and he replied in the same tongue as if he'd been born to it.

Without a pause in his speech and hesitating only briefly in his stride, he reached over and yanked her from her dhoolie onto her feet. The unfamiliar feel of his large hands on her waist stunned Pauline. Her brush with death—and her unexpected encounter with the stranger—weakened her knees and she nearly collapsed.

"Damned delicate woman," the man said, giving her a small shake. "Don't show your fear. That's what they're counting on."

Delicate woman? In all her nineteen years, no one had ever called her delicate. She was the tough one, strong and capable and needing no one! Her strength returning in a rush, she shoved his strong, callused hands from her waist. Before she could fire back a response, he strode away from her to join the argument.

Pauline hurried to the side of Lily's chair. "What's going on?"

"The bearers demanded more payment to continue the journey. When the commissioner refused, they threatened to throw us over the edge. I'd heard of such tactics, but never experienced it until now." She gripped Pauline's hand. "I'm so sorry they chose *you* to threaten. You must have been terrified."

Pauline shrugged. "Don't worry about me. I'm fine." She couldn't even think about her fear, which had seemed so real moments before. Her attention was riveted to the stranger, the White Tiger, who had come to her rescue. Who had touched her.

And insulted her, she fiercely reminded herself.

In a few short minutes, he had settled the dispute. The commissioner shook the White Tiger's hand, then gave a stern command to his *dhoolie wallahs*. The bearers responded by lifting the chairs and moving back into line to continue up the mountain. No money changed hands, and Pauline guessed that the bearers had failed in their attempt to extract a higher-than-agreed-on payment. Her own bearers acted as if they hadn't just threatened her life. They simply moved her *dhoolie* to the center of the trail for her to remount.

The White Tiger and his manservant continued up the path on foot, outpacing the slow-moving bearers hauling passengers and their luggage. Pauline returned to her *dhoolie,* the feel of the stranger's hands lingering on her waist.

TWO

Simla, India

"Stop fidgeting, sweetie. I can't adjust your flounce if you don't stand still."

Pauline propped her hands on her hips and rolled her eyes. Her sister Lily was arranging the back of her skirt and didn't see Pauline's irritated reaction to her fussing.

She stared at her reflection in the looking glass in Lily's bedroom, trying to feel comfortable in the satin-and-silk ball gown. The pale primrose confection was decorated with a plethora of flounces and ruffles and lace. Pauline hated ruffles almost as much as she hated lace. But she didn't want to hurt her sister's feelings. Lily had specially ordered this gown from Paris to show off Pauline's "assets." Lily cared about highlighting assets. Pauline did not.

"You've filled out since I last saw you," Lily said, coming around the front and tugging her low sleeves even lower on her shoulders, to reveal more of her chest. "You're still as tall and slender as a reed, but now you have curves."

"And that's important because . . . ?"

"Don't be rude," Lily said mildly, adjusting one of

a dozen pale pink bows that lifted the voluminous skirt in a series of swags, revealing an ivory under-skirt. "Men enjoy curves, and a good shape makes fashion so much easier to wear."

Fashion. If Pauline found anything duller than fashion, she couldn't imagine what it might be. Even so, she had to admit that Lily had wrought an amazing transformation in her appearance. So amazing, she could only stare at the young woman in the mirror and wonder who she was.

Her straight, light-brown locks had been twisted, woven with pink ribbons, and pinned atop her head in an elaborate style that Lily claimed was all the rage. Tendrils teased her cheeks and neck, tickling her skin. Pauline had to resist the urge to swipe at them. "I don't even look like myself," she said.

"Don't be silly. You're a lovely young woman. It's time you started looking like it." Lily gave her a gentle pat on the cheek, then dropped to her knees to toy with the gown's hemline again.

"I see no reason to dress up."

"Of course you must dress up. We're going to a ball!"

The whirl of Simla social life suited Lily, and her lively, stylish sister obviously enjoyed every minute of it. Although Lily, three years her senior, didn't obsess about marrying her off as their mother did, she talked of little else but the clothes Pauline would wear, the parties she would attend, and the bachelors she would meet.

All this courting nonsense annoyed Pauline in a way neither her mother nor her sister understood. Did being a young lady have to be so demeaning?

She'd already suffered through a Season in New York, during which her mother had dragged her to one event after another, introducing her to the most tedious young men. Thank goodness she'd been able to scare most of them off. Through it all, she felt like a horse being looked over by potential buyers, all of whom weighed only her looks and her family's immense wealth in their decision whether to court her.

"This gown arrived none too soon," Lily said. "We'll show them just how pretty and feminine my little sister can be!"

Pretty? Pauline had never been considered pretty. She lacked that round, feminine face and delicate features of girls considered pretty. At most, she might be considered handsome. "Why does it matter so much? I don't care what the fellows around here think of me," she said fiercely, determined that it should be true.

"Oh, Pauline, I'm only worried about your happiness while you're here. Life at Simla is all about being social."

"And I've been social." Since arriving at Simla three weeks ago, she'd participated in every sport available, from archery—her favorite—to riding.

Pauline adored sports. It was one area where she could shine. Besides the sheer fun of exerting and challenging herself, she didn't have to worry about keeping every hair in place while playing badminton or tennis. She'd also competed in a treasure hunt, visited the gymkhana, and enjoyed a picnic—each with games more frivolous than the last.

"Yes, you have been social. In sports. I'm referring

to the gentler pursuits. You're incredibly competitive. I fear you may be overdoing it."

"What do you mean?"

"Well, you know you're more skilled than many of the young men."

"It's not my fault Lieutenant Bingham lost the tennis match. He needed to be taken down a peg anyway." The lieutenant had bragged about his ability and mocked her own claims. So she'd proven him wrong.

Besides, she couldn't imagine being interested in a fellow who couldn't hold his own against her on the tennis courts or the archery field. At the very least, he shouldn't be bothered that she excelled in those areas or even surpassed him. "I can't help it that he's a poor sport."

Lily gave a long-suffering sigh that would have done their mother proud. "Pauline, I believe the man was trying to flirt with you."

"If he didn't intend to play a serious game and risk being bested, he shouldn't have challenged me."

"Very well, if you say so. I'm sure what people are saying about you doesn't matter a whit." Lily had an annoyingly effective ability to garner the response she desired from whomever she was conversing with.

Her curiosity aroused, Pauline asked nonchalantly, "Now you're being coy, and you know it. What are they saying? Not that I really care, mind you."

Lily finished adjusting her hem, then rose and patted Pauline's shoulder. "Never mind. Just enjoy yourself tonight, dancing and meeting handsome men." She began adjusting a bow at her waist.

Pauline stayed her hand. "Tell me, Lily."

Lily lifted her dark eyes to Pauline's. "Very well. Alex told me that some of the young men are a little intimidated by you. Men like women who make them feel . . . *manly.*"

Pauline wrinkled her nose. "They shouldn't need my help for that."

"Yes, but *you* don't want to be considered mannish, either."

Pauline's stomach knotted. Mannish? They thought of her as mannish? "Is that what they're really saying about me?" she asked hesitantly, not sure she wanted to hear any more about it.

Lily shrugged her delicate ivory shoulders. "Of course it's an exaggeration, and these fellows don't really know you. But you hardly give them a chance."

What a withering condemnation! Pauline fiercely reminded herself she didn't care what others thought about her. She decided to ignore her hurt feelings. After all, she was used to scaring off men. The one boy she'd thought had possibilities, even risked her precious reputation to spoon with, had been too intimidated by her family's position to kiss her properly. "Oh, piffle. I don't care. But to make you happy, I'll go to the ball and dance with whoever you want me to."

"It's not me, sweetie. I want you to be happy. And I know how much of a lady you can really be."

Pauline sighed. "The parties and entertainments are no better here than in England. They still have one goal in mind—to marry me off."

"And that's so bad?"

"Yes!"

Lily sighed and rose to her feet. "Mother wrote to

me that you insisted you didn't want to marry. I thought—or hoped—you were merely tweaking her nose; she can be so obsessive about finding us quality matches." They met each other's gazes in the mirror and smiled in understanding. "After all, you can't really mean it. Hannah didn't think she wanted to marry, either, and now she's very happily married with two children."

"That's Hannah."

Lily anchored her hands on Pauline's waist. "Trust me, you look like a dream. Absolutely gorgeous. You're so tall and slender. Men love tall women. They'll be begging for dances from you."

The idea failed to spark even a hint of enthusiasm in Pauline. Which wasn't Lily's fault.

Impulsively Pauline grasped Lily's hand. "I appreciate what you're trying to do for me," she said, wishing she could communicate to Lily what she truly felt. "I do. I'm sorry I haven't given you much to work with."

"Oh, sweetie, don't sell yourself short. Yourself or India. You'll find the men here different from those in New York. They're men of action."

"Oh?"

"Give it time. You'll see how exciting society here can be—and the men."

Exciting . . . An image of the White Tiger played before her eyes, all broad sinew and casual intensity. He most definitely was not cut from the same cloth as the New York swains she'd avoided. Was he the sort of man Lily meant? Not that he would have any interest in a "delicate woman" like her. *Delicate.* The condemnation still stung. If she ever saw him again, she'd convince him just how wrong he was!

Pauline's tonga driver pulled up to the entrance of the Club and stopped. Lily's husband, Alexander Drake, stepped from his own two-seated tonga ahead and helped his wife down, then came over and handed Pauline out.

Pauline could not imagine a couple more dazzling and sophisticated than Lily and Alexander Drake. Alex was on his way up in the foreign service. He had just been named to head up the Famine Commission, which brought relief to starving natives through irrigation projects. And everyone loved Lily's ability to draw people of diverse backgrounds together in a variety of causes and entertainments.

With Lily at his right, Alex tucked Pauline's hand into the crook of his left arm. "I'll be the envy of every man there, escorting two such lovely ladies," he said in his impeccably charming manner.

"Please don't worry about entertaining me," Pauline said, feeling like a third wheel. She rarely felt otherwise while in the company of these two. Neither Alex nor Lily did anything to make her feel uncomfortable or unwanted. Still, the way they gazed at each other made Pauline quite aware that they relished each other's company above anyone else's.

"It's hardly a worry, Pauly," Lily said. "As soon as the men set their eyes on you in that gown, they'll be begging for dances." She leaned closed and whispered, "Even the men you bested in tennis. Remember, there are three gentlemen for every lady in India."

If Lily thought such odds would excite Pauline, she couldn't be more mistaken. "Let's cut to the chase. Line them all up and let me inspect them before making my choice."

"Pauline!" Lily said.

Pauline shrugged. "It's no less than the treatment we ladies receive at their hands."

"You needn't be outrageous every moment. Try to show your more ladylike self. She must be in there somewhere." She arched a teasing brow.

Pauline sighed. She did enjoy dancing, so she decided to behave and do her best to make Lily proud.

A footman opened the door, and they entered the lobby, then moved down the hall to the large ballroom. As she expected, the crowded ballroom was stuffy, crowded, and hot. Despite Lily's promise that she would meet adventuresome men, not a single man looked anything like the White Tiger. About half wore white ties and tails, while the rest wore Army uniforms. Yet even the military men looked soft compared to the blond, tanned giant she'd seen when she'd arrived in Simla. She spotted the faces of several men she'd already met—and successfully discouraged—at previous outings. The lieutenant Pauline had shamed at tennis met her gaze, then immediately turned his attention elsewhere, as if she didn't exist.

Though it was less grand than the ballrooms of New York, the ladies of the Club had worked for hours hanging colorful swags and preparing delectable refreshments. Despite how remote Simla was, the English managed to import their favorite foods, including smoked salmon from Scotland, pâtés from

France, and Mediterranean sardines. The viceroy and his wife, who would host a similar ball at their residence later in the season, held court at one end of the room, meeting and greeting the guests.

Lily and Alex led her toward the viceroy and the vicereine. As they passed the guests standing along the walls, dozens of voices greeted the Drakes. And dozens of curious eyes followed Pauline. Pauline caught a few whispered words: "Carrington . . . sister . . . heiress."

Lily took the attention in stride, smiling and nodding to everyone there, as if each one were a personal friend. *And I'm the ugly duckling following in the swan's wake,* Pauline thought, a rueful smile curving her lips. She could almost hear the men's thoughts as she passed: "Rather pretty, but demmed tall" . . . "Too skinny for my tastes" . . . "That hair—is it brown trying to be blond, or blond trying to be brown?" . . . "I'm desperate for a wife, any wife. She'll do."

Being evaluated on her looks alone annoyed her to no end. She decided to have a little fun and gave any man who stared too long an equally bold stare. To a man, they looked away first, and a few of them even turned red. A rebellious sense of victory filled her.

Despite her efforts to repel the men, before long Lily had managed to fill her entire dance card. The gilt-edged card dangled from her wrist by a silk cord, along with a handy pink pencil. One side listed the dances; the opposite bore dotted lines filled in with the names of strange men of nearly every age. Lily explained that officers under the rank of captain were encouraged to dance with married women, saving the single ladies for their older, still unmarried fellow officers. Which meant in some cases that Pauline danced with men as old as her father.

As Colonel Samuels swung her around in a reel, light from the chandelier glinted off his bald, moist pate. He was at least a head shorter than she. "I noticed you at the gymkhana. You're quite an accomplished athlete. I've never seen such a physical young woman." His smile grew as his gaze focused on her bosom. "Indeed, a fresh face is a rare and wondrous thing in Simla."

"Then why aren't you looking at my face?" she asked tartly.

The man blushed, then hemmed and hawed as he fought to change the subject. "So, you're Mrs. Drake's sister, eh? Does she have any more . . . that is, are there others?"

Irritation filled her. Already the man had dismissed her as a potential mate. Not that she minded. Yet she'd received similar reactions so often, she was starting to believe something was seriously wrong with her. "I have four sisters, and only two are married."

"Indeed?" he said with enthusiasm. "And are they rather like you, or your sister?"

He wanted to know if her shy sister, Clara, and Meryl, the baby of the family, were gorgeous like Lily or average like her. The nerve! "Neither. One has a terrible condition where she screams uncontrollably at the sight of men. The other laughs like a hyena and never combs her hair."

He looked so shocked, his eyebrows reminded her of thick, gray caterpillars crawling up toward his bald head. Though the music hadn't ended, Pauline had reached the end of her patience with ballroom talk.

She pressed the back of her gloved hand to her forehead and said theatrically, "Thought of my poor, bedeviled sisters has left me feeling faint. I need to rest."

The colonel led her off the dance floor and wasted no time extricating himself from her company.

Another young man began to head in her direction. Pauline suddenly felt trapped in the claustrophobic, rigid atmosphere of the ballroom. She looked around for Lily, but she and Alex were dancing—again—gazing into each other's eyes as if no one else were in the room. Pauline didn't have the heart to interrupt them merely to complain about how bored she was.

Before the young man could reach her, she turned and darted out of the room toward the ladies' retiring room.

This room was no better. Seven or eight women had gone there to freshen up and to talk about their potential conquests. The room buzzed with their high-pitched voices discussing their dance partners. Pauline recognized a few of the ladies as fellow passengers on the ship that had brought her to Bombay. They were part of the infamous "fishing fleet," young ladies who traveled to India to find husbands. If they failed, they would receive the embarrassing label of "returned empties." Pauline shuddered to think people believed her to be one of them.

Since she had a mazurka scheduled, she made her way back to the ballroom. Pausing near the wall, she glanced about, wondering what Major Jenkins looked like. The faces of the men she'd been introduced to—and who had signed her dance card—blurred together.

In the conversation surrounding her, her own name sounded clearly. Two men on the other side of the potted palms were chatting about "Miss Carrington." Remaining silent, she leaned closer to the palms to listen.

"You're giving up so soon?" one man asked.

"Afraid so," his companion replied with a heavy, fatalistic sigh. "I'd get out of it if I could, after hearing how she's treated her other dance partners."

"She can't be all bad, Colonel," the first man said. "She's handsome enough, though I would hardly want a woman towering over me, I admit. Certainly her substantial dowry would cover a vast array of detriments."

"Oh, the money would be lovely, indeed. An American Carrington! She must be worth millions! But putting up with that tongue . . ." Pauline could almost feel him shudder. "I prefer to keep my manhood intact, thank you very much." His friend joined him in a congenial laugh. "Well, the next dance is about to start. I had best head into the fray, before my cowardly impulse to flee takes hold. Wish me luck."

Pauline watched the colonel head toward the ballroom, his gaze scanning the ladies along the walls and on the dance floor, looking for her. *He won't find me,* Pauline decided, turning and fleeing back down the hall toward the ladies' retiring room. *None of them will find me.*

She blinked back a surge of moisture building in her eyes. Her tears surprised her. How annoying! She didn't care what these people thought of her.

She wanted as little to do with them as they did with her. Except for her money. That's all the men saw when they looked at her—a walking bank account. *Well, they'll never have it*, Pauline decided right then and there. *I will never, ever marry.*

Sometimes she wondered what drove her to rebel against her family's expectations. Her mother seemed to think it had something to do with being the middle of five children, implying that she was going overboard to keep from becoming lost in the crowd.

Pauline knew she lacked the gifts that people valued in her sisters. Her oldest sister, Hannah, was brilliant, and Lily was gorgeous. As for her younger sisters, Clara's natural goodness and kind heart set a standard Pauline consistently failed to meet. And Meryl—she was the petite, blond, spunky baby of the family, whom all of them loved to coddle.

She paused outside the open archway leading into the retiring room. The ladies' gossip drifted out to her. She couldn't bring herself to enter. She wanted out—out of the crowd, away from these people. Lifting her skirts, she headed away from the ballroom, deeper into the once-private men's club. When she reached the end of the hall, she was met with a staircase leading to the second level. A sign posted on the wall stated bluntly, "Women not admitted beyond this point." Pauline ignored it and began to ascend.

As soon as she reached the landing, she heard men's voices, their laughter and exclamations echoing down the hall. The noise spilled from a room on her left. After a moment, the group chatter gave way to a single man's voice, gravelly and deep. "After it began to stalk me, I knew my minutes on this earth were numbered."

Recognition froze her. The White Tiger. He was here?

Her heart began to pound with anticipation. Despite knowing almost nothing about him, she knew adventure followed in his wake. Or he followed adventure. He seemed to be telling a rousing tale of how he'd put down a dangerous man-eating tiger. Hearing his story promised to be the most interesting event of the evening.

She approached the door and peered in. To her dismay, his tall-backed mahogany chair was angled away from her so she couldn't see him. Except for one strong hand, which rested on the chair arm, cradling a glass of whiskey. A dozen refugees from the ballroom surrounded him, hanging on his every word.

Near the door stood a servant in a starched white uniform with a striped belt and turban. As soon as he saw her, he stepped into the doorway to block her entrance. "So sorry," he said tersely in his rich Punjabi accent, "no memsahibs are permitted within."

"I thought the club was no longer off limits to women," Pauline said. Lily herself had spearheaded the effort to open the club to everyone, and had succeeded despite the old guard.

"Allow me to direct you to the *moorghi-khana*, the ladies' retiring room on the first floor. This is smoking room, for gentlemen only."

Lily had explained that *moorghi-khana* meant henhouse. How disparaging! As for gentlemen, she could do without *their* company, but the White Tiger was hardly cut from the same cloth. *He* had something interesting to say, as their avid attention to his story proved. "Maybe I'd rather smoke than retire," she shot back.

The servant arched his brows at her impertinence but didn't budge so much as an inch. "Again I say, so sorry," he said, sounding not at all sorry.

Pauline sighed. It would be fruitless to argue, so she retreated from the door. She hovered in the hall, trying to catch snatches of the story being told, but the servant's stare unnerved her. Turning, she headed back downstairs.

At the foot of the stairs, she still couldn't bring herself to return to the ballroom. Instead, she pushed through a door leading outside. She found herself following a path around the building, lit by Chinese paper lanterns hanging from bamboo poles.

The path led across the lawn behind the ballroom. Music and light spilled from the double doors, filling the air with gaiety, and—for most young ladies—excitement. A surprising sense of envy filled her. The other ladies were so happy to be here, to be dancing at a ball and meeting men. Why couldn't she find even a fraction of that enthusiasm within herself? Why couldn't she give in to her fate and behave as everyone expected her to?

Because it would be a lie. If she lived a lie, she could never forgive herself. She'd be just as bad as the posturing gentlemen and simpering females she scorned.

But what other option did she have? She'd been in India only three weeks. The restrictions on her freedom were just as tight as they'd been in New York. The men were just as shallow, all determined to treat her like a helpless female. She could definitely do without men. She shuddered, recalling the caustic opinion of her expressed by the colonel and his friend. *Men.* They only wanted painted hothouse flowers, not women who could stand on their own two feet.

She continued around the corner, and the sounds of the ball receded. A cluster of male voices spilled from the floor above. The word "tiger" leaped out at her, and she paused.

She stared upward. The men's smoking room. It was right above her.

On the second level, a pair of closed doors led onto a stone balcony. Golden light from inside the room shone through the glass doors, but curtains obscured the interior. She couldn't see a thing, and she could barely hear. Now and then, laughter lifted on the breeze.

Frustration filled her, fueled by a deep yearning that grew stronger by the day. Here she was in India, the exciting land of Rudyard Kipling's tales of adventure. Yet she was doing nothing differently than she had done back in New York.

If she hid on that balcony, in a shadowed corner, she could hear the exciting stories the men were telling and no one would be the wiser. She spotted a vine-covered trellis leading from the ground well past the balcony. How convenient! She'd used the trellis beside her bedroom window back home as a ladder for months before her parents caught her at it and removed it. The trellis would be so easy to climb. If she were so inclined.

Pauline, you're crazy for considering it! If Lily found out

. . . Well, she'd taken bigger risks back home. Her fancy gown might make the climb a little awkward, but she could manage. Before she could talk herself out of it, she'd approached the trellis and tugged on it. It was bolted in place and would make a fine ladder. She bunched up her skirt in front of her and placed her foot on the lowest rung. When she placed her other foot, the expensive fabric of her dress became crushed against the flowering clematis. A twinge of guilt shot through her. If Lily could see how she was treating her fancy dress, she'd have a conniption fit. Oh, well. Any damage to the gown had probably already been done. "In for a penny, in for a pound," she murmured, and once more began to climb.

Despite her having to fight with her gown, the climb couldn't have been easier. Soon she found herself even with the balcony. She would have to climb higher in order to step over the balustrade. She lifted her foot and began to ascend once more.

A sudden snap jarred her, and she lost her hold. She began to fall. With her last bit of leverage, she hurled herself toward the balcony, hands extended, and prayed.

THREE

The crack of wood and rustle of branches drew Nate Savidge's attention from his story. Despite the friendly surroundings of the smoking room, he was always alert for strange noises that might indicate danger. Though not loud, this sound was definitely strange.

"Excuse me." He set down his whiskey. Rising, he adjusted his tweed jacket. Though the brown herringbone was the finest suit he owned, it was a step down from the uniforms and tailored suits worn by the gentlemen surrounding him. He didn't mind. Nor was he concerned that his country accent revealed his lack of a truly English education. He crossed to the curtained double doors leading to the balcony.

"It's probably just those dastardly monkeys again," called Captain Quint Robinson. "Come back and finish your tale."

It could be monkeys. The pitter-patter of their feet across the roof was an intermittent background noise that residents learned to ignore. Except that the sound of wood breaking seemed out of place.

Nate swung open the doors and stepped onto the wrought-iron balcony. He heard another rustle, and a very human grunt. Leaning over the balustrade, he saw a most unusual sight. A young lady hung from the balcony floor by only her fingers, her feet kicking fruitlessly in the air. Her legs tangled in the voluminous folds of her dressy ball-gown, and her breasts—they were practically spilling from her neckline. Or perhaps it was merely the advantageous angle from which he viewed her predicament.

"Funny, you don't look like a monkey." He leaned over the edge, reaching out to pull her to safety.

To his surprise—what was one more surprise after this!—she shook her head frantically and mouthed "no." Her large, dark eyes darted toward the inner room, then back to his face, pleading silently with him not to reveal her presence.

Quint appeared in the open door behind him. "Was it something interesting?"

"Not at all. Just a monkey causing trouble. He's gone now. I'm going to stay here a moment, catch a breath of fresh air."

Quint made a move to join him. "I say, that's a jolly good idea. Perhaps you can tell me—"

"I'll rejoin you in a moment," he shot back.

Quint took the hint. He nodded his head. "Very well. But you hardly ever visit. You left us in a most precarious position with that story of yours."

"Precarious. Yes, indeed. Never fear, I'll resolve it eventually," he said, talking more for the dangling girl's benefit. Assuming she was still hanging on and hadn't fallen. Yet he'd heard no thump on the ground.

"I'll see you inside, then." Quint retreated through the door.

"Close the door behind you, please," Nate said.

The door clicked into place, finally leaving him alone with the oddly stubborn female. He peered over the edge. She still hung there, her eyes even larger with panic.

"Are you alone?" she gasped out, while struggling to refresh her grip on the rough stone.

Her sheer grit impressed him, and he wasn't easily impressed. "I'm quite alone."

"Then hurry up and help me!"

"If you insist," he said mildly. He reached over as far as he could without losing his own balance. Grasping her forearms, he pulled her across the railing. She sucked in a breath and struggled to swing her legs over. Though overt familiarity with ladies was frowned upon, he never put much stock in impractical rules of etiquette. Sliding his arm around her waist, he lifted her to her feet.

There were definite advantages to a lack of gentlemanly pretense. For a moment, he allowed himself to enjoy the feel of her lithe, long-limbed body in his arms. Taller than most women in his experience, she came to just under his chin.

She didn't allow his enjoyment to last. She shoved away from him, stepping into a shaft of light from the curtained door behind her. The light illuminated a stunning figure. She looked like a fairy princess from a storybook, fluffy cotton candy and sugared marzipan. Yards of fabric spread about her, draped with pink ribbons and lace. Her hair was no less elaborate. Tiny ribbons secured bobbing ringlets and looped tendrils, several of which had sprung free.

Her amber eyes, high cheekbones, and determined mouth struck a familiar chord. "By God, you're the same chit I assisted on the road. Are you determined to fall to your death?"

She crossed her arms defensively, but her tone was defiant. "This never would have happened if this club didn't have ridiculous rules about excluding women."

"You were trying to break into the smoking room?"

"Don't be silly. I had no intention of joining you. I merely wanted to listen. Before I could secure a footing on the balcony, the trellis snapped."

To think a young lady—or at least a chit dressed like one—would dare to skulk about the bushes, listening in to men's talk! Amazing that a lady would take such risks. Her reputation could be ruined, along with her marriage prospects. He could tell by her accent she was no milksop English girl accustomed to doing only as her governess told her. Perhaps that explained it. "Do all American chits eavesdrop? I'd heard you Yanks were short on manners."

"There's no need to be rude." She rubbed her hands together, and he realized she had probably hurt herself.

Grasping her wrists, he dragged her into the light to better see her injuries. Which brought her within inches of him. The feminine scent of roses teased his nose. He'd been in the bush so long, surrounded by dust, insects, and the musk of his fellow men, that he'd forgotten such delicate smells existed. Or such soft skin . . . Unable to resist, he ran his fingers along her satiny wrist and hand. Soft, yet her palms bore calluses. Perhaps she wasn't as well-to-do as her expensive gown suggested. Certainly, her strength in holding onto the balcony for so long proved she wasn't unaccustomed to using her body, possibly in backbreaking labor like his own mum. Who on earth was she, and what could she be after?

An inexplicable shaft of tenderness filled him. "Silly female," he grumbled. "Scaling the walls in a ball gown. Whatever possessed you?"

Probably because of her brush with death, only a single breathless word made its way past her trembling lips. "Tigers."

"Tigers? That's why you were skulking about out here in the dark, eavesdropping on our conversation?" Lifting her palms higher, he began to study them. She resisted him, making fists. Without a word, he began prying them open, coaxing her to submit.

A shiver passed through her, and she finally relented, her hands relaxing in his.

A half-dozen scratches and a drop or two of blood marred her palms. He smoothed the scratches with his thumb, and she flinched. "Not deep. You'll live."

She yanked her hands from his. To his consternation, he immediately missed the physical connection, despite how meaningless it had been. "I never asked for your opinion."

"Nor for my help, but you're lucky I was here to provide it."

"Are you always so arrogant? Or are you expecting me to worship at your feet, like the natives do?"

"People are generally grateful when you prevent wild animals from eating their women and children." He smiled wryly, recalling how she'd watched him intently from the station platform in Kalka. He knew he'd attract attention bringing his kill into town at that busy hour. Since the British were interlopers in this land, impressing the natives with the help he could provide was always a good idea. As for the Anglos, he usually ignored those who gawked at his handiwork. Yet he'd noticed the slender, fresh-faced girl who'd seemed so riveted by the sight of his dead tiger—and of him.

Until now, he'd assumed her fascination had been one of morbid disgust at his kill. Now he began to wonder if she hadn't been interested in *him*. "*You* certainly stared hard enough," he finally said, enjoying the prospect of angering her. "You looked positively awestruck."

"Not by you. By your tiger."

Her voice was filled with so much derision, he nearly laughed. So, he hadn't caught her fancy after all. How utterly deflating. "My tiger. I see. Most ladies turn up their pert little noses at the sight of animal carcasses."

Her thin, golden brows leveled in irritation. "My nose is hardly pert."

He studied her. Indeed, she was right. Her nose was long and straight, her features neatly sculpted. She lacked the delicate, pampered look so many European women cultivated, the better to be a burden on their menfolk. Instead, her unique beauty seemed to come from an inner strength, or at least defiance. How curious. "Why are you so interested in tigers?"

His perusal seemed to bother her, for she broke eye contact and looked out over the balcony toward the star-filled sky. "I want to come face to face with a ferocious tiger intent on eating me, and win."

She couldn't have surprised him more if she'd announced she intended to fly. "Hunt a tiger? *You?*"

She glared at him, her eyes shooting fire. "Yes, *me.* I'm an excellent marksman. Markswoman, I mean."

"Indeed?" Since the Mutiny of '57, in which hundreds of British men, women, and children were slaughtered, most Anglo men in India were wise enough to teach their women to handle a gun. Some ladies took to it and became excellent shots, though few sought to hunt big game, restricting their endeavors to target practice and bird shooting. "What do you carry? A Winchester?"

She shuffled her feet and wouldn't meet his eye. "Not exactly, no."

"Well, what, then?"

"A bow and arrow."

"A bow and arrow? You propose to kill a ferocious tiger with a bow and arrow? Bloody ridiculous." He started to chuckle, unsure why he was even wasting his time with this girl, who was clearly out of her mind.

His reaction infuriated her. Her complexion began to pinken and she drew in a sharp breath, luring his eye to her breasts swelling above her gown.

"I intend to *learn* how to shoot, if I can find a proper teacher," she insisted. "A woman can be just as good a shot as a man. Haven't you ever heard of Annie Oakley, the greatest shot in the West?"

Nate had heard of Buffalo Bill's Wild West Show.

He wasn't surprised this girl found such rehearsed demonstrations exciting. "Ah, yes, the gal who shoots corks out of bottles for an audience. Tigers aren't so cooperative."

"Don't be so rude. Annie can handle a rifle or a six-shooter better than anyone alive, including you!"

"Let's hope it never comes to a contest between the two of us, then." He found it impossible not to smile, despite seeing how it infuriated her. Maybe *because* it infuriated her. "Somehow, you don't strike me as a frontier woman. Who are you, exactly?"

She muttered something so low under her breath, he couldn't catch it. "What did you say?"

"I *said*, I'm Mrs. Alexander Drake's sister."

"Mrs. Drake's sister? You mean *you're* the Carrington heiress?" As soon as he'd arrived at the Club tonight—his first visit since arriving in the area—he'd been told about this new arrival, an unusually aristocratic member of the husband-hunting "fishing fleet." Moreover, he'd been told how unapproachable the girl was, despite the efforts of every eligible man on the station to attract her interest.

His gaze skimmed her expensive, elaborate, and highly impractical gown. No wonder she looked like a princess. For all practical purposes, she was as close to a princess as an American could get. And she had no business bothering him.

A sudden desire filled him to push her away, to send her running back to the dandies in the ballroom downstairs who longed to get their hands on her money. Throwing away all pretense of gentlemanly manners, he leaned back against the railing and boldly studied her. He slid his gaze down her curves in an attempt to fluster her and spark her maidenly fears.

He failed miserably. Resting her hands on her hips, she lifted her chin and said with a queen's haughtiness, "If you don't stop looking at me in such a rude and undisciplined manner, I shall slap your face."

He grinned in triumph. "Ah, there she is. The haughty heiress. I wondered if you would ever show yourself." Reaching inside his suit jacket, he extracted his worn and dented cigarette case, snapped it open, and extracted a smoke. He held the case out to her, but she shook her head.

He crossed his ankles and tapped the cigarette against the railing. "An heiress. A genuine sterling-silver American princess. My, my. I've met a lot of people over the years, but never a female worth a fortune. Do you wear solid-gold shoes? Do servants brush your golden-brown hair? Are you a terribly spoiled young lady who gets whatever she demands, even tiger hunting?"

"You are despicable." She glared at him, her dark eyes sparking. "You know nothing about me."

He'd definitely angered her. It felt good to throw up a wall between them, to remind himself how far removed his life was from women like her. To remember how much he enjoyed his freedom—no encumbrances, no refined ladies, no demands on his time. His mother had made a choice long ago to leave such a pampered life behind. Though they had struggled over the years, every day he thanked her for his freedom.

He smiled with arrogant assurance. "I know that your aristocratic parents wouldn't approve of their darling daughter climbing around the Club at night, peeking into gentlemen's private rooms."

"That's none of your business." Her glare hadn't diminished, yet for some reason she'd drawn closer—or had he inched closer to her? Barely three feet separated them. He had a sudden urge to close the distance entirely, to yank her hard against his body and give her the sort of attention other men wouldn't dare.

To distract himself, he propped the cigarette between his lips and patted his pockets for his matches. Her gaze seemed riveted to his cigarette—or his mouth. It was incredibly disconcerting.

He spoke around his cigarette. "You've damned well made your business mine, more fool me."

"I hardly think—"

"Savidge?" Quint's voice called as the door began to swing open. "Are you coming back inside, or are you planning to camp out here?"

The girl had the good sense to scurry into the shadows by the wall, positioning herself behind the door as it swung open and Quint's head emerged. "What are you up to? You've left us hanging."

Nate sighed and pulled his cigarette from his mouth. "Quint, you must learn to entertain yourself," he said wryly.

Quint had carried his whiskey glass with him. He took a sip. "I couldn't possibly compete with your tales of the bush. I have to say, though, Ganning gave a remarkably funny account of a lady whose bosoms tumbled out of her ballgown, right in front of him! Against all odds, he maintained his composure." He leaned against the railing, as if he intended to stay a while.

Nate tensed, knowing that if Quint peered over his shoulder, he would probably see the girl. And he wasn't ready to share her.

Quint chuckled as he continued his story. "Ganning actually said, 'My dear, these are far too exquisite to share with everyone.' Then he grabbed her boobies and stuffed them back into her gown. I don't think the lady appreciated his gentlemanly manners. She gave him a good, hard slap. Poor fellow is still recovering."

"Wonderful tale," Nate said dryly.

"Well? Are you coming back inside? I know you had a disagreement with the DC, but—"

"I'm not concerned with the district commissioner," he said, trying to hide his annoyance. The DC was pressing him to host an organized tiger hunt for an important visitor. In such a hunt, a dozen beaters would pound drums at the edge of a field while the hunters, safe atop their elephants, would advance from the opposite side, easily picking off whatever game ran from the noise. In one shoot Nate had attended, so much game had been slaughtered, much of it had been left to rot in the sun. Worse, the DC wanted to ensure that the guest— some earl from England—actually managed to shoot a tiger, even if that meant baiting it with an opium-laced buffalo.

And these men called themselves hunters! He'd like to see the earl try to hunt like a real man—on foot, when one false move could mean his own life. Earls. He hated them. He hated all noblemen with a passion exceeded only by his hate for cowardly hunters.

So he had refused the DC's demand, causing an uproar in the viceroy's offices.

Quint pressed him again. "It's just that we so rarely see you."

"I appreciate that. Please. Another moment." He nodded toward the open door, and Quint finally took his leave. Nate tapped the base of the door with his foot, closing it behind Quint.

Nate turned back to the girl. "Well, it's been . . . interesting, to say the least." Tossing his cigarette on the balcony, he ground it out with his heel—only then realizing he'd never lit it. Where was his head?

He focused on the cause—the strange Carrington chit, who was now hanging over the balcony staring at the trellis, her fanny in the air. Despite his better sense, he imagined cupping her rounded bottom. A jolt of heat swept through him.

Don't be ridiculous, he scolded himself. This pampered princess held absolutely no appeal for him.

Unfortunately, she'd embroiled him in her intrigue. How was he going to explain her sudden presence to the men inside—and the fact he'd been out here alone with her? The men already believed he had a woman in every village from here to Calcutta. The last thing he needed were rumors linking him to a wealthy, inexperienced debutante. Her father would probably call him out, and he'd have to shoot the fellow to defend himself. Not a fatal shot, of course—just a wing shot. Then he'd have to head deeper into the hills.

"I suppose I'll have to invent a story to explain

your sudden arrival from the balcony. The men inside are bound to be curious."

"You won't have to tell them." Hiking up her voluminous skirts, she swung one leg over the railing and balanced there, riding it astride as she might a horse—or a lover. Any moment she could lose her balance and tumble off, twenty feet to the bone-jarring ground.

Panic filled him. "By God, are you out of your mind?" Dashing forward, he grasped her arm. "You broke the trellis, remember? If you put your weight on it again, it might snap."

She shook him off and gave him a cool look. "Only a single board snapped on this side. The far side appears solid."

She was serious! His panic intensified, became a clawing beast within his chest. "Don't be daft. Get down from there before you fall to your death."

His stern command failed to frighten sense into her. She gave him a curiously victorious smile. "My goodness, such concern! Are you afraid for me?"

"It would be a better idea to face the men inside—"

"So much for the courage of the legendary White Tiger."

He reached for her, but his fingers only grazed her silken shoulder before she leaped off the railing toward the trellis, her skirts spreading like bird's wings. With as much agility as a monkey, she snagged the crosspiece and clung there. Flexing her arms, she lifted herself until she found her footing. Her physical strength, her fearless audacity, stunned him.

Amazed, he watched her scramble down, her footing sure, her skirts making only the softest rustle against the vines. He realized that if the trellis hadn't broken earlier, he never would have known she was out here. Never would have met her.

In seconds, her slipper-adorned feet touched the ground. Lifting her wrinkled skirts high, she dashed into the night. Even after she'd disappeared into the shadows, Nate continued to stare after her, wondering whether all American heiresses were as wild, as unpredictable. And positively unforgettable.

FOUR

"Such concerns are groundless. The Indians are perfectly content in their positions." The commissioner's wife blithely sipped from her teacup. "God designed the savage races to serve those above them."

Behind her, virtually ignored, a uniformed servant stood silently, his dark-skinned face impassive. "An Indian is standing right there," Pauline said under her breath to Lily, sitting beside her at the linen-covered table.

"Shhh," Lily said, shooting her a warning glance.

Pauline sipped her tea, fighting the urge to say what was really on her mind. Hours ago, Lily and she had arrived by tonga at the viceroy's hillside mansion to attend the vicereine's weekly tea. The expansive lawn held no fewer than ten linen-covered tables, each served by a uniformed Indian servant proffering lettuce-and-tomato sandwiches, curry puffs, and iced cakes. A military band played selections from Gilbert and Sullivan softly in background.

The event could be no more elegant had it been held in Newport. Pauline sighed, toying with the cucumber finger sandwich on her plate. She felt as if she'd never left America.

At her table, the conversation continued along painfully predictable lines. Nothing was more torturous than ladies' gossip. Lily and her friends talked about nothing but marriages and no marriages and would-be marriages and ought-to-be marriages, and gentlemen's attention and ladies' flirtings, and what Mr. This said to Miss That, and what Miss That did to Mr. This . . . Could anything be more tedious?

Pauline hadn't spoken softly enough. The commissioner's wife lifted her lorgnette to her eye and peered at her. "I say, if you have something to share, please do so. And say it loudly enough for us all to hear."

"It was nothing," Lily began.

"Yes, it was," Pauline said. "I hardly think the Indians are below us. They're simply different, and—"

"Impertinent chit! Your opinion is of no import. You need to learn that a true lady holds her tongue before her betters."

"Pauline didn't realize—" Lily began.

Pauline cut her off. "I can speak for myself. Mrs. Winston, you are hardly one to talk about holding one's tongue. An Indian servant—a gentleman—is standing right behind you, yet you talk about his people as if he is oblivious to every word you're saying!"

Mrs. Winston's face began to turn red. Her hand shook. "Why—what an impudent girl! Your poor Yankee breeding is showing. India is the jewel in Queen Victoria's crown. This is now *our* country. It is our Christian duty to reform these wretched, idolatrous heathens. If the blacks did not consent to our God-given superiority, we would not be here."

"Are you so sure they consent?" Pauline shot back. "What about the Mutiny of 'fifty-seven?"

Mrs. Winston looked as if she'd seen a ghost. The other ladies shared shocked looks as a dread silence descended.

"Do not ever bring that subject up in polite company," Mrs. Winston finally said, her words filled with ice. She turned her accusing gaze on Lily. "Mrs. Drake, you must learn to control your sister, or she will be most unwelcome in polite society. From now on, she is certainly unwelcome in mine."

"I'm so sorry, Mrs. Winston. We'll take our leave." Lily rose and grasped Pauline's elbow. "Come, Pauline, it's time we returned home."

Pauline leaped to her feet and yanked her arm away. "No, Lily. You stay here and enjoy the company of your friends—something I cannot manage to do. I shall find my own way home." *Or go somewhere else, anywhere else.* Before giving Lily a chance to reply, she threw down her napkin and strode toward the gate leading to the avenue.

"Pauline!" Lily called behind her. In a moment, she caught up. Grasping her arm, she swung her around. "You're creating a scene."

Pauline wanted to rail at her sister. "I can't simply sit there while they say such mean things."

"Please, Pauline. Show some sense," Lily said. "I don't agree with them either, but you must learn to hold your tongue."

"Why? Because she's important? I don't care who she is. You know I didn't want to attend this boring tea party anyway." Turning, she began striding away.

Lily caught up again and rounded on her.

"Pauline! Stop running away. You're not even trying to get along. In the past month, you've managed to alienate nearly everyone on the station. I do my best to mend fences, but—"

"Don't bother."

"Pauline, think about your future! What will happen to you? Mother worries so about you, and now I understand what you must have put her through."

Pauline threw up her hands. "Lily, I'm not like you. Please, just let me be who I am." Hiking up her skirts, she broke into an unladylike sprint, drawing the shocked gazes of all those she passed. Before she reached the gate, a servant swung it open for her, and a moment later she found herself on the street, in the middle of the bustling afternoon traffic.

The late-afternoon sun sinking behind the buildings and trees drew deep contrasts between shadow and light along the winding avenue. *And which are you: shadow or light?* Pauline asked herself, afraid she knew the answer. Rather than return home, she headed in the opposite direction, toward the edge of town. Soon she was climbing the path to the top of tree-covered Jakko Hill.

Lily's distraught words pursued her up the steep, winding track. Now that she was alone, with time to reflect on the conversation, she could admit to herself that Lily was right. She hadn't tried to get along. Her efforts to change, to be someone else, always felt false, and she couldn't bring herself to pretend. As a consequence, wherever she went, she felt like an outsider. *You don't belong here, any more than you did in New York. You don't belong anywhere.*

The cool mountain breeze pressed Pauline's skirt

against her legs as she walked the last few yards to the summit. Ahead rose the Monkey Temple, a tiny whitewashed, tin-roofed shrine swarming with bickering, noisy brown monkeys tended by patient priests. The creatures instantly swarmed her. Two of the monkeys began tugging at her skirts with their cold, muscular hands.

"I brought nothing for you. I'm sorry." She held out her empty palms. To Pauline's relief, a chocolate-skinned, robed priest stepped from behind the temple. He scolded his furry congregation and shooed them away. The monkeys retreated to the temple area, swinging into the trees overhead. The priest bowed and retreated, leaving her alone.

Pauline smiled her thanks and caught her breath. This odd monkey temple was worth writing home about, one of the few unique experiences she'd had since arriving in India.

She crossed to the far edge of the hill, well away from the chattering monkeys, and leaned against a rocky outcropping. Her eye turned to the horizon, where lush green valleys led to even higher hills. Beyond that rose the jagged, snow-capped Himalayas—the roof of the world. Below her, Simla clung to the hillsides in a crescent.

Bisecting the town's center was the mall, surrounded on both sides by Bavarian-style wooden buildings containing shops selling European goods, hotels, cafés, libraries, even stone churches with spires and Gothic arches. Unlike Indians, with their homes of mud bricks, Simla's British residents lived in pitched-roof houses just like those in England, constructed of brick and timber and with glass windows and fireplaces.

At this time of day, it seemed everyone was about on the mall, Anglo and Indian alike. Most of the Indians in sight were waiting on the Anglos, carrying their goods, or pulling them about in rickshaws.

On the highest ridge above the mall rose the homes of the well-to-do, including Lily and Alex's villa, its drawing room and bedrooms decorated to match those in New York. Below the mall was the crowded Indian bazaar, which Lily had promised they would soon visit. Past the bazaar, the tin-roofed shanties of the natives clung to the hillsides in tightly packed knots.

Pauline's eyes returned to the mall and the Central Hotel, a sprawling, multitiered edifice. She'd heard Mr. Savidge was staying there. Thoughts of the man were never far from her mind. Was she terribly spoiled, as Mr. Savidge claimed? She sometimes felt she was being unreasonable, at the very least.

Why couldn't she be satisfied with her lot in life? Why did she keep disappointing her family, even hurting them? Any other young lady would dream of being in her shoes as a daughter of privilege. Yet she'd come to India with dreams of adventure, and all she'd found was an imitation of New York society, with a few British traditions thrown in for good measure. It was just as restrictive, certainly. The Brits carried on as if they preferred to forget they weren't in England. She was appalled that so few of the Anglos took advantage of the opportunity to see and experience this vibrant, colorful land.

Then again, she was no better. She herself had yet

to truly take a risk, to live life to the fullest. Her fate was to marry a high-ranking officer or administrator with an aristocratic—or better yet, noble—heritage. As an unmarried lady, she had few freedoms. Once married, her freedom would depend on her husband's forbearance, her behavior dictated by his wishes.

You must accept your future, Pauline, she told herself sternly. *You have to give up your dreams of adventure. You'll only be miserable if you don't.*

The screeching of the monkeys grew closer. Pauline looked toward the temple just as a bold creature approached and snatched her platter-shaped hat from her head. Its lavender veil fluttered in the breeze as the monkey scurried with his prize across the clearing.

"Why, you furry little thief!" Pauline leaped to her feet. Hiking up her skirts, she sprinted after the monkey. It swung into a tree, then along a branch above her head. Pauline leaped up, stretching her arm as far as possible, but the monkey remained out of her reach. It grinned down at her and gave an annoying cry of victory, taunting her with its prize. Pauline gathered her strength and leaped again but fell short. She was contemplating climbing the tree—despite wearing a lacy tea gown—when a stand of trees on the far side of the temple rustled, drawing her attention.

The man never far from her thoughts stepped into the temple clearing. He appeared to have formed from the mists lingering between the shadowed branches. He was more ruggedly handsome than she remembered, if that was possible.

Pauline's blood warmed and her pulse raced with a delicious excitement she'd felt all too rarely here in India. What power did this man possess that made her believe adventure would follow in his wake, even here on Jakko Hill? His eyes caught hers, and she noted with great satisfaction that he paused in his stride. The hesitation was so brief, if she hadn't been staring at him she wouldn't have seen it.

He stepped farther into the clearing. That's when Pauline realized he wasn't alone. A short yet shapely native woman followed close behind him. Her flowing magenta sari clung to her voluptuous figure in ways Pauline's own clothes never could. Numerous bracelets, necklaces, and long silver earrings adorned her. She was the physical opposite of Pauline—petite, busty, and dark. *So this is the sort of woman he prefers,* she thought. *And it isn't you.*

Nate and the woman drew to a stop five feet from her, and Pauline changed her assessment. Mr. Savidge's companion wasn't a woman. The moon-faced girl couldn't be more than fourteen or fifteen, the age of Meryl, Pauline's youngest sister.

Yet her large, dark eyes conveyed a depth of awareness and self-confidence Pauline couldn't begin to match. The girl exchanged a look with Mr. Savidge, then stared boldly at Pauline, her eyes openly questioning. Though young, she carried herself with poise and confidence, unafraid of the Western woman before her. Unafraid of her own femininity despite the nearness of an incredibly attractive man.

Pauline smoothed her palms down her skirt, feeling ungainly and overdressed in her impractical petticoats and layers of fine cloth. She could at least pretend a confidence she didn't feel. Lifting her chin, she coolly greeted them. "Mr. Savidge. And miss." She nodded formally at each of them.

A smile flickered on Nate's rugged face. "Miss Carrington. How do you do?" He tugged at the brim of his pith helmet in what should have been a respectful greeting, but Pauline couldn't help feeling he was secretly laughing at her.

"I'm quite well, thank you."

He glanced about. "You're alone?"

"Is that a concern?" Of all people, she didn't expect this man to care about propriety.

"It's merely surprising. This *is* a popular assignation spot."

Pauline flushed. He thought she might have hiked up here to spoon with a beau? Was that what *he'd* been doing?

Her gaze flicked to the native lady beside him. The petite girl didn't even reach his shoulder, making Pauline feel taller and less feminine than usual. "I don't believe I've had the pleasure of meeting your companion."

His eyes continued to shine in silent laughter. "Not surprising you've never met. She's never been to Simla." Leaning closer, he said softly, "I only purchased her today."

Despite her desire to appear sophisticated, his remark stunned Pauline and her mouth fell open. She echoed stupidly, "You *purchased* her?"

"At the Seepie Fair, seven miles from here. Don't fret, Miss Carrington. I assure you she's excited to have been chosen."

"I'm sure," she said dryly. How arrogant could the

man possibly be? Did he truly think every woman longed to be bedded by him? Worse than his arrogance was his utter disregard for women! How dare he actually buy one for himself! "Why, that's—that's nothing short of prostitution," she bit out.

He arched a brow. "Hardly that. Amritha could not find a husband in her village. It's the tradition in her tribe for several brothers to share a single wife, to keep their population in check. Their hill land can't support but a small number of them."

"They share a wife?" She'd always prided herself on being open-minded, but her Christian sensibility fought against accepting such a barbaric practice.

Nate continued, his tone so matter-of-fact, he could have been speaking of the weather. "Naturally, this means they have a surplus of marriageable maidens."

"And you've taken advantage of this." She choked out the words.

"Of course. She cost a mere two hundred rupees." He had to know how his words appalled her, yet he seemed to revel in that fact. "Goodness, Miss Carrington, their traditions aren't so different from your own."

"How can you possibly compare—"

"You're here in Simla seeking a worthy husband, one who will pay the necessary price for *you.*"

Pauline paled, fighting to think of something to say, some way of disputing his words. She could think of nothing.

Unconcerned with her inner struggle, he continued, "Bhaga has been fretting over a demon he fears he's swallowed and now lives in his stomach. Only the sweet touch of a new wife will relieve him of his suffering." He lifted his gaze to the branches above her head. "That fellow is certainly enjoying your offering. Or did you want it back?" Without waiting for an answer, he crouched down and began exploring the ground with his palms.

"A demon?" Pauline said dumbly, stuck on his arcane explanation. His words and actions made no sense to her. Did he mean the girl was intended for another man? Had he actually said something about a demon? And now he was digging about on the ground!

"Yes, a demon," he said. "You must learn to keep up."

Rising, he clutched a small stone and looked at a high branch a dozen feet away, toward the monkey thief. His appearance in the clearing had caused her to forget about her hat, still in the clutches of the furry fiend on a high tree branch. He hefted the stone once, weighing it in his palm, then hurled it toward the monkey, at the same instant screeching in perfect imitation of the monkey's cry. The bizarre, unexpected sound shocked Pauline—and the monkey. The stone hit it squarely in the chest.

The monkey dropped her hat and scurried higher into the branches. It turned back and screeched in high dudgeon. Then it disappeared for good, along with most of its fellows.

Nate stooped and retrieved her hat, then tossed it to her. She snagged it and clutched it to her chest. "Thank you," she muttered, annoyed beyond belief that he'd succeeded where she'd failed. And so easily.

As if reading her mind, his blue eyes twinkled.

"Don't be too hard on yourself. I have an advantage. I grew up in these hills."

"You have no house in Simla. You're staying at the Central Hotel."

"Aren't you the knowledgeable one. My home is in Naintal, in the next province over. I manage to return there a few weeks of the year." He turned again to his female companion and spoke in swift, flawless Punjabi. He must have told the girl it was time to go, for she strolled toward the path leading to town. Her sari flowed against her shapely body as she stepped down the rocky path, graceful and surefooted. Envy filled Pauline at the young girl's freedom, and the obvious attraction she held for men—including Mr. Savidge.

Nate nodded his head in farewell, then turned and followed the woman he'd purchased.

"He *bought* a young girl, can you believe it? He actually paid money for her. He's no better than a slave owner."

Pauline returned the silk scarf Lily was showing her to the table before her. After they'd each apologized for their spat, Lily had suggested a visit to the bazaar to lift their mood. Lily insisted things always looked brighter after a shopping excursion.

Despite the noisy, colorful stalls that surrounded her in the Simla bazaar, Pauline couldn't focus on shopping. Even the strange sight of a snake charmer luring forth a cobra from a woven basket failed to chase away thoughts of Nate Savidge.

As the women strolled along the crowded track,

the air vibrated with sound. Music from a stringed sitar joined with voices speaking native Punjabi, Hindi, and Urdu, peppered with English. The heady scents of jasmine and sandalwood mingled with pungent tobaccos, the tang of spices, and the acrid smoke of burning cow dung.

In one stall, young boys used hammers to pound designs into brass pots, while next to them a wizened, dark man weighed papayas on a small brass scale for a portly household servant. Nearby, potters of the *kumhar* caste worked the same magic their forefathers had, turning soft, malleable clay into vessels of use and beauty, from cooking pots to containers for temple offerings.

"A slave owner. That's a little harsh, isn't it?" Lily said, frustratingly unwilling to understand Pauline's disgust with Mr. Nathaniel Savidge. "You said the girl was from a hill village, one with a surplus of females."

"Are you defending him?"

Lily seemed more interested in admiring a three-strand ivory-and-coral necklace than in debating the merits of Mr. Savidge. "Things are different here than in New York," she said mildly, holding the necklace against Pauline's neck. "I thought that's why you wanted to come."

Pauline sighed. "Not different enough."

Lily set down the necklace and gave Pauline her full attention. "Oh, Pauly. It's not what you do. It's who you do it with. Once you find the man you're interested in, you'll see. Even the simplest outing will take on grand significance. Besides, you must admit Mr. Savidge is hardly the sort of fellow you were used to in New York."

"To put it mildly."

"He's very well-respected. He's saved hundreds of natives. They practically worship him."

"I'm sure that does his ego no good."

"I thought you rather liked him." Pauline opened her mouth to protest, but Lily blithely continued, "In any case, you'll have the opportunity to tell him what you think to his face. He's coming to dinner tonight."

"You invited him to dinner?" Pauline struggled against the burst of excitement in her chest at this news.

Lily lifted another scarf from the table and held it up to Pauline's dark-blond hair. "This one is lovely for you. You hate ladies' teas, but I trust you'll be at dinner," she said dryly. "You can wear it then." The teasing glow in Lily's eyes gave Pauline the strong feeling her sister suspected her attraction to the hunter, an attraction she herself only vaguely understood.

"I'm hardly about to dress up for him! He already thinks I'm nothing but a soft, silly female. Not that I *care* what he thinks. He's nothing but an unsophisticated boor, all rough and unmannered and . . ." *Dangerous and exciting.* Her string of insults exhausted, she turned her annoyance on her sister. "To think *you* think I care what *he* thinks, why that's—that's—"

"Mrs. Drake, I'm sorry to interrupt." The familiar gravelly voice shocked Pauline into silence. Slowly she turned around and found herself facing Mr. Savidge himself. How much had he heard? Thank God he wasn't looking at her. "I regret I must decline your invitation to dinner after all."

"I'm sorry to hear that." Lily shot Pauline a look of

irritation, no doubt believing her precipitous words had changed Mr. Savidge's mind.

"I've received a telegram from the maharajah of Rawa, in the central provinces. It seems my services are needed there."

"Why, what's happened?" Lily asked.

He hesitated, and Pauline realized to her annoyance that he was being far more mannerly with her lovely sister than he'd ever been with her.

"I'm not afraid of the truth," Lily said. She placed her gloved hand on his arm. She had the remarkable ability to make any man—young, old, married, single—do as she wished.

Savidge's expression darkened. "There's a rogue tiger in the district which needs to be put down. The creature has already killed more than fifty villagers, and a few Anglo soldiers who tried to hunt it. I'm going to bring it down, collect a nice bounty."

A man-eater. Pauline's heartbeat accelerated. The most dangerous creature in India, or perhaps all of Asia. A tiger with a taste for human flesh. It was the adventure of a lifetime. And she was stuck here in Simla, preening for stuffy administrators and pudgy officers. What she wouldn't give to be part of it! She could experience India in ways she never would in the care of her sister.

Her task was clear. She would have to convince Lily—and Mr. Savidge, of course—to allow her to accompany him. It would take time, but if she proved herself to Mr. Savidge, showed him that she could take care of herself . . .

"When do you leave?" Lily asked.

"At first light, once I've hired porters."

"So soon?" Pauline burst out. She would have no chance to convince anyone of anything!

Mr. Savidge finally looked at her. Pauline caught her breath at the strange look in his eyes: a mixture of humor and, oddly, anger that sent a chill up her spine. His lips turned up in a cool smile. "You sound disappointed, Miss Carrington. I thought you'd be glad to be rid of an unsophisticated boor such as myself. If you'll excuse me." He bowed slightly to Lily but not to Pauline and continued down the crowded bazaar.

Pauline pressed her gloved hands to her face. "He heard me," she moaned, thoroughly disgusted with herself. "Mother always tells me to moderate my words, but I never listen."

"I'm sorry, Pauline. I know you liked the fellow. I was happy to see you take even a passing interest in a man, though I can't say he was all that suitable."

"What do you mean?" Pauline asked, suddenly alert.

"He's not the sort of fellow mother was hoping I'd introduce you to. He grew up here, but I gather he was from a very poor family, one that socialized freely with the Indians."

And she'd called him unsophisticated! Could she have been more cruel?

Lily tucked Pauline's arm in hers and began to propel her down the street to a rickshaw stand. "It's almost time for tea. You must put thoughts of Mr. Savidge completely out of your mind. I highly doubt you'll ever see the fellow again."

* * *

"You must put thoughts of Mr. Savidge completely out of your mind. I highly doubt you'll ever see the fellow again."

Never see him again? Pauline bit down her smile as she walked softly down the hallway toward the room that the front desk clerk had identified as Mr. Savidge's. Lily should have known better than to make such a decisive statement. Pauline's nature rebelled at any limitations. She couldn't help but take it as a challenge.

After dinner, she'd gone for a stroll. Rather than enjoying the English-style gardens planted outside her sister's villa, she'd hiked up her skirts and sprinted down the hill to town and the Central Hotel.

Halfway down the hall, a dark-skinned, turbaned gentleman passed her. Pauline realized he looked familiar, but before she could place him, she found Savidge's door. It hung partly open, golden light spilling onto the hall's parquet flooring.

Sucking in a breath, Pauline peeked in the door. All she could see was a booted foot, stretched out from someone sitting. Pauline was surprised to realize she recognized that scarred, well-worn leather boot. Even this small detail of Nate Savidge's appearance had impressed her.

Gathering her courage, she opened the door wider and boldly stepped into the room.

FIVE

Nate Savidge swept his oilcloth along the twin barrels of the .450/.400 rifle propped between his thighs. He always gave his favorite rifle a thorough cleaning before a hunt, and with the difficult task ahead, nothing was more important than a smoothly working weapon.

Taking down the man-eater would mean a hefty bounty from the government, a nice income for the season. Other hunters had already tried and failed to bag the creature, but most of them weren't born Anglo-Indians, as he was. He lived and breathed this land, understood its wildlife in ways few men did. He was certain he could manage the task, barring any unforeseen difficulties.

He sensed the presence of another person in the room. "Back already, Bhaga?" When his syce didn't reply, he glanced toward the figure by the door.

And froze.

He must have drunk too much whiskey after dinner. Nothing else but an inebriated brain could possibly explain the vision of Miss Carrington in his room this late at night.

He'd been pursued by women enough times. Females from the hill stations and the Indian villages who, drawn by his notoriety, readily made themselves available to him. But not *her* sort. Never the daughters of wealth, reared to expect nothing but pampering and comfort from their men. Never young ladies bred to believe that high excitement was attending church followed by a Sunday picnic.

The girl was an enigma, as difficult to understand as a tigress abandoning her cubs. Worse, he'd wasted far more time puzzling over her than he ought. Leaving Simla would put an end to that.

As if confronted by a wild animal, he moved carefully, so as not to frighten her—or succumb to her attack. He set his oilcloth and rifle on the floor beside his chair and slowly rose to his feet. "What are you doing here?" he rasped out.

"Excuse me, Mr. Savidge. I hate to intrude, but . . . is your manservant returning soon?" She gestured to the door, then closed it and turned the lock.

By God, she'd locked herself in with him! Did she intend . . . ? What else was he to think, but that she meant to . . . His eyes slid to the canopied bed across from the fireplace. In an instant, he saw it all: her lacy garments falling to the floor atop his sturdy khakis. Her milky-white skin so soft and pure, such a contrast to his own scarred hide. Her flushed, damp face against the pillows as he slid deep inside her—

"I want to go with you, to hunt the tiger."

Reality returned, along with a brief flash of disappointment. Of course. He should have realized. The girl had made no secret of her self-professed "skills" with her bow and arrow. She was only interested in him as a means to an end. For some bizarre reason, she fancied herself quite an outdoorswoman, and he was her ticket to adventure.

"You want to go with me?" he said lamely, scrambling to find a strategy to deal with this creature before him.

"Yes. Please. I know it seems strange, but—"

"Strange? You think it seems strange?" What an understatement!

His words seemed to give her hope. She clutched her hands before her chest and stepped closer. "Well, not that strange, really. You should welcome someone like me. I'm . . ."

"As daft as they come."

She ignored his gibe, her dark eyes sparking with more determination and enthusiasm than he'd seen in seasoned hunters. "I'm very capable of taking care of myself. I learn fast, and I promise I won't be any trouble."

How typical of the wealthy to expect everyone else to be at their beck and call! "You're walking trouble. Toddle off, now. I have work to do." He reached for his rifle and plopped back in the chair, determined to send the message that he wanted nothing to do with her—even though the bed behind him continued to beckon. God, it had been so long . . .

To his dismay, Miss Carrington adjusted her yellow satin skirt and crouched at his feet, her hand on the arm of his chair. She was inches from him, her sweet scent mingling with the smoky aroma of the fire.

"Please don't dismiss me out of hand. I'm not like other girls. Other *women,*" she corrected.

By God, the chit still thought of herself as a girl,

she was so recently out of the schoolroom. He had no business being alone with her.

"I've never fit in with balls and parties and feminine things. But I know this is something I can do. I know it." Her hand fisted on his chair arm.

Slowly he lifted his hand and laid it over hers. Her eyes lit up with hope. Hope he was about to dash. Squeezing her hand in his, he rose to his feet, bringing her up with him. Her hand opened in his, and suddenly they were holding hands, like a pair of lovers. It would be so easy to slide his arm around her and pull her close. He resisted that notion, instead walking with her toward the door.

She dug in her heels. When he continued to drag her, she tore her hand from his. "You haven't heard me at all."

He turned and settled his hands on his hips. "I've heard more than enough. A man-eating tiger is not a toy, and hunting it is not a game. This is hardly a pleasure hunt arranged for your enjoyment. I have a job to do and don't intend to host a female, any female, particularly one such as you."

"What is that supposed to mean?"

He slid his eyes pointedly up and down her figure. Her lemon-yellow dress was designed for a formal dinner. Beneath her wrap, her shoulders were bare. She was ripe and ready for a garden tryst with a lover, not a difficult journey into the bush. Ripe and ready . . .

As if reading his mind, she tugged the ends of her wrap closed and lifted her chin. "I won't wear a dress, of course."

He took a step closer, then another. Ever defiant,

she remained rooted to the spot, until she had to tilt her head back to look in his face.

He slid his hands up her arms, his palms tightening securely on her upper arms so she couldn't wriggle free. "You are a goddamned lady," he rasped, his voice low and intense from a physical desire he hadn't expected to feel. "A *lady,* bred to enjoy the finer things."

Her lips trembled at his assault, and he had the incredibly strong urge to taste them. He resisted with more words. "Do you know what people will say about you if you go gallivanting across India with an *unsophisticated boor* like me?"

"I'm sorry I called you that," she murmured softly, laying her hand on his bare forearm in a soothing gesture. Rather than soothe him, her touch burned his skin. "I don't care if you lack manners. I don't care if you're rough and uneducated. I don't care at all, even though I should."

He lacked manners, did he? That was true enough, considering the thoughts spinning in his mind. No doubt she believed him beneath the refined swains who courted her. That thought annoyed him more than it should. He had no interest in impressing this flighty female.

He gave her a small shake. "Damn it, miss. You have a reputation to consider. A family name. Did that cross your addled brain even once?"

"They don't have to know," she said, her voice barely a whisper. "Only Lily will know, after I write her a note, and she won't tell a soul."

His thumbs traced the lace pattern of the expensive silk shawl draped over her arms. "By God, you have an answer for everything."

"Yes, I do."

He studied her angular face, so filled with fire and determination. She wasn't easily rattled, that was clear. Yet she had little idea of the real dangers in the wild. Worse, she was oblivious to the dangerous yearnings she sparked deep within him. "There's another obstacle, woman, and it's quite out of your control." He pulled her nearer, bringing his mouth just above hers. "Do you truly fancy I wouldn't take advantage of the situation?"

"Don't be silly," she scoffed, shoving against his chest to put distance between them. "This isn't about romance. It's a hunting expedition!"

Her audacity astounded him. How could a woman of such limited experience be so bold and self-assured?

A devil took control of him then—a demon determined to knock her off her feet, to rattle her composure so badly she would never bother—never tempt—him again. Grasping her waist, he yanked her hard against his body. "Who said anything about romance?" he bit out. Then he pressed his mouth to hers.

A shock of desire startled his senses. Pure bliss . . . softer and more giving than he'd dared imagine. He'd gone so long without a hint of comfort or softness in his life, what he'd intended as a single punishing contact ignited a ravenous hunger deep within him. Barely realizing what he was doing, he grasped her head in his hands and opened his mouth over hers, his tongue tangling with hers. He drank of her as if he could never get enough.

A sensuous moan drifted from her mouth as she slid her hands up his back. Her strokes brought him to his senses. She was enjoying this! He forced himself to tear his mouth from hers and step back. She swayed on her feet, then caught herself, her eyes meeting his calmly, even though her lips were swollen from his kiss.

"There," he said, fighting to hide how breathless she'd made him. "That should do it." On unsteady legs, he crossed to the door and yanked it open. His syce was standing quietly on the other side.

"Bhaga! You're back. Good." He rubbed his palms together and fought to project a completely normal countenance. "Good. So, you put out the word we need porters?"

"Yes, sahib. Those interested in serving you will gather outside the hotel at first light."

"Good," he said once more. He paced back into the room and picked up his shaving supplies from the bureau. "We have a lot to do and no time to waste."

Crossing the room, he retrieved his satchel, a canteen, and his jacket from a chair. He tossed his things on the bed, forgetting for the moment he'd be occupying the bed before the end of the night.

"Good evening, miss." Bhaga bowed before his visitor, who remained quiet, hopefully so shocked by his boorish action that she couldn't find her voice.

"Would you be so kind as to show my guest to the door?" Nate asked. He glanced over the collection of items he'd thrown on the bed, and realized he hadn't meant to pack until morning. The girl had him so rattled, he couldn't think straight.

"Yes, sahib. This way, miss." Bhaga gestured to the door, but Pauline remained rooted to the spot.

"I take it you still refuse?" she asked, her voice as firm as ever. By God, his kiss hadn't rattled her in the least! He fancied himself a decent lover, but apparently this woman was immune. He tried not to allow that truth to sting. Worse, she remained stubbornly oblivious to the damage he could do her. Frustration swelled within him. "Of course I refuse!" he bellowed. "Get out!"

His outburst had the desired effect. Head held high, she strode from his room with the haughty demeanor of a queen.

As soon Bhaga closed the door behind her, Nate sagged on his bed, his hands fisted on his knees. He suddenly had no energy for packing.

"Since we had planned to finish packing in the morning, will you be requiring anything else this evening?" Bhaga asked, his black eyes dancing at Nate's expense.

Nate frowned at him. "Just wipe those thoughts clean out of your mind, you rascal. That isn't what happened."

"It is not for me to understand the strange customs of the white man," Bhaga said.

Nate glared at him. Bhaga often adopted the attitude of "humble sage of the East" to yank his chain, despite the fact he'd been educated in an English-run school and grown up around white men. They'd known each other far too long for Nate to successfully keep secrets from him.

"Yes, sahib." Bhaga gave him a mockingly deep salaam. "Now, I must discuss business of great import with you."

Nate set down the canteen he'd been fiddling with and gave Bhaga his full attention.

"This sounds serious."

"As you say. I deeply regret that I shall not be able to continue in your employ."

"What?" Bhaga had worked for him for five years, and Nate couldn't imagine being without his ready assistance.

"Now that I am a married man—a happily married man, due to your beneficence," he added with a wide smile, "my beloved wife, Amritha, needs me to remain with her."

"You're setting up housekeeping?"

"I have been told a gentleman with such fine manners as myself will have no difficulty finding employment fit for my abilities."

Nate smiled and nodded, despite his keen disappointment. His shoes would be difficult to fill, and as a friend, Bhaga was irreplaceable. He could certainly survive without a syce, but having Bhaga reliably by his side made his life so much easier. He would attempt to find someone to take his place as soon as practical—which may not be until after he found and put down the man-eater. He would put out word among his British friends, perhaps ask the prince once he reached Rawa.

He studied Bhaga. The man's face glowed. "I hope your pleasure extends from the bliss of your connubial state rather than seeing the last of me," Nate said dryly.

"Very much so. I am among the happiest of men with my new wife, thanks to you. Yet, at the very same time, I am most devastated to be leaving your service."

Nate barked out a laugh at the contradiction. He couldn't begin to express how much he would miss this man, who had become so much more than a servant to him despite the social gulf that separated them. Rising, he clasped Bhaga's hand in both of his, aware that his reticence to share his true feelings hampered him now, as always. "I wish you all the best," he said with sincerity. He had the irrefutable sense that, with the departure of his closest friend on this earth, his life would change forever.

Pauline's steps slowed as she entered the street outside the hotel. Finally alone, in the deep shadows cast by a cluster of deodar trees, the reality of her encounter with the White Tiger struck her and her knees turned liquid. Collapsing against a tree trunk, she dragged in a steadying breath.

"What nonsense," she murmured, annoyed by how winded she sounded. Her voice wasn't the only evidence of their shockingly intimate encounter. Her lips still burned with the heat of the White Tiger's potent touch. He'd kissed her, in one blazing moment bringing forth a surge of passion she had hardly dreamed she could feel.

Until now, she hadn't understood the confusion of feminine feelings that would catch her when she least expected it.

Oh, she had kissed other men—or rather, boys. But Michael O'Shaunessy's tentative, careful kiss had felt nothing like *his*. When the butcher's son had climbed the trellis into her room, they'd barely touched lips before the upstairs maid discovered them. She was only experimenting. She never would have allowed the boy to touch any other part of her. Yet all hell had broken loose, as Pauline had known it would if she was discovered. Still, she'd taken the risk, danced close to the fire despite the threat of being burned.

Just like tonight.

Her parents' warnings echoed in her head. "Once you start down that carnal path, you can never go back," her father had told her, his face pale. "You'll be lost to us, a disgrace to your family and yourself."

"No daughter of mine will be known as a trollop," her mother had cried, her cheeks splotchy and red from tears and anger. "As I live and breathe, I will not allow you to bring ruin upon our heads!"

Still, she risked everything, to keep from giving in and becoming someone she wasn't. Deep inside Pauline lurked desires she didn't begin to understand, an untamed beast that, if given its head, would most assuredly drag her to ruin.

What will become of me? She wondered, gazing at the stars above. She would surely destroy her family's reputation if she continued on the path she seemed determined to take. *Why do I have such fearful, dangerous desires inside me?* And how could a man like the White Tiger tap into them so easily?

You're a poor excuse for a Carrington, and you know it, she scolded herself. She seemed destined to hurt her family, destined to make the worst choices imaginable. Her family didn't think she realized how much trouble her wayward nature could cause them all.

Oh, she was well aware. She longed to play with fire. When the fire dared to share its heat, she hadn't backed away. Instead, she'd embraced it.

She was well on the road to ruin, and powerless to resist its siren call.

Panic began to engulf her. She would fall and drag her family down with her. It was only a matter of time. *I can't remain here, playing the part of the sweet lady, not when I'm anything but. They don't need me cluttering up their lives and threatening their social standing.*

She would have to leave. If she could figure out a way, she would depart tomorrow, with Mr. Savidge. But how? She knew she could never convince him to take her along. After he hired porters, he would be gone, traveling alone except for a few servants.

Then an idea occurred to her. Preposterous as the thought was, she nurtured it, turned it into the beginnings of a plan. Perhaps she could manage it.

But only if she hurried.

Pauline swiped the shoe black across her face and stepped back from the bureau to examine her reflection in the mirror. No, too dark by far. Searching among Lily's enormous collection of face powders and rouges, she selected a buff-colored powder. After a little experimentation, she realized she could create a nice mocha color by blending the powder into the shoe black.

Somewhat nasty stuff, but it did the trick. In a few minutes, she had darkened her skin significantly. She wondered briefly whether the color would permanently stain her complexion, then shrugged. If her plan worked, the potential benefits far out-weighed any damage to her so-called beauty.

Thank goodness she had found a solution to the trickiest problem. She didn't have much time. The sun had already broken over the eastern hills. Lily and Alex had already gone down to the mall to see off the White Tiger on his latest adventure, along with half the hill station. Pauline had begged off, claiming to be ill. No doubt Lily thought she was still angry with the man for buying a woman. She still *was* angry, she reminded herself. But not because he'd bought a woman.

Because he kissed you.

"No, that's not it at all," she told her reflection as she wrapped a plain cotton turban around her chest, flattening her breasts. Before securing the long cloth, she shoved her face paint, silver-backed hairbrush, and a few other personal items into a silk purse and tied it to the wrap so that it would hang hidden under the tunic at her waist. Then she slipped on the ankle-length sheath that would hide her figure from the probing eyes of men like Nate Savidge.

Because he refuses to believe I'm capable—that's why I'm angry with him.

After tying up her hair, she grasped a second blue cloth and began wrapping it in the traditional tur-ban style worn by Sikhs who lived in the area. Lily's house servant had shown her how to manage the long cloth a few days ago, as a lark.

Pauline's plan was simple. After last night's tu-multuous encounter, her plan provided the added benefit of putting distance between her and the ex-pedition's leader. Once Mr. Savidge believed her to be a man, he would have no desire whatsoever to pull her into another lusty embrace. She would be completely safe from his potent attentions.

She gave her reflection a last once-over. Yes, it just might work. If she hadn't been able to make a worthy disguise, she would never have attempted such an outrageous deception. The image staring back at her could belong to one of a thousand native fellows found in the bazaars and hills of India.

Relief mingled with excitement in her chest. This was going to work after all. No one would ever suspect the truth. No one would ever imagine that a white woman would disguise herself like this. Barring some unforeseen circumstance, she would never be discovered. Her femininity had been banished.

But her disappearance couldn't be hidden as easily. A twinge of guilt caused her smile to fade. She hated the thought that Lily might waste even a moment worrying about her. Certainly, her absence might cause concern at first, but Lily would be much better in the long run without her disagreeable sister muddying up the works.

Opening her desk, Pauline slid out the note she'd carefully composed the night before and propped it on Lily's bureau. The note asked her sister not to worry about her, and to forgive all of her mistakes.

She secured her quiver of arrows across her back and slid her bow over her arm. With a single backward glance at her reflection, she raced from Lily and Alex's bedroom and down the hall, startling the house servant, who shrieked and cried an alarm over the strange man in the house.

The servant's reaction gave Pauline fresh resolve.

Her disguise was convincing. That was exactly what she needed to know.

As soon as Pauline reached the mall, she spotted the crowd in front of the Central Hotel. More than thirty people had gathered to see the White Tiger off, Anglos and Indians alike. A knot of native men, in garb similar to hers, crowded close to the steps of the hotel veranda, gossiping among themselves.

On the veranda stood Mr. Savidge, his feet planted shoulder-width apart, hands on hips, like a king surveying his land. A hotel clerk under the watchful eye of his servant Bhaga carried out two well-worn satchels. He placed them at the base of the stairs beside a pile of supplies—tins of food with "BRITISH ARMY" stamped on the side, coils of rope, and canvas tents, probably delivered by other porters from the general store.

Pauline's stomach clenched. This was real, not a schoolgirl's fantasy of adventure. This man was about to depart on a journey into the jungles of the central provinces in search of a man-eating tiger.

And, if her courage didn't flag, she might be lucky enough to accompany him without his ever knowing it. He had said he needed to hire porters. She was strong; she could easily fill such a role—if she could convince him to hire her. She'd be in the thick of the action, carrying his supplies, cleaning his guns, tracking the beast . . . and no one would ever know that a brash American girl had taken part.

Approaching the back of the crowd, she spotted familiar faces in the gathering, including her dance

partner Colonel Samuels, and beside him, Lily and
Alex. Instinctively she ducked her head, hoping Lily
wouldn't look her way, wouldn't see past her disguise.

She squeezed through the crowd to join the gathering of native men. Nate was speaking to them in
fluent Punjabi. He gestured to a fellow who then
moved toward the stack of supplies to join two others waiting there. So far, three men had been chosen
to serve him as porters. She had no idea how many
he would select, but at least she wasn't too late. Yet
what would possibly make him notice her among all
these men, much less choose to hire her? She shifted
her feet, anxious to think of something to make certain he saw her and her enthusiasm for the job.
Then a man beside her spoke.

His words were completely incomprehensible to
Pauline. In her month in India, she'd picked up only
a smattering of Punjabi, the most commonly spoken
local language.

In that instant, the full import of what she was
attempting slammed down on her. She might look
the part, but how could she possibly act it? She
knew scarcely two words of Punjabi! She smiled at
the man and looked away, hoping to put him off,
but he persisted, saying something else in his quick,
musical tongue. He was missing his two front teeth,
and his weathered face reminded her of a monkey's.

Pauline smiled again, this time adding a nod, as
if in agreement with whatever he said. Apparently,
she shouldn't have agreed. The man glared at her
and turned away in a huff.

What had she done? What was she doing here, attempting such an outrageous stunt? Her thoughts darted frantically through a number of scenarios, which, in her excitement over coming up with a plan, she'd forgotten to consider. If her deception actually worked, if Mr. Savidge hired her as a porter, how could she possibly fool him without giving herself away? How could she live such a ruse twenty-four hours a day, every day, for days on end?

And there were more practical considerations she'd forgotten about, until now. How could she keep her face paint a secret? What if it smeared? Worse, how would she bathe with it on? Or, for that matter, with it off? And what about the nights? Would she be forced to bed down beside strange men?

Mad. She was as mad as a hatter. The impossibility of her plan jolted sense into her and she became frantic. She had to leave, *now*, before anyone realized what she'd attempted. "Excuse me," she muttered in English, and began forcing her way through the crowd.

"Hold on there." The loud, commanding voice caused her to freeze. Savidge. No, he couldn't mean her. She began once more to push through the crowd.

His voice, once more speaking English, stopped her progress. "You, there, with the bow. Are you any good with it?"

Everyone's eyes turned to her, Anglo and Indian alike. Pauline froze. Though her back was to the hotel entrance, she knew Nate Savidge was staring right at her. She'd lost her chance. It was too late to back out now.

Slowly she turned around and faced him.

SIX

Nate barely managed to contain his shock. That a woman would go to such outrageous lengths to escape the comfortable life she'd been born to completely floored him.

He'd been scanning the crowd with only moderate interest. Being a porter required little more than a strong back and a willingness to work. He had hardly paid attention when a new fellow arrived, a lanky man with a slight figure.

Then he focused on his face.

A shaft of surprise had cut through him, one so strong it nearly floored him. Miss Carrington? The well-bred heiress? By God in heaven, she was done up like a Punjabi! She actually wanted him to hire her as a porter! He knew she was different; he knew she was determined. But to go to such lengths to fulfill her dreams of adventure . . .

Mad. She was, quite simply, as mad as a hatter.

No face paint could disguise those features, that long, proud nose, that full mouth he'd so recently kissed.

As she stood unsteadily before him in her turban and face paint, her dark eyes wide with concern, he realized with unaccountably deep satisfaction that the shoe was on the other foot. The woman was now dancing to his tune, waiting for his reaction to learn if her ploy had fooled him. Fool him? Not possible. Not after he'd spent the better part of the night with her visage in his mind. Not after tasting those lips, now frowning with concern.

A look of concern flitted across her face. She had to be worried that he would recognize her and call her out, humiliating her in front of her social set. Nate decided on a more satisfying tactic.

"Well, boy? I asked you a question," he said in his gruffest, most commanding voice. "Do you know how to shoot that thing, or do you merely carry it to make yourself look manly?"

Miss Carrington flinched, but only momentarily. She straightened her shoulders and looked him right in the eye. "I am an excellent shot, sir," she said with a surprisingly good imitation of a Punjabi accent.

"You're rather scrawny. You don't look strong enough to be of much use. Why should I trust you as one of my porters?"

Determination flashed in her eyes. Stepping forward, she reached down and lifted the satchel at his feet, then hoisted it over her shoulder with one hand. Crossing to the pile of supplies at the foot of the steps, she tossed it on top. She turned to face him, a triumphant look in her amber eyes.

Nate fought the urge to burst out laughing at her show of defiance. God, it was fun to play with the girl. He couldn't help being impressed by her determination. To go to such lengths to be part of his hunt . . . "Very well. You're hired."

At his pronouncement, Miss Carrington grinned,

her face lighting up despite the dark paint, her joy so strong, Nate felt as if the sun had come out from behind the clouds.

She hurried over to help the other three bearers transfer the foodstuffs he'd purchased to carrying packs.

Nate stared after her, trying his damnedest to figure out what had possessed him. *You're hired?* Had he actually said that? The words had been uttered in a rare burst of insanity; that was the only explanation. The prospect of toying with her—even better, of having her completely in his power—had been so irresistible . . .

"Sahib, are you well?" Bhaga asked, his eyes far too perceptive.

"Of course I'm well," Nate snapped. "Don't coddle me, damn it. Go on, you have a job to finish before we part."

Bhaga tried to hide a smile as he turned away to oversee the bearers.

As Nate stared at Miss Carrington, now industriously working beside the other porters, the reality of his situation began to settle in. He couldn't allow this to continue. He had no interest in borrowing trouble, no interest in dragging Miss Carrington along on a potentially dangerous journey. Of course, he couldn't leave Simla with her.

Where was her sister? Scanning the crowd of Europeans watching the activity, he spotted the tall, dapper form of Alexander Drake, then his perfectly turned-out wife standing beside him. He leaped off the steps of the hotel and moved through the crowd toward them. The crowd parted as he passed.

"Drake," he said to Alex. "With all due respect, I need to borrow your wife." Grasping Lily's elbow, he pulled her out of the crowd and toward a side alley, seeking privacy.

"Mrs. Drake, I have a problem that only you can solve."

The lady gazed up at him with a curious expression on her perfect features. She remained composed despite his odd request. "What is it, Mr. Savidge?"

"It's your sister. She's . . ."

Mention of Pauline brought a crease to her forehead. "She's what?"

"She's determined to come with me. So determined, she's posing as a Punjabi right now. She's over there." He pointed toward his men. "The slender one."

Mrs. Drake's eyes followed his finger. "Oh, my goodness. That's Pauline? That's Pauline!" A laugh burst from her. "What a creative plan. Well, it didn't work, did it?" Her gaze swung back to him. "You caught her out immediately. I didn't realize you knew her well enough to recognize her under that disguise."

He wasn't about to reveal just how familiar they'd been with each other. "Yeah, well, the point is, I can't take her with me."

"I see . . ."

"I mean, someone has to break it to her. It's going to hurt her, no doubt, but—"

"Can't you?"

"Break it to her?"

"No. Take her with you."

"What?" Her suggestion stunned Nate. To allow her

sister to spend time in his company unchaperoned! These Carrington women were strange indeed, or perhaps it was because they were American.

Mrs. Drake continued, "Pauline believes her plan worked. Would it hurt so much for you to take her along, just for a few days?"

"Take her along," he repeated, still finding it hard to believe her well-bred sister would suggest such a thing.

Mrs. Drake shrugged. "Let her work as a porter. When you reach a town with a rail line, put her on the train and send her back here."

"Why? Why would you even consider something like that?"

She sighed heavily. "It's simple, Mr. Savidge. I've tried my best to interest her in life here in India, but I've failed."

"Life in *your* India," he said pointedly. Though he and this delicate lady were both Anglos, his own experiences in his birth land could hardly be compared with hers.

"Life in my India," she conceded. "And by rights, Pauline's. My sister is still young and lacking maturity. I fear her unfulfilled longings may overpower her common sense and lead her into awful trouble."

Nate tried not to imagine the nature of an untried girl's "unfulfilled longings." Certainly, her sister didn't have to spell out the sort of trouble a young lady could get herself into. "I don't see what this has to do with me."

"If Pauline feels she's actually gotten away with her deception, at least for a while, it will satisfy this wild need she has to risk her neck. I trust you to keep her safe, despite herself. And when she returns home, she'll have experienced the adventure she craves."

"And, you hope, be ready to settle down and marry one of the young society blokes."

"Exactly." Stepping closer, she laid her hand on his arm. Her familiar touch startled him, but he found himself falling under her persuasive spell. "Mr. Savidge, I know it sounds mad, but you don't know what we've been through with Pauline. My mother was at the end of her rope with concern for her. And I'm starting to feel the same way. Pauline came to visit me as a last resort. I thought in India she might find whatever she's so desperately looking for." Glancing around to be sure they were alone, she lowered her voice. "Ever since she left school a year ago, she's been no end of trouble—sneaking out in the middle of the night, smoking, even stealing liquor from Father's study. One night she was caught with a young man in her room."

Indeed? Just how experienced was this girl? This probably explained why he had failed to shock her with his kiss. "Were they . . . up to something?"

"Not yet, no, thank goodness. But the damage to her reputation if anyone outside the family had heard of it . . ." She gave a delicate shudder.

"Right."

"If she were a boy . . ."

"She'd be considered normal," he finished for her. "Or at least he could be sent to enlist in the army to learn a little discipline."

Lily nodded. "You do understand. Pauline has a rebellious nature. She balks at every effort to turn her into a lady, to help her take her proper place in society. She doesn't mean to hurt us, but she can't seem to rid herself of this notion that she needs to live an adventurous life, as unconventional as that may be. But she has a picture-book idea of adventure, with no understanding of the risks and hardships. If you could show her the reality of your life, the dangers inherent in any adventure . . ."

This insight into Miss Carrington intrigued Nate. Didn't most adventurers have that longing to live life outside the norm? He certainly did. Tasting adventure had only made him long for more. "So, you think she'll come to her senses then?"

"I pray she will."

"And I'm to be her nanny?"

"Just treat her like your other bearers. Don't go any easier on her. But of course, I expect you to keep her as safe as possible."

"While knocking sense into her."

"Exactly."

By God, this might be fun. Not that he'd ever agree to the additional burden of hauling the girl around with him. Still, he couldn't help feeling a sense of excitement at the prospect of teaching her a few of life's harsher lessons. Of teaching her a good deal more, even, about the dangers of men like him. The danger of arousing his passions . . .

Mrs. Drake's next words caused him to flush inwardly with embarrassment at the direction his thoughts had taken. "I know I needn't say it, but I'm confident you'll behave as a gentleman around her."

"No, you needn't say it," he said more harshly than he intended. Despite how the chit set fire to his baser instincts, he had no intention of laying a hand on her. She was far too much trouble. Giving in to his animal drives would only compound that.

Mrs. Drake continued, "If I doubted for a minute that you were trustworthy, I would never even propose—"

"You actually expect I'd be willing to put up with a spoiled female just to do you a favor?"

"Of course not, Mr. Savidge. I'll pay you whatever you want."

"You socialites," he mocked. "Think you can buy anything with money. You couldn't pay me enough for all the trouble I'm sure she'll cause."

She ignored his protest. "How does one thousand pounds sound to you?"

One thousand pounds? Nate tried his damnedest not to allow his shock to show. That sum made the government bounty on the tiger look like small change.

He thumbed up the brim of his pith helmet. "I'm not sure about—"

"Very well. Two thousand."

Two thousand? *Don't be a fool, Savidge,* an inner voice whispered. *You need the money.*

Yeah, but if anything happens to her, your neck will be on the line.

Nevertheless, he heard himself saying, "Okay, ma'am. Two thousand it is." He extended his hand and Lily shook it, with as much confidence as any businessman.

She began to turn away, but he called her back. "Wait, ma'am. How do I get rid of—rather, how do I return her to you? I'm not returning to Simla."

She cocked her head, a thoughtful look on her

lovely face. "Where are you headed, after you finish your task for the prince?"

"I have no idea. I can send her back on the train, but I can't escort her all the way back here."

"Are you going near Agra? I have friends who can meet her there. In case she balks, that is. Which she's bound to do."

"I wouldn't be too sure of that." He smiled. "I have a feeling she'll be more than ready to come home." Once he was through with her, she would be begging to return to the comfortable circle of her wealthy family.

SEVEN

Pauline had never been so tired in her life. She considered herself physically fit—goodness, the matrons were always harping on her "athleticism" as if it were something bad. But despite that, nothing had prepared her for hour upon hour of walking down a steep, winding track with a heavy pack on her back.

At least it was downhill. Pauline shrugged the pack higher, trying to relieve the pressure on her shoulder blades. She longed to ask for a break but wouldn't dare take the risk that she would appear weaker than the other three men—or Mr. Savidge, who was striding along in the lead with an even heavier pack.

To think four men had carried her up this steep hill! And she'd taken their efforts for granted. She recalled how they'd demanded higher payment, and how the commissioner had refused. If it were up to her, she would give them all a generous bonus.

The sun had almost set by the time their group, with Pauline, perspiration-soaked, entered Kalka. Rather than heading to the railroad station, Nate paused outside a small hotel. The bearers relieved themselves of their packs and gathered around him, their hands extended. Saying *"Bhala hove,"* the Punjabi words for "thank you," Savidge fished out some rupees and gave them to each of the men.

Pauline watched the exchange, dread welling up in her stomach. This was the extent of her adventure? He had hired porters only to take him from Simla to Kalka? Of course. Why would he take these local men miles from their home when he could easily hire porters once he reached his destination? How foolish she had been to assume they would accompany him on the tiger hunt! To assume *she* would accompany him. Now she would be stranded alone, here in Kalka, until she somehow managed to make her way back up the mountain, her tail between her legs, her adventure over before it began.

Hesitantly she extended her hand, determined not to reveal her identity, desperate to maintain the pretense despite how foolish it had made her appear.

The other three porters took their pay and departed, chattering among themselves in their colorful language.

Mr. Savidge stared at her and her outstretched hand but made no move to place any coins in her palm. Pauline shifted her feet.

"Well, boy, I take it you speak English."

"Yes, sahib."

"And you're interested in using that bow and arrow on game."

"Yes, sahib." Why was he prolonging her torture? Why didn't he simply pay her off as he had the others?

"I'm in need of a syce, a manservant."

"You are?" Hope bloomed in her chest, along with a healthy dose of trepidation. As one of a group of bearers, she had been invisible. As a personal manservant . . . Mother would die! Yet her adventure would continue.

"Bhaga got it in his head he likes his wife's company, which leaves me without a syce." He clapped her on her back so hard, Pauline nearly lost her balance. "What do you say? Want the job?"

"I—yes, sahib," she said, suddenly out of breath.

"Excellent. Let's get a room, then. The train leaves at eight in the morning."

A room? A hotel room? A single hotel room? Pauline found it impossible to move her leg. She watched Mr. Savidge stride up the steps, his powerful legs and broad back taunting her with their sheer maleness.

She'd done it again. She'd jumped before looking, and now she was not only in his employ but in the role of his personal servant. Servant to a *man*. A strong, physical being she scarcely understood. She would be expected to cater to his every whim. She, a well-bred female inexperienced in the ways of the world and of men. But how she wanted to learn!

You can do it, Pauline. You can do it.

"Hey! Boy!" he called from the top of the steps. "What is your name, anyway?"

"It's . . . I am known as . . . Manu," she blurted out the first male name she could think of, the name of Lily's head cook.

"*Ma*nu," he said, stressing the first syllable. Why did he keep smiling at her as if something was funny? Was he onto her? "You can't be more than—what? Sixteen years? You haven't any beard." He tapped her cheek with his finger.

Pauline jerked back, worried that he would smear her face paint—and notice her secret thrill at his touch. His hand came away clean, thank goodness. "I have no beard yet, sahib, but I am stronger than I appear. And I work hard. For my family. We are poor, sahib."

He arched a single eyebrow, and humor continued to dance in his eyes. "Poor?"

Pauline wondered why he found her statement so hard to believe. Many Indians suffered from poverty. "Very poor. Terribly poor."

"Well, Manu, you poor little thing, move your scrawny legs. Put all my bags in our room. Then I'll want dinner served, and a bath before I retire. So get to it."

"Yes, sahib," she muttered with a trace of sarcasm, unable to disguise her annoyance at his high-handed attitude.

He seemed oblivious, merely turned and headed into the lobby and toward the registration desk. Lifting two of the heavy packs, she followed him inside.

The door clicked softly behind Nate, leaving him alone with his new servant in a room only eight feet square. She stood hesitantly on the other side of the room, as far away from him as possible, her eyes darting nervously about. No doubt she'd never been in such a shabby hotel.

Poor! He'd nearly choked at her lie. As a pampered heiress with servants to tend to her every whim, she had no concept of what it meant to be poor, to hunt game to feed a family, to put in a hard day's backbreaking labor.

Today had been merely a stroll. He'd barely begun to knock sense into her, to exhaust her, to teach her a lesson she would never forget. Over the next few days, he would punish her until she screamed for mercy and ran back to her comfortable life.

The chit had been born under a lucky star, yet she was foolish enough to turn her back on her lot. Nate firmly believed that everyone belonged where God had put them. Miss Carrington—*Manu*—was no exception. Raised in the lap of luxury, that's exactly where she belonged. She had no idea how to serve anyone, except as a pretty ornament. No idea how to make herself useful. No idea how to meet his needs.

A truth she was about to learn.

"Don't just stand there," he snapped, causing her to start. "Get fresh water so I can wash up. My toiletries—they're somewhere in my pack."

She turned first toward the ewer and basin on the bureau, then spun around toward his stack of bags. Deciding to get water first, she picked up the ewer and began heading out the door.

Nate decide to confuse her even further. "Where do you think you're going? Take off my boots." He plopped down on the bed and stuck out his feet.

She set the ewer back on the bureau so hard it threatened to crack. Without looking at his face, she knelt before him and carefully took one of his feet in her hands, as if afraid it might bite her.

"Hurry up, or we'll be here all night," he said. "My feet are sore from the hike."

She lifted her face to his, her amber eyes wide. "Yours, too? I thought only mine . . ."

Despite his determination to be tough on her, he couldn't help feeling a pang of sympathy. Her tender, delicate body must be suffering right now. He studied her, noticing the fatigue reflected in her face, the slowness of her movements. Contrary to his every intention, the pang of sympathy grew into a desire to comfort her. "The hike took a bit out of you, eh? Feet hurting?" He patted the bed beside him. "Take a seat and let me see."

Instantly, she reverted to her servant demeanor. "No, sahib, it would not be—"

"I won't bloody well bite you."

"No, sahib, but—"

"Do as I say," he snapped.

Bowing her head, she gingerly settled beside him. The mattress sagged, pressing her hip against his. Reaching down, he lifted her foot into his lap, easily scooting her around so she was facing him. She was wearing a pair of locally made *chaplies,* sandals which would have been fine for a household servant. For the bush, however, they were ridiculously inadequate. She'd worn a hole nearly clean through the sole under the ball of her right foot.

"If you plan to work, you must learn to wear proper attire," he muttered, trying to sound distant and authoritative despite cradling her graceful foot between his palms. He unlaced the sandal and tossed it to the floor, then stared at her foot in shock. Red welts had risen along her ankles and soles. At the back of her ankle, the sandal strap had rubbed the skin nearly raw. "By God, look what you've done to yourself! You must have been in agony all day."

"No, sahib. Only . . ."

"Well?"

"Only a few hours."

She was speaking so softly, he had to strain to hear. "How many hours?" he demanded.

"Five or so."

Five hours? Good God. His mind flashed back to their meeting on the balcony of the Club. That evening, he'd tried to tend to her scratched hands, but she had resisted. Why did this girl, raised in the lap of privilege, allow herself to become so beat up without a word of complaint? What madness drove her to such lengths?

And why did her pain bother him? He detested high-born females with a passion, with their expert flirting and shallow greed, and the ease with which they exploited gullible men. But this one—perhaps she truly was different, as she claimed. All those hours in agony, footstep after footstep, and not one word of protest. Amazing. He ran his thumb across a blister and she sucked in a breath.

"Please, I'm fine. Really, I am." She tried to jerk her foot away, but he kept hold of it.

He stroked her foot, marveling at the softness of her skin, at its delicate strength. "You're hardly fine," he said gruffly. "Bloody little fool. You should have worn proper boots. And you should have said something, let me know you were in agony."

"What good would that have done, sahib? I had a job to do."

"The brave little soldier, are you? It's a blessing

we're taking the train tomorrow. You can give your feet a proper rest. You're no good to me crippled."

"I'm hardly crippled. Besides, you ought not to worry about me," she said primly. "As your syce, I mean. If you waste your time worrying, I will add to your burdens rather than help to carry them."

She was right, but he didn't want to discuss the facts, couldn't bring himself to treat her as he would a male servant. Her heavy face paint could not hide her features, appearing golden tan under the gas lantern on the bureau. He was captivated by the angles of her face, and he could not forget kissing those tender lips. He wanted the intimacy to continue, to keep her here, with his foot in his lap. "You speak English remarkably well."

"I—I like to practice when I can."

She looked so vulnerable just then, his heart squeezed in his chest. Without conscious thought, he reached out to her, his fingers stroking the edge of her jaw.

She flinched and he yanked his hand back. So quickly he had forgotten their roles! He had nearly cupped her chin in his hand to draw her closer, perhaps even to kiss her. She would either figure out that he was onto her, or she'd think he preferred the company of boys! He had to keep his head, treat her like his servant, or the charade would be ruined. He would have to send her back to her sister.

And he wasn't nearly through with her yet. Sure, she'd found this first day difficult. But it was only a single day. Her sore feet were only the first lesson.

"Very well," he said tightly, releasing her foot. "We'll keep speaking English, then." No reason to make things harder on the girl, after all, by pretending she could speak Punjabi or Hindi. Besides, he enjoyed the strange challenge of talking to her, of trying to figure out what made her tick.

Never in a thousand years had he pictured this situation. His life had been gritty, hard, and dangerous. To find himself in the situation of being tended to by the very type of woman he detested most—either this was heavenly justice at work, or hell's joke.

Don't think of her as an heiress, or a woman, he counseled himself. *Think of her as a boy, or you'll never survive this.*

A lady manservant. Damned ridiculous situation, it was. All the way into Kalka, Nate had puzzled over what to do with his unwelcome burden. Since Bhaga had left his employ, he'd realized the only logical answer was to hire her in his place, filling the gap until he could find a suitable replacement. What better way to keep a close eye on her?

Which was all well and good. Until now, when the practical problems loomed before him, such as sleeping arrangements. She would have to share his living quarters, as Bhaga had. Which meant sharing the same hotel room.

If her sister had realized this, she never would have agreed, he reflected. Then again, Mrs. Drake assumed he was a gentleman, a man who would never take advantage of the situation. *And you sure as hell won't,* he reminded himself.

But he couldn't help the direction his thoughts took as he watched her kneel before him and unlace his boots with her long, graceful fingers. To have such a lovely young lady at his beck and call surely didn't play to his better nature. Even this simple task challenged him. He was aware of her touch through the scarred leather. When she slid off his boot, a jolt of awareness sizzled up his leg.

She wrinkled her nose. His foot had to smell like the dickens. His male pride took over and he yanked his foot from her grasp. He could peel off his own sock, thank you very much. "Quit dawdling and find my soap and towel," he barked out. "You move as slowly as a water ox."

"I have no idea where you keep your things. I'm trying to learn," she said in frustration, sounding more like a put-out female than a properly obsequious servant. "How could I possibly be expected to—"

"So, you're a slow learner, then," he said, simply because he knew it would annoy her. Sure enough, her eyes narrowed, her expression just this side of a scowl under her brown face paint. The paint had streaked from her perspiration, but he'd hardly given her a chance to primp in a mirror. He would have to give her an opportunity to take care of her female business sometime before bedtime.

When she'd be sleeping right beside him, all warm curves and feminine heat—

Bloody hell.

"Try the brown leather satchel," he said finally, ready to have this awkward encounter reach its conclusion. After a good night's sleep, he'd be able to put this strange situation in perspective. He'd get used to thinking of her as his servant.

Or die trying.

* * *

Don't stare. Act like a man. You've seen men before. You are a man. A man. With the same sleek shape. The same . . . parts.

It wasn't working. Despite trying to think like a man, Pauline could not will her eyes from Nate Savidge's bare torso. He stood before the bureau in nothing but his trousers, splashing water on his face, oblivious that he was sharing his room with a lady.

No, not a lady. A lusty young woman who longed to experiment with her awakening femininity.

As he leaned over the washbasin, Pauline's gaze followed the play of finely carved muscles along his back, sides, and shoulders. Even his stomach showed defined muscles in gentle ridges. His body was huge, like a slab of granite. He filled the room. Everywhere she turned, he was there. She'd struggled through fixing them a cold dinner from provisions in their packs, struggled through washing out his shirt. At no time could she escape his alert gaze, which seemed to follow her every move.

Until now, when the tables had turned, and she could finally study him with impunity.

He froze, his hands halfway to his face. Pauline lifted her gaze to find him looking into the mirror— and straight at her. She jerked away and wrapped her arms around her torso, glad that her face paint would hide her blush.

"Not used to white men?" he asked, arching a thick, blond brow. "Or do you find something interesting in my scarred hide? Maybe you wish you had muscles like mine?"

Pauline couldn't decide whether to slap him or melt into the floor. Such blatant arrogance! The fact she had been staring at his body didn't excuse his rudeness. And here she was, forced to cater to his every need, his every whim. "White men are all the same to me," she said, knowing she sounded belligerent. "Most of them think far too much of themselves."

He barked out a laugh. Turning to face her, he clapped her hard on the shoulder, nearly knocking her down. "Don't worry, Manu. Someday you'll finish growing into a man. If you work hard serving your masters, you may even develop a decent build."

He turned back around. Pauline glared daggers into his back.

Pauline lay awake on the bedroll on the hard wooden floor, listening for the man in the bed beside her to fall into a deep, even breathing that might indicate sleep. She had been waiting for hours.

Her situation was so precarious, so dangerous, it frightened even her. Less than a full day had passed, and already she had experienced more adventure than in her entire previous life. What tomorrow would bring, she could only guess.

Before they had retired, she had been allowed to go alone to the WC at the end of the hall. As crude as the facilities were, she had been thankful for the chance to be alone.

In all other ways, she felt tied to Mr. Savidge at the waist. Whatever he wanted, she was compelled to do. It was a strange feeling. Except for obeying her teachers and parents—which she only did on occasion—she had given orders, not taken them. She'd taken her servants for granted for her entire life. Somehow, she sensed Mr. Savidge enjoyed her distress.

Perhaps he was merely a cruel man, though she'd seen no sign of true cruelty in their previous awkward—and heated—encounters. He was an enigma.

Moonlight fell through the open window across his bed, highlighting his bare back. At least he'd waited until she put out the light to remove his trousers and slide under the sheet. But the sheet had dropped to his waist, leaving his half-naked body visible to her.

To pass the time, she stared at him, amazed that any man could be so perfect. Her gaze played up and down his sculpted arms and back, the corded muscles well-shaped even at rest.

Her body began to feel warm all over, so she forced herself to look away. She wondered if she would burn in hell for being alone in a room with a nearly naked man.

After a while, Savidge began to breathe deeply, evenly. He was finally, blessedly asleep.

Folding back her blanket, she slid out of the bedroll and stealthily approached the bureau. She grabbed a towel, a bar of brown soap, and the ewer of water, then silently slipped out of the room.

Pauline's skin felt stretched and uncomfortable under the heavy face paint, but her plan depended on never being seen without it. In the privacy of the pine water closet, she poured water in a basin and washed her face, scrubbing away the smeared makeup, caked dirt, and perspiration that had clung to her like a second skin. She removed her tunic and hung it on a hook behind the door. Sighing in relief, she unwrapped the cloth binding her breasts and ran her hands under and around them, massaging her aching skin. How good it felt to be free!

She washed up as well as she could under the circumstances. She hadn't dared try this in the room. Mr. Savidge would probably begin to think she never washed, but she could see no way around it. She would have to stay up late and rise before him to take care of her personal needs and restore her face paint.

Her hair—how was she going to wash her hair? She had actually crawled into her bedroll with her turban on, drawing a curious comment from Mr. Savidge. She shot off some excuse about her tribe's traditions. What else was she to do but leave her turban in place?

Carefully, she unwrapped the long cloth and shook out her hair. A deep, satisfied sigh rose up from her chest as she brushed out the locks with her fingers. She debated leaving her hair free. Since Savidge was asleep, she could get away with it until morning. Unless he awoke and saw her inexplicable light-brown hair. Unfortunately, to be safe she would have to tie it back under the turban. Gathering her hair atop her head, she secured it with its silk ribbon and rewound the turban in place. Rewrapping her breasts, she pulled on her tunic, gathered her things, and exited the WC.

She hadn't taken two steps before running into a wall.

Not a wall. Savidge.

EIGHT

Standing face to face with Savidge in the dark hall, Pauline couldn't think of a thing to say.

To her dismay and secret fascination, she realized he wore nothing but a pair of loose undershorts. And she wasn't wearing her face paint. She prayed the dark would keep her secret hidden.

"I wondered where you'd got off to." He grasped her upper arms, bringing her within a few inches of his muscular chest.

Memory of being held in his arms, of being so ardently, unashamedly kissed, returned to her in a heady rush. How she longed to taste him once more! She imagined placing her palms on his chest and feeling his hot, bare skin, seeing again that hunger in his eyes. *Stop it, Pauline!*

Her self-control was so poor, she feared her passion would burst forth any moment and cause her to do something unthinkable. "What are you doing here?" she bit out in defense. She averted her face, staring at his bare feet so he wouldn't see how light her skin was.

"I was beginning to worry."

A dart of pure pleasure shot through her. He was concerned about her.

No, not her. Manu. If she remained this close to him here in the dark, he might be able to read her secret desires. She squirmed out of his grasp. "Excuse me, sahib. I am supposed to take care of *you*, not the other way around. Or did you think I was already leaving your employ? You are not that difficult a taskmaster."

He settled his hands on his hips, his undershorts a slash of white in the darkness, and peered at her. "I'm not?"

"Of course not. You are as . . . as nothing. As the wind—yes, the wind. And I am strong, like . . . like a tree." She couldn't tell whether he was grimacing or smiling at her attempt to spout Eastern wisdom, as so many of Lily's servants did.

"A sapling, maybe. All twigs and soft branches and—sap."

She could hear the laughter in his voice but bit down her retort. He obviously enjoyed torturing her with his teasing. What did he expect her to do, engage in witty repartee? She was supposed to be an Indian youth, not a lady trained in the fine art of conversation. "I will return to my bed now. Good night, sahib." With as much aplomb as she could muster, she strode down the hall to their room.

Entering the room, she slid into her bedroll and threw the blankets over her head. She fought to catch her breath at how close she'd come to exposing herself. He had seen her without her face paint! Yet he hadn't caught on. If the hall hadn't been so dim . . . if she hadn't rewrapped her hair in the turban . . . Never again would she risk going without her face paint or her turban.

The floor creaked as Savidge crossed to his own bed and began climbing in. Under the suffocating wool, she could scarcely hear his movements over her heartbeat pounding in her ears.

Pauline shifted on the hard seat, trying to hide her discomfort from the man beside her. He kept watching her from the corners of his piercing blue eyes.

She had always scoffed at girls who acted like delicate flowers in need of pampering. Nevertheless, like it or not, she *had* been pampered. She and her family had always traveled in high style, with the finest accommodations and the best service. She'd occupied a first-class cabin on the steamer from London, then stayed overnight in a suite at the palatial Taj Mahal Hotel in Bombay. On the three-day train trip to Kalka, Lily and she had shared a sleeper car with padded seats.

For the past several hours, she and Mr. Savidge had been squeezed together on a single hardwood seat in second class. His broad shoulder pressed against hers, making the seat seem even smaller.

She brushed at the fine layer of coal dust spewed from the engine's stacks that now coated her tunic and pants. Closing the window beside her would help, but the cool breezes relieved the stifling air inside the car. She had never been so sticky and uncomfortable, even when wearing a corset with stays.

Children's cries echoed through the car, punctuating dozens of conversations in at least five languages and dialects. Curious, Pauline studied the other passengers, people from all walks of life. A native woman in a bright orange sari nursed an infant, her breast exposed for the world to see. No one seemed to notice. Two Sikhs shared a thin pipe that caused a blue-gray cloud to form above their heads. And the small, dark children—she couldn't resist looking at them, they were so adorable with their enormous black eyes.

This was the life of India, the life her family's good intentions had protected her from. If they could see her now, what would they think? Would they finally cast out their black sheep and wash their hands of her? After all, she'd spent the night with a man.

And Lily . . . Pauline prayed Lily would forgive her. She knew Lily would worry, but after a time, she would forget about her wayward sister. Wouldn't she?

She stared at her companion, so strong and mysterious. She had thrown her lot in with him, despite knowing almost nothing about him except his near-legendary reputation as a hunter. What was he like as a man? Her gaze traced the scar that ran from just under his left eye to his jaw. Some time in the past, some wild creature had lain his skin open, nearly blinding him. Was he as scarred on the inside, too?

She knew instinctively a man like Nate Savidge wouldn't give up his secrets easily. But she had never been shy about getting what she wanted. She formulated a properly submissive way to bring up the subject. "Sahib? I beg leave to ask a question."

He gave her a careful look, then nodded.

"The scar on your face. Was it from an encounter with a dangerous beast?"

He stiffened and his eyes flashed darkly. "That's one way of putting it."

"A tiger?"

He shook his head, then turned his attention to the window. He crossed his thick arms over his chest, hunched his shoulders, and lowered his worn pith helmet over his eyes. Pauline knew she wouldn't learn anything about his scar today. "Perhaps, then, we can pass the time with stories of your adventures," she suggested.

He studied her from the corner of his eye, a secret smile dancing on his lips. His hawklike gaze made her shift uncomfortably on the hard bench. "What makes you think I have any?"

"You are a great *shikari*, the White Tiger. You must have many stories. Tell me about your first man-eater."

Shrugging his shoulders, he said, "It was a leopard. I tracked it; I found it; I shot it."

"Sahib, if I may say so, I am quite certain you can do better."

He began to relate the story, but in the most basic terms. Pauline had to ask numerous questions to draw the details out of him. For a man as tough and worldly as he, she found his obvious reluctance to talk about himself endearing. Why, he was modest!

After a while, he began to lose himself in the tale, an absorbing account of his first encounter with a deadly creature that had developed a taste for human flesh. She became riveted by his account and understood why his stories had been so in demand at the Club. Unlike many men's braggadocio, his tales had the ring of truth. He described his mistakes as well as his triumphs, giving her the feeling she was right there beside him when he came face to face with the leopard after a month-long search and emerged victorious.

A month . . . Would she be gone from Simla that long? Would she ever return? What would happen to her in that time?

As hour after hour rolled by and the train chugged toward Satna, Pauline's excitement transformed to a fidgety boredom. The trip south to the central provinces seemed endless, despite the frequent stops that provided opportunities to stretch her legs. Their only side trip had been a rushed visit to the army store in the Delhi cantonment to buy her proper boots.

She hoped that the inaction strained Savidge as much as it did her, but if so, he refused to admit it. At the Agra station, she had wanted to take an hour or two and visit the Taj Mahal mausoleum, but he had shot down her suggestion, reminding her that they had a mission to complete.

As evening drew on, the other passengers began nodding off. Pauline couldn't. She shifted in her seat once more, bumping up against Nate.

"If you want to be a decent hunter, you need to learn patience and stop fidgeting," her companion said, his deep voice vibrating through her.

"Yes, sahib," she said with a sigh. She uttered that phrase a hundred times a day. She was already so sick of it, she wanted to scream. It wasn't like her to be patient or circumspect. How much longer could she keep up this pretense of servitude without doing or saying something rash?

Her stomach growled, drawing a curious gaze from her companion. "A little late for dinner, isn't it?"

"Excuse me, sahib," she said coolly. "I did not partake of dinner."

He arched his blond brow. "Why in hell not? I left food with you." Nate himself had gone to the dining car, alone. Indians weren't allowed there.

She opened her mouth, but couldn't begin to tell him how her stomach remained in tense knots. She was too worried about hiding her identity to think about food. That morning at the hotel, she'd risen early enough to make certain her face paint and costume were in place before he awakened. She would risk no more close calls, as she had last night.

Then, she'd been hard pressed to transport all of his gear to the train station without collapsing in an exhausted heap. Her muscles still screamed from the hike downhill and a night spent on the floor. Never had she imagined herself to be so weak. She was worse than the princess in the fairytale who could detect a pea under ten mattresses!

But the physical strain was nothing compared with the mental strain. Every moment in Mr. Savidge's company, she hoped she would grow more comfortable, be able to relax. Yet she couldn't. Any moment she could say the wrong thing and make a crucial mistake. If he learned how she'd duped him . . . She shuddered. How awful it would be to lose his esteem! His gentle teasing would end. He would look at her in disgust and fury, wash his hands of her entirely. Just thinking about it made her queasy.

Leaning over, he slid out a pack crammed into the narrow space under the seat before them. Untying the flap, he pulled out a mango and tossed it to her. She scrambled not to drop it.

"Learn to eat when I eat, sleep when I sleep, and

smoke when I smoke," he said slowly, as if talking to a child. Extracting a cigarette from a dented silver case, he slid it between his lips. Pauline tried not to look at his mouth, which had kissed hers only days ago. Striking a match, he set the flame to his smoke and inhaled until it caught.

"You are offering to share your smokes?" she asked in her false Punjabi accent.

Reaching into his pocket, he pulled out a second cigarette and held it out to her, his eyes sparkling with humor. Apparently, he thought her too young to have experience with cigarettes.

Pauline took the proffered cigarette, then snatched the cigarette from his mouth. "Hey!"

Ignoring his protest, she pressed the ends together until her cigarette lit, then returned his and took a defiant pull on hers.

His smile faded at her act of bravado, just as she'd hoped it would. On more than one occasion, she'd stolen cigarettes from her father's study. She didn't love the taste, but the prospect of trying the forbidden had been too enticing to resist. Now she was glad she knew how to smoke like a man. Taking a long drag on the cigarette, she blew a stream of smoke right into Savidge's face.

To her shock, Savidge reached out and snatched the cigarette from her fingers. "You're too damned young to smoke," he growled, then tossed the offending item out the window.

"You're worse than my parents," she shot back. Crossing her arms, she sank into the corner and stared out the window.

"Bloody hell. So I'm babysitting, am I? Only children whine about their parents. Adults accept their lot in life."

He was lecturing her! "I hardly need your advice."

"You'd darn well better listen to someone, before you ruin yourself completely."

At his unusually serious tone, Pauline slid her gaze toward him, looking for the spark of humor that always seemed to linger in his eyes. This time, it was absent. What did he mean, ruin herself? Why would he think that?

She knew he believed her to be an inexperienced Indian youth just beginning to make his way in the world. So why didn't he at least extend her the courtesy of treating her like a man instead of a foolish child? The man was insufferable, and she found it a wonder Bhaga had remained in his service for so long.

"I have all the experience a man like you could ever need," she finally replied, knowing it was more than a stretch—it was a total fabrication.

"*All* the experience?" Leaning back, he stretched his arm along the back of the seat, so it settled right behind her head.

Pauline's muscles grew even more tense than they already were. Was this normal behavior for a man toward his servant? She had the urge to slap his arm away but didn't want to be caught behaving like a prissy lady. Still, her body noticed his nearness. Blood pounded under her skin, making her warm and prickly all over.

Pauline again turned her gaze to the window, to the moonlit plains where jackals called to each other in the dark. They were passing villages surrounded by cultivated fields and croplands. The ruins of a mysterious fortress atop low hills were silhouetted against the enormous moonlit sky. Farther on, a domed pavilion with slender pillars stood as a last lonely remnant of a forgotten city from long ago.

Imagining who might have lived there, Pauline closed her eyes. Gradually, the rocking motion of the train lulled her to sleep.

Nate gazed down at the lady sleeping on his shoulder. A strand of her honey-brown hair had slipped from under her turban. Despite knowing he might wake her, he tucked it back in place.

Daft woman. Two days now and she still hadn't given up her charade. And he hadn't been able to forget for a moment that she was all female. Sitting so close beside her, he found it impossible not to remember their stolen kiss and imagine further intimacy. He longed to taste her mouth under his, feel her lithe body in his arms, banish her bravado with passion only he could stimulate. Yet his kiss hadn't affected her at all, he reflected ruefully.

Frustrated and needing distraction, he'd resorted to expressing his needs with brief touches—a hand on her shoulder, a brush against her arm. Yet instead of providing satisfaction, the physical contact only made his hunger grow stronger. And, from what he could tell, had left the girl unmoved.

What an idiot he was. The last thing he needed was to feel drawn to a lady who didn't return his feelings.

They had left the village of Jhansi behind when

the train wheels suddenly squealed, throwing him forward. Instinctively, he threw out his arm to prevent Pauline from flying off the seat.

She awoke with a start as the train continued to decelerate. "What—what's happening? An accident?" She looked out the window, where a hint of dawn could be seen in the east. "This isn't Satna, is it?"

In her half-asleep state, she had neglected to adopt her formalized, Indian-sounding accent. He ignored the slip and patted her knee. "Don't know yet. Stay put and I'll find out what's up."

Few of the other passengers seemed to think anything was amiss in the train's sudden stop. Despite having instituted a remarkably broad network of rail lines, the British had yet to ensure that the trains ran on time and without incident. Most of the natives took the frequent delays in stride. Nate wasn't nearly as sanguine. With a man-eater on the prowl, every day that passed risked more people's lives.

He had to travel through three crowded, smoky railcars before finding a conductor and learning that the train had stopped because of an accident farther up the line.

Nate sighed in relief that their own train hadn't been involved in the accident, whatever it was. He couldn't imagine his fate if Pauline were injured in a train wreck while under his care.

"How long will we be sitting here?" he asked the conductor.

"Only Allah knows," the uniformed fellow replied unhelpfully. "Perhaps half a day, perhaps three days."

"Three days! No. No, that won't do." He had no intention of waiting here one minute longer than necessary. Sitting next to Pauline hour upon hour had already strained his good intentions to the breaking point.

"As Allah allows," the conductor replied, then turned and continued his stroll down the train car.

"Bugger that. Damn Muslims, leaving it up to fate," Nate muttered to himself. He could never leave anything to fate. He was a man of action, and he intended to take his future into his own hands, thank you very much.

Besides, he realized, there was an added benefit. His "servant" had so far experienced nothing more dangerous than sleeping in a hotel room and riding in a train. Hardly the sorts of experiences that would scare her into behaving like a proper young lady. He needed to separate the men from the women, as it were. Force her to really rough it. Rattle her safe little world so hard she fled in terror back to her sister—and away from him.

Returning to his seat, he found Pauline awake, her dark eyes large and wary. "What has happened?" she said, this time affecting a much better Hindi accent.

Nate pulled her pack from the rack above the seat and tossed it on her lap. "We were going to travel to Satna via Jabalpur," he explained, "which would have wrapped us around to the eastern side of the prince's province. Instead, we'll get off here, on the northwest side."

"Get off? You mean walk from here?"

"Righto." He yanked down his own pack and shrugged the straps over his shoulders.

She rose and accepted her bow and quiver from him. "But your provisions. All those bags I carried to the station. You were going to hire more porters at Satna, weren't you? What about . . . ?"

"The bags can make the long trip around without us," he said, slinging his rifle over his shoulder. "Once we reach the prince's palace, he'll send porters to the station for them. I won't need the food or other tents until I get there, learn the situation, and form a proper hunting expedition. Come on, the day's a-wastin'."

"Wasting! It's still dark out."

Ignoring her typically female protest, he strode toward the end of the car. Outside, the stars overhead fought against the coming daylight. A turquoise line on the eastern horizon beckoned him toward a scrabbly forest that thickened a mile distant. He climbed down the steps and hopped to the ground.

Pauline had followed him to the end of the car but was making no move to climb down. "Are you sure this is wise? Won't it be quicker to wait?"

"Up to three days? Rawa isn't that far off, sweet." The endearment tumbled out without a thought.

Her brows began to lower in confusion, so he rushed to correct his slip. "*Sweet* mother of God, quit whining. It isn't much farther hiking into the forest from this side than traveling by train to the eastern edge. Only take a few days."

She remained on the platform. "But where will we sleep?"

Leave it up to a lady to worry about her personal comfort, he thought in annoyance. He patted to the rolled canvas tied to the bottom of his pack. "It's called a tent."

A worried light entered her eyes. "Then we're camping outside."

"Makes more sense than camping inside."

"Oh. Very well." Turning around, she began to climb down. "I've never—that is, it can't be much different from conditions in my family home. We live in very rustic conditions."

"I'm sure," he said dryly.

She reached the bottom step and paused.

"What now?" His patience had strained to the breaking point. He ought to walk off and leave the chit here. If he hadn't promised her sister, he might do just that. "Well?"

"It's just that you have—"

Nate lost his patience. Without waiting for another protest, he grasped her waist and yanked her down. She lost her balance and fell against him, her soft, yielding body sliding along his. A shiver of pleasure sparked against his skin where their bodies touched. Too soon she was firmly on her feet, facing him.

She gazed up into his face, her eyes wide, her breathing shaky. "Only a single tent," she finished.

A single tent. Christ almighty, she was right. He knew in his gut her sister hadn't expected *this* situation. Nor had he exactly clued Mrs. Drake in on how intimate things could get. Of course, he should have, but the prospect of two thousand pounds—enough to make him comfortable for years—had been irresistible. With two thousand pounds in the bank, he would never again have to take the district commissioner, or any wealthy sahib or prince, on a "hunting" expedition designed to slaughter animals senselessly.

He needed that money. He needed to deal with Miss Carrington. They had shared a hotel room and he'd kept his hands off of her. A tent wasn't that much different. Only smaller. Much smaller. And privacy would be all but nonexistent.

Then it struck him. *She's worried about being alone with me.* She couldn't be concerned about *his* amorous feelings toward *her,* a "boy." So she must worried about her own feelings, for him. He tried to wrap his mind around that truth. He found it difficult to grasp, considering the way he'd treated her. To think she was attracted to him . . .

She continued to gaze at him, as if looking for something. Reassurance that nothing untoward would happen? Reassurance that he wouldn't let her make a terrible mistake? He ought to be pleased at her concern. Unmarried ladies *should* think of their virtue. Her sister would be proud.

Then again, if Miss Carrington felt tempted by him, she might want to explore her feelings, as she had with the butcher's son. *Don't even think about it,* he sternly told himself.

"There are only two of us," he said carefully, trying to sound reasonable. "It's a big enough tent. Plenty of room."

"Oh." She backed out of his arms, putting a good five feet between them. She wrapped her arms around her chest. "Forgive me, sahib. You must think me a terrible coward to be so concerned."

"No," he said firmly. He thought her quite possibly the bravest woman he'd met, besides his mother. Abandoned to her own devices, his mum had managed to carve out a life for them in this exotic and difficult land, without the help of his oblivious father.

"I am foolish for questioning your judgment. I do not know what has gotten into me. I am looking forward to traveling"—she risked a glance in his direction—"with you."

Her throaty voice caused a physical shock to go through him. He had a sudden desire to take her in his arms again. Which he must never do.

"Fine, then," he bit out. "But you'd better not complain again, or you'll be on the first train home." Turning, he began hiking away from her, toward the forest looming several hundred yards distant.

Without looking, he knew she was following him. In a matter of moments, she was striding right beside him, her long legs matching his step for step.

Now the real test would begin, he thought as the scrub brush crunched under his feet. She'd been pampered too much on the hotel and on the train. She thought she wanted a life of adventure, and he was quite capable of giving it to her. As long as he felt he could protect her, he'd allow her to remain with him—despite his ridiculous physical response to her.

Then, when they drew closer to the man-eater's territory, he would send her back home. The prince of Rawa could arrange rail passage and an escort—this time, a proper Indian matron.

He could only hope the man-eater remained on the eastern side of Rawa and didn't venture in this direction.

He'd have to play it by ear, as he always did.

They had just entered the thickest part of the forest, following a well-worn deer track, when a low growl sounded from the bushes on their left.

NINE

Pauline's blood turned to ice. She had roamed the backwoods while vacationing in the Adirondacks with her family. She knew the smells and sounds of a New England forest. But this? She had no idea what might be lurking in the bushes to their left. Though the sun was breaking over the horizon, the light barely penetrated the heavy shadows on the forest floor.

Savidge stretched out his arm and urged her behind him. Without making a sound, he slid his rifle off his back and lifted it to his shoulder.

Pauline gladly took her cue from him. Not only did she remain silent, she removed her bow from her shoulder and nocked an arrow to the string. Her action drew a glance of disbelief from Savidge. He probably thought her weapon useless—or her skill with it—but she knew otherwise.

In fascination, she watched him crouch low to the ground. She followed his example before he gestured for her to do so. Savidge studied the ground, then the surrounding bushes. He pointed out a fresh paw print in the forest floor. He mouthed a single word: "Leopard."

It took Pauline a moment to stop focusing on his sensuous lips before the meaning of the word sank in. She tensed and stared into the shadows under the canopy, looking for the creature, for any sign of movement. She saw something—its eyes?—glimmer, but for such a brief flash that she might have imagined it.

The leopard growled again, sending prickles up Pauline's spine. Savidge tugged on her arm, drawing her attention. He pressed his fingers to her lips, signaling her to remain silent. As if she needed the reminder! As silently as a predatory cat himself, he rose to his feet and gestured her to follow suit.

He gave her a small push in the direction they'd been heading, then slipped protectively behind her, his gun aimed at the shadows. She didn't want to move without him, but he began backing away in the same direction. In this way, they left the animal behind.

He didn't begin to relax his posture until they had put fifty yards between themselves and the predator. Savidge slung his rifle back over his shoulder and once more took the lead.

"How much danger were we in back there?" she asked.

"Only some. The beast was feeding off a fresh kill. He thought we might be threatening to steal it."

"Raw meat isn't my idea of a delicious breakfast," she said wryly, then caught herself and added quickly, "I prefer rice cakes and chutney, the way my mother makes it."

He gave her a strange look, which she couldn't interpret. To change the subject, she asked, "How did you know it was feeding?"

"Smelled it. Nothing else smells like blood. And I

expected it. Dawn and dusk are prime hunting hours for wildlife."

A look of worry must have crossed her face, because he gave her a gentle smile. "No worries, mate. We'll be perfectly safe if we keep our wits about us. Besides, isn't this what you wanted, adventure?"

"I have to admit, now that the danger has passed, it *was* exciting," she said.

"Gets your blood pumping, doesn't it?" His enjoyment at living on the edge showed in his eyes.

"I know exactly what you mean," she said enthusiastically. No one she had ever met understood her need to experience that thrill. "Waiting with bated breath, the seconds stretching out . . ."

"The blood singing in your veins. It's right exciting."

She spontaneously grasped his arm. "Yes, sahib. Dangerous and exciting."

"Exciting," he repeated. His gaze on her intensified, sending a queer feeling surging in her stomach. She'd seen that light in his eyes before, when they had argued in his room, right before he'd kissed her. But they weren't arguing now.

He cleared his throat and looked away. "As long as you don't die."

The harsh truth of his words struck home. "I have no intention of dying."

He ran a finger down the side of her face in a tender gesture. "Can't have one without threat of the other, love."

"Love?" Had he just called her that? His young syce?

"Love adventure, that's what you have to do," he said in a rush, as if covering for a verbal slip. He turned away and kept walking, leaving her more than a little confused.

Did he know she was a female? How could he? Had she made some mistake, provided a clue? Certainly, if he knew she was Miss Pauline Carrington, he would immediately send her back to Simla, so at least that fact remained a secret.

Yet, if he knew she was female, why was he putting up with her? If he knew, he never would have allowed her to come with him. Unless he wanted her for something that had nothing to do with her duties as his syce. Like being his mistress.

The thought annoyed her. Yet she shouldn't be surprised. The man purchased brides, after all. More telling, the rogue had kissed her, a lady, in his room at the hotel!

Nevertheless, she couldn't fight off a forbidden thrill at the prospect. After all, she didn't feel uncomfortable with him, nor at all in danger. She ought to fear the danger he presented. A lady was supposed to prize her virtue above everything else. Yet if she had been at all worried about her virtue, she never would have accompanied him in the first place.

She was, quite simply, hopeless where her virtue was concerned. Ever since she'd begun to transform into a woman, she had felt secret longings toward men of a certain stripe. Not the dandies who tried to impress her at society parties, with visions of her daddy's money dancing in their eyes. No, she preferred dangerous men, *real* men who didn't care that she was worth millions.

Men like Nate Savidge. He fascinated her: the way he walked, the way he talked, the way he treated her like less than a lady. The way he kissed her, setting fire to needs that had never been satisfied. How she wanted that satisfaction! How she wanted to be wanted by such a powerful, confident man.

Right then, she made a decision. She would no longer give heed to her virtue, regardless of what society said. She wanted to experience life, and if that meant the White Tiger wanted her as his mate . . .

A flush began to creep up her face at the intimate, carnal thought. She walked behind him, reveling in the sight of his broad back and powerful thighs as he strode over rocks and scrub. She imagined him kissing her, touching her, bringing to life all the secret pleasures she longed to feel.

"Manu, keep up the pace."

Savidge called over his shoulder to her, and she realized her daydreaming had caused her to lag behind. She hurried to catch up to him along a short, rocky rise. They ascended the crest and began down the other side into an open, gentle valley. The forest resumed on the far side.

"Growing weary?" he asked.

"Not unless you are," she hedged. She wasn't about to ask for a rest break, though she could definitely use one.

He paused and looked into the sky, gauging the position of the sun. "It's a couple of hours until noon. Let's push on a bit. I believe there's a stream not far off. We can stop there for dinner."

"You mean luncheon."

He gave her a pointed look. Too late she realized her slip. The British called the midday meal dinner. If she was an Indian who had learned English in a

British-run school, she ought to be calling it dinner, too.

He continued on wordlessly, and she decided not to try to explain. She couldn't begin to think of an explanation anyway. She would simply hope he paid no heed to her mistake.

Dust had begun to cake in the natural creases of her skin. She felt as if she were walking through a furnace. For hours, they had been traipsing into ravines and up rocky hills covered in deciduous scrub, each footfall sending up a puff of dust.

"It's hot as Hades." Nate paused and drank a swig of water from his canteen. Pulling a handkerchief from his pocket, he dampened it and swabbed his face. He held the cloth out to her. Though she was tempted, she shook her head. If she wiped her face with anything, her dark "skin" would blacken his handkerchief. She hated the glop on her face. At least her man's costume was a far sight more comfortable than a lady's dress could ever be.

Except, of course, for the cotton binding her breasts. She tried holding her arms at a different angle, but the cloth still chafed the skin under her arms.

"How hot is it?" she asked, dabbing judiciously at her forehead with the end of her turban. Sure enough, it came away streaked with makeup.

"Probably ninety, ninety-five. The River Ken is a few more miles. We should reach it by nightfall. Make for a good camping spot."

"And we can wash off in the river," she said, already

imagining how she would soak in the cool, flowing stream.

"Sure, if you can avoid the crocs." Without waiting for her reaction, he turned and continued hiking.

As the morning dragged to a close, Pauline began to wonder how many more steps she could take before collapsing in exhaustion. Her pack seemed to grow heavier with every step she took. She admitted that while an adventurous life was exciting, it could also be hard and uncomfortable. Still, despite her sore feet and tired back from hauling her pack, she loved the experience, one so far removed from fancy dress balls and tea parties. She adored the forest, the rise and fall of the changing landscape, the sounds of life all around them in the trees and bushes. As the sun rose higher, the colors changed, grew more intense, and she spotted yellow orchids in the trees.

"It's so beautiful here," she said to him. "More vibrant, more intense than the woods back home."

"The Simla Hills?" he said. She glanced over at him, noting the dry tone to his words.

Yet again she had forgotten who she was supposed to be. "Well, yes, of course, sahib. It is drier here. Hotter. Yet so full of life. I can feel it all around me, in the trees." Impulsively she made a pirouette, her eyes on the canopy above. She felt remarkably giddy. The forest, the fresh air, and her compelling companion all worked their magic on her. She had never felt more alive.

He gave her an appreciative smile. "You can feel that? Even though you can't see it?"

"Oh, yes. I think the animals are watching us, curious at such strangers in their midst. But I don't feel unwelcome. Far from it. It's as if we're part of the essence of life here in the wild, the truth of life, away from all the buildings and roads and everyone telling you what to do and how to act."

She felt so free out here. While she thought of her family often, and missed them, she did not miss in the least the pressures they had put on her to conform to the life she'd been born to. How lucky for Nate to be free to choose his own course!

She grinned at him. "You must be the luckiest man in all the world."

He arched a brow. "Me?"

She threw out her arms in an all-encompassing gesture. "You live here!"

He chuckled and she drew closer to him, not even trying to resist the urge to touch him. She stroked his rock-hard biceps in a flirtatious manner that surprised even her. "You, Mr. Savidge, are a reflection of this land. All hard and gritty and filled with mystery." How she longed to unlock his secrets!

He grasped her arms, pulling her toward him. Pauline had the strong sense he wanted to kiss her. *Please* . . . she silently begged, not sure whether she longed for him to release her or to fulfill the potent promise in his glinting blue eyes.

He shoved her from him. "By God, you're chatty today. Just like a female."

Turning, he strode away.

Pauline sighed, a deep pain welling in her chest. Her yearnings grew with each passing moment in his company. A need to be seen as a woman, desired as a woman. Yet what had she expected? And when would she make an irreversible mistake and reveal herself?

Perhaps, she thought dangerously, not soon enough.

The longer Nate knew the strange Miss Carrington, the more pleasing he found her company.

She hadn't been able to maintain the pretense of subservience for very long, which made his job more difficult. Miss Carrington had spent a lifetime being taken care of. It was a wonder she had lasted as long out here as she had.

She came up beside him, matching his stride as they crossed a flat, dusty, scrub-filled plain. He studied her from the corners of his eyes, noting the high color in her cheeks, the excitement in her chocolate eyes.

She hadn't merely lasted; she was thriving on it. His assumption that she would crumble at the first difficulty had been completely obliterated. Her comment about loving adventure had struck a familiar chord in his own chest. He was in the company of a fellow being, someone who understood what drove him, at least on one level.

And she seemed determined to find out the rest of his secrets.

"Who taught you to hunt?" she asked, her tone still dangerously familiar despite how he'd shoved her away. "You still haven't told me."

"A boy grows up learning to hunt, when his family's survival depends on his ability to put food on the table."

"Yes, but the tracking. They say you're the very best *shikari* in India. Surely, someone taught you his secrets."

He sighed but found himself answering her question. "There was an old poacher. Name of Rajeev. He showed me a few tricks."

"Such as?"

Did she really want to know? He studied her avid expression, noted how intently she gazed at him. He couldn't bring himself to deny her. He began telling her the basics of tracking, which led to more questions. Her interest was surprisingly genuine, and the more he shared, the more she wanted to know. The lesson continued for at least two miles, during which he often paused to point out a track, a dropping, the numerous telling signs and sounds that told him the story of the forest.

When they stopped for a rest and dinner on the bank of a narrow, tree-lined stream that fed into the River Ken, her questions turned personal.

"Were you the only hunter in your family? Did you have any brothers to help?" she asked after swallowing a portion of the ox meat he'd given her from one of his army tins. Despite her sophisticated palate, she ate his camp food with a voracious appetite worthy of a man.

Carefully pouring water from the nearby creek through his portable water filter, he considered her question. *Brother* . . . That word could mean so much, or in his case, so little. He never thought of that man in England as his brother, so he finally replied, "Just me and my mother."

"What brought her to India?"

He passed her a cup of water, then snapped open a second tin of army food, dug out a plum, and popped it in his mouth. "She was born here. She was the postmaster's daughter."

"And your father?"

He hesitated. He hated discussing his father, preferred to think he never had one. He certainly would never tell who his father really was. No one needed to know that. "A British . . . gentleman," he finally said. "He took my mother back to England briefly, but it didn't last, so she came back here to her homeland to live."

"With you."

"You could say that."

"Your father. He let her leave with you?" She seemed surprised. Most English gentlemen prized their sons. But until Nate reached manhood, his father hadn't even known he existed. If he had known about Nate, he never would have let his mother leave England, and his life would have turned out much differently. Every day Nate thanked his mother for bringing him here, to his beloved India.

"You're truly Indian yourself, then, aren't you?" Pauline persisted.

Nate found himself nodding. "I am, yes. India is in my blood, my soul. I belong here."

"Have you ever been to England?"

"Land of fog and rain and bone-chilling cold? Cities of crowded streets and factories belching soot? Yeah." He ground out his cigarette butt on the earth. "Yeah, I've been."

"So, you hated it."

He gazed at her. She didn't seem shocked, and he felt she just might understand. Here was a woman who also hated the posturing and posing of the upper crust. Who wanted honesty, though she was taking a dangerous route to finding it. "With a passion," he said.

She nodded. "I can't begin to imagine you enjoying stuffy drawing rooms and stilted conversation. I like you better here."

She liked him. Here. He ought not to care what she thought of him, but her appreciation warmed his heart. A female voice heard long ago echoed in his head: *You cannot truly believe I would be pleased to live in your awful, savage India. You're little better than an animal, Nate. You must realize you're beneath me, despite your fortunate birth.*

Beatrice had been no better born than Miss Carrington, he realized with a start of satisfaction. Yet this lady before him approved of his life. Approved of him. Even without knowing who he really was.

His cynical side argued him down from his height of satisfaction. There was no doubt Miss Carrington was an odd bird. That explained it. A true society belle would have nothing to do with a man like him—and that was exactly how he liked it, he reminded himself.

"Mr. Savidge?"

Pauline's gentle words drew him from his reverie. Her gaze searched his, no doubt seeing uncharacteristic emotion on his face. He'd be damned if he would let her under his skin, allow her to touch him with tender words and understanding gazes. Only a fool revealed his vulnerability. To expose one's weak spot, one's white underbelly, was to invite disaster. To suffer defeat.

He shot to his feet and shouldered his pack.

"We've cooled our heels long enough. Ought to put in another five miles before making camp."

She rushed to shove her tin cup into her pack and pull it on. Still her gaze remained on him, and he had the uncomfortable feeling she had seen far more than he'd intended to share.

That evening, they made camp where the stream they had been following emptied into the River Ken. Rather than give in to his urge to watch Miss Carrington putter around their makeshift camp, Nate focused on cleaning his rifle. He sat on the ground and leaned against a stump well away from the fire pit, where she crouched poking the flames with a stick. He'd shot down a pheasant right before they'd made camp, and cooked it over their campfire. The food had been fresh and filling. True to form, Miss Carrington hadn't complained once about the simple fare.

He'd kept her occupied dressing the bird, duties she'd willingly embraced. She had plucked the feathers in record time and whacked off its head and feet without trepidation. From her questions, he knew she'd never done such gritty chores before, but her willingness and enthusiasm made up for her lack of experience. He was coming to the conclusion that her sister's plan was an utter failure. Nothing rattled this female. But she was most definitely rattling him.

From her position tending the fire, she cocked her head to the side and gave him a studious look, as if trying yet again to read him. "You could teach me how to care for your weapon."

Her throaty invitation went straight through him. He thought of her "caring for" quite a different weapon in his armory. Blast the girl. One would have thought her ridiculous face paint—now smeared by perspiration, leaving her looking something like a diseased trout—would be off-putting enough. And those ripe breasts he remembered from that evening at the Club . . . They must have been all corset and padding, since he could see no evidence of them on her chest now. Still, he wanted to hold her, to kiss her ripe lips.

"I can handle my own gun, thank you very much," he said, hearing the strain in his words.

She knelt beside him, rocking back on her heels in a decidedly feminine manner that drew his eyes to her rounded hips under her tunic. "Teach me how to shoot."

He shoved the bristle-tipped cleaning rod into the barrel and spun it around. "My bearers don't have to shoot. When I close in on my prey, I send them away for their own safety."

"But I should know how to handle a gun. To protect myself. And my family."

"Your family?" The image of Miss Carrington standing in a fluffy ball gown, aiming a rifle at the gentlemen and ladies of the Club, nearly made him laugh out loud.

"I have four sisters. They need my protection. And my parents, too."

"The ones back in Simla."

"Yes, of course."

"Of course."

Her hands fisted on her thighs. "Why are you repeating everything I say? Why do you find it so hard to believe that I would need to care for them, to—"

He set his gun aside. "Enough of this nonsense. I'm heading to the river for a bath." He jerked to his feet and looked down at her. "I won't be gone long. If you stay by the fire, you'll be safe. If something does menace the camp . . ."

"Use your gun?"

"Scream real loud." Turning, he headed down the bank.

Furious, Pauline snatched up the rifle. Taking a bead on a tree branch above his head, she slowly, carefully pressed the trigger.

The blast sent a shock wave through her body and she fell back a step. But her aim was true. The branch, severed from the tree, fell at Savidge's feet. He remained frozen, staring the direction he'd been heading for a long, terrible heartbeat. Pauline sucked in a breath, her pulse slowing, her anger abating. She'd actually done it. What a risk! She could have shot him in the back. But she hadn't.

He turned around, slowly, like a predatory animal bent on revenge, his fists in tight knots at his sides. His eyes held cold fury. He strode up to her and snatched the rifle from her grasp. "That was a bloody stupid thing to do. Bloody stupid! I ought to spank you."

Pauline stared at him with a mutinous expression. "You keep saying things are dangerous around here. Then you had better not leave me alone unless you teach me how to protect myself."

His blue eyes slid over her, his mouth a tight, thin line. "Were you aiming for that branch? Or for me?"

"The branch, of course."

His expression remained hard and unforgiving. "Then turn around."

Pauline remained rooted to the spot. She could feel the anger vibrating off of him in waves. Did he really intend to spank her? He wouldn't dare. Then again . . .

"Turn around!" His sharp command sent her spinning away from him.

A moment later, his arms settled around her. Pauline barely managed to breathe. He pressed his rifle into her hands and lifted her arms so that she was holding the gun in the correct position. "Rest the butt against your shoulder. That's right."

Pauline listened with only half an ear to his instructions as he tightened her fingers on the trigger. A delicious lethargy slid over her, making her feel weak as a kitten. His hard chest pressed into her back, and she longed to melt into his strength. She watched his muscular hands slide along the gun barrel, imagined them sliding along her limbs, caressing her, learning her . . .

He tapped the sight on the top of the rifle. "Look through here to take a bead on your prey. You have to learn to hunt not only standing up, but crouching. Even on your stomach." His voice was low and deep in her ear. Despite the prosaic nature of his words, she couldn't help feeling he was seducing her. She felt so ready, even though she could barely imagine what she might be ready for. All she knew was that her charade couldn't last much longer, or she would go completely and utterly mad. She wanted Nate Savidge to see her as a woman. Touch her as a woman.

Leaving her to hold the gun, he lowered his hands to her stomach, anchoring her against him. His touch heated her through. "See that flower up there in the branches?"

Lifting the rifle, she centered the yellow orchid in the sight.

"Shoot it from the tree, if you can."

"Of course I can." Goodness, if his hand slipped much lower, he would be touching her most private of places. The thought nearly made her melt into a puddle at his feet. "I'll try anything. You should know that about me by now."

"I hear you loud and clear, love," he said, his voice a deep, intimate murmur. "Now, a good shot is all about the build-up. The preparation. Your state of mind. You have to want it. Really want it, deep in your gut." He swirled his palm on her abdomen, and her knees threatened to buckle.

"I want it," she breathed out. Her arms had begun to shake from a need that had nothing to do with hunting.

"Then take it."

Closing her eyes, she squeezed the trigger. The recoil pressed her against him even harder. A moment later, she cracked open her eyes to see that the flower remained untouched, but some very annoyed monkeys had begun screeching at them.

Savidge released her and stepped back, snatching his rifle from her frozen hands. With a smug look on his face, he said, "Beginner's luck, just as I said." Leaning the rifle up against the stump, he turned and once more strode toward the stream bank.

Pauline stared after his retreating figure, her con-

fusion transforming into fury. He must have done
that on purpose! Rattled her so badly she was bound
to miss. He would not have taught a young syce how
to shoot in such an intimate, suggestive way.

Damn him. If he knew she was female, why didn't
he say so? Why didn't *she*?

She sank onto the stump and rested her face in
her hands, thinking hard. It was a very good question. Why didn't she?

Finally, she understood what she needed to do.

TEN

Nate pulled on a clean, dry shirt. He only had two shirts, and he had laid the other to dry on a rock after a quick wash.

Bhaga had taken care of the laundry, but Nate's sense of propriety had kept him from telling Pauline to wash out his sweat-stained shirts.

He had spent longer than usual in the stream. It had felt good to wash the grit off his skin—and get his mind off of Pauline. He couldn't relax when he was around the girl. He either wanted to spank her or kiss her.

He felt better, his head clearer, now that he'd spent time away from her. While he was gone, dusk had settled on the land. Grabbing up his boots, he headed the short distance back to camp. He didn't want to leave Pauline alone for long, despite her newfound ability to fire a gun. Or perhaps because of it.

He strode into the clearing and stopped in his tracks.

The tent was filled with golden light. Pauline had lit his camp lantern, revealing her silhouette through the canvas in all its feminine beauty.

Mesmerized, he watched her dark outline and realized she was unwinding a long cloth from around her torso. Though he couldn't see her skin, he imagined her slowly exposing herself to the warm night air, understood how good it felt after a hard day to free oneself of clothes.

She yanked the end of the cloth away. From the side, he saw her full breasts fall free, a tantalizing sight he couldn't tear his gaze from. She ran her hands up her rib cage, no doubt relishing the freedom from the binding cloth. She lifted her breasts high in her hands, massaging beneath and above them. Nate drank in the innocently erotic sight, his breath ragged in the still night.

Then she turned her back. Keen disappointment pierced him.

He closed the distance to the tent, his steps slow. He shouldn't come any closer, but he was drawn to her like a moth to a flame.

He rationalized that coming upon her this way would end the tension, the pretense that kept him from thinking straight. She would shriek and grab for her tunic to cover herself, but the subterfuge would finally end. Once her identity was out in the open, he could deal with her in a straightforward, uncomplicated manner. No more sensuous encounters disguised as shooting lessons. Their roles would become clear.

Or so he told himself.

Slowly, carefully, he lowered to a crouch in front of the tent flap and drew it aside.

An expanse of feminine skin filled his gaze. Pauline sat on her bedroll, her legs crossed, wearing nothing but her baggy cotton trousers. Her back—that delicious white vee of skin—lay exposed to his gaze. Her

flawless skin, washed in the golden-glow of his camp
lantern, couldn't possibly look more delicious.

She ran a brush through her hair—where had she
concealed that silver-handled implement?—and
tossed back her newly washed golden brown mane.
It tumbled down her back, caressing her skin, silk on
silk. She must have slipped away to the river by herself, despite his warnings, for her skin glowed
cleanly, her face bearing not a trace of brown paint.
She looked positively luscious, making it impossible
for him to be annoyed with her.

A low, intense heat swelled in his abdomen, building hotter by the second.

He knew when she sensed his presence.

A shiver slid along her body. She jerked her face
toward him, her eyes bright over one creamy shoulder. Her gaze met his and a gasp escaped her parted
lips. She pressed her shirt to her chest but didn't say
a word. Her eyes remained on his, and he saw there
a reflection of his own desires.

The tension between them grew stronger and more
potent with every beat of his heart. As if it were the
most natural thing in the world, she turned to face
him, allowing him to indulge in shameless perusal of
her. He reveled in the sight of her ivory complexion,
its small imperfections—a tiny mole on her lower
cheek, a slight sunburn on her nose—only making
her more appealing. His gaze slid to her creamy neck,
then to the gentle hollows of her collarbone.

His heart throbbed, each beat heavy in his chest.
Only a few feet separated them. He longed to reach
out, to slide his palms along her bare arms and drag

her closer, to toss aside the shirt she pressed to her chest.

She must have sensed his desires, must have known how he longed for her. Slowly she began to lower the shirt protecting her modesty. The rounded tops of her breasts slid into view. Still she didn't stop revealing her soft feminine curves to him. And only to him.

Her tunic dropped to her lap in a final flutter of cloth. Cherry-pink nipples topped generous breasts, more sensuous than in his dreams. She didn't need a corset to make them higher or rounder. She was built that way, built for a man's loving.

He had told himself he could resist her, that they could share a tent without difficulty. What a fool he had been! He hadn't counted on her brash audacity, on the desire for him reflected in her own eyes.

Her invitation was clear. And irresistible to any warm-blooded man. His manhood swelled painfully hot and hard in his trousers, throbbing, demanding satisfaction.

"Damn it, Pauline," he rasped, the words thick and hard in his throat. Still he forced them out. "Have the grace to cover yourself in my presence."

Yanking down the tent flap, he jerked to his feet and headed into the night.

Pauline watched his shadow move away from the tent, into the darkness. Her fingers curled around the tunic in her lap and she once again dragged it to cover her chest.

Humiliation washed through her. The way he had

gazed at her—she had been certain he wanted her as she wanted him. His insult rang in her ears, mocking her. Now there was no question who she was. She may not be a man, but she had proven that she was no lady. That wouldn't have mattered if he had accepted her invitation. If he had chosen to share in her heady exploration. But to be turned down as if she were nothing but a tart! How dare he?

He had been so calm, staring his fill, looking but not touching. He hadn't seemed the least surprised by her actions.

Not only that, but he recognized her. He called her by name. And he hadn't been confused that she was here, in his tent.

Part of her wanted never to face him again, she was so humiliated by his rejection. But she had never been one to run from conflict. Pulling on her tunic, she flipped open the tent flap. She saw no sign of him in the clearing beyond the tent. Had he left her here, alone? Was he that disgusted with her?

From the depths of shadow cast by a thick patch of cedars, a small red light caught her eye. The tip of his cigarette.

Wrapping her arms protectively around herself, she approached him. "How long have you known?" she murmured.

He stepped into the moonlight. His rugged face revealed none of the anger or shock she had expected should he discover her identity. "From the moment you joined the crowd in front of the hotel."

He had known. All along he had known, yet he had said nothing. He had merely let her go on pretending, every moment in his company. The trouble she had gone through to keep up the pretense had been pointless. Every time he'd spoken to her, he had known. Every time he touched her, made her feel . . .

Fury bubbled within her, hot and unbridled. In two swift strides, she reached him. Raising her hand, she slapped him hard across the face.

The sound reverberated in the night air like a gunshot. He rubbed his cheek, his smile cold and tight. His eyes glinted in the moonlight, as brittle as ice. "There she is. Back at last. The haughty heiress. Thinking the world revolves around her, and everyone else should be dancing to her tune. Whereas I'm the one who ought to be slapping *you.*"

He took a menacing step toward her. His powerful form had never terrified her, until now.

She held her ground. "You wouldn't dare," she bit out, not at all sure he wouldn't.

His jaw was so tense, it creased his scar into a deep hollow. "You were attempting to play me for a fool."

"You let me try! You let me go to all this trouble, with the outfit and the name and the accent. You let *me* make a complete and utter fool of myself."

"Don't be so addle-brained. You got what you wanted. You're here, aren't you?"

"Why didn't you say anything?"

"Why didn't you?"

"Don't play games with me."

"All we do is play games." His words were harsh. "From the moment we met, you've been dancing to your own tune, oblivious of anyone or anything else."

"That's not true."

He brought his face within inches of hers. "Oh, isn't it? I've never met a more spoiled female in all my years."

"How can you call me spoiled? I haven't complained once—"

"You attach yourself to me, desperate to get what you can from me without a thought to the difficulty your interference poses to me. I call that bloody selfish." Flicking his cigarette to the ground, he ground it out with his boot.

Pauline continued to glare at him, but his harsh words cut close to the bone. She began to see her actions in a different light. Every rebellious thing she'd done had hurt someone—her parents, her sisters. She might tell herself they remained unscathed by her actions, but she knew the truth.

Nate stepped around her and headed back toward the tent. "The tent is yours. I'm sleeping outside."

Pauline stared after him as he began laying out his bedroll beside the tent. His words had stung; his rejection had hurt. But she would be damned if she'd let him see it. Keeping her chin high, she marched past him to the tent. Stooping low, she entered and secured the flap behind her. She crawled onto her bedroll and curled into a protective ball, trying hard to cope with how completely her adventure had shattered around her.

After their fight the evening before, Pauline wasn't sure how to approach Nate Savidge. He was angry with her; that much was clear. But why had he taken her with him in the first place?

When she woke, she found him sitting on a log before the fire pit, poking the small fire that he'd built there. Their cook pot rested in the middle.

Unsure of her welcome, she approached tentatively, circling around to sit on a fallen log on the opposite side of the fire pit.

"There's tea in the pot. Darjeeling straight from the plantation," he said without inflection.

At least he was willing to be reasonable this morning. She took that as an encouraging sign. Still, she moved slowly, deliberately, as she crossed to the pile of camping gear to retrieve her tin cup. Returning to the fire pit, she poured herself tea, then took a seat across the fire from him.

"Thank you," she murmured, sipping the lukewarm brew. She preferred American coffee but resisted telling him that.

"Happy to be of service."

She couldn't tell if he was being sarcastic, and she wasn't in the mood to ask.

Despite how he had walked out on her the night before, this morning he seemed undeniably interested in her body, probably because she no longer wore her disguise. Without the pretense of the turban, her hair hung in a single braid to her waist.

Nate spent several minutes studying her face, as if reminding himself what she looked like without the face paint. She knew she looked less than her best; her small hand mirror had revealed as much when she'd washed away the face paint at the river the night before. Her nose was sunburned and peeling, and the face paint and turban had caused blemishes along her hairline. Yet, from his interested expression, he didn't seem to find her less attractive for her flaws.

His gaze slid lower, to her chest. Though he had already seen her without clothes, his stare still caused her to blush.

"Having second thoughts?" she said tartly.

"I can't avoid what's right before my eyes."

"Or imagining what you can't see."

"Who said I'm imagining?"

What did he mean? Puzzled, Pauline peered down at her chest, trying not to be obvious. The tips of her breasts were peaking against the cloth. She hadn't realized her body could react so strongly to nothing more than his gaze. When dressing that morning, she had left her breasts unbound, a curiously freeing feeling after a lifetime of corsets. Nate had already seen her naked, so she saw no reason to suffer the tight cloth binding her chest.

She resisted the urge to cross her arms. It was far too late for that. Sucking in a breath, she straightened her spine and threw back her shoulders. *Let him look. Let him hunger for me; let him long for me until he screams in frustration!*

He took another sip of his tea, and Pauline caught a smile twisting his sensuous lips. His sparkling eyes caught hers, and she didn't need words to read his silent appreciation of her audacity.

She loved trying out her feminine wiles on him. No other man had intrigued her like this one, no other man had responded so boldly to her teasing. Even more, she adored that Nate didn't scold her or shun her for being less than a lady.

He tossed the dredges of his tea on the fire, and

it sizzled in a plume of smoke. "Time to move on. Pack the gear while I break down the tent."

"Fine." Pauline rose to her feet with a slow, sinuous motion. Lifting her arms over her head, she stretched deeply. She arched her back, causing her breasts to strain against the cotton fabric.

"Damn it, Pauline. Were you put on this earth to torture me? Is there a demon following me? Is it bad karma for something I did?"

"Caramel?"

"Karma," he said in exasperation. He yanked the branches supporting the tent from the ground and freed them from the fabric, then tossed them aside with more energy than necessary. "It's the Hindu way of explaining the forces of the universe. What goes around comes around. If you do something bad, you get bad back. For me, that must mean you."

His words hurt her more than she could ever reveal. Feeling as if the wind had been knocked from her, she sank to the log by the fire. "I seem to play that role for everyone else. Why not you?"

The tent fabric bunched in his hands, he turned toward her, his expression softening. He tossed the tent to the ground and approached her.

"You can't believe that." He sat beside her, his shoulder brushing hers. "You know better than to listen to a no-account like me."

"It's not you," she said.

"Your sister and mum, they don't understand you. That doesn't make you bad."

"I didn't realize my reputation had reached you. I shouldn't be surprised, after I ruined Mrs. Winslow's tea."

"Mrs. Winslow? That old biddy? What happened?"

"Well, I sort of made a rather dreadful scene." She found herself describing that afternoon's events, how a proper ladies' tea had served as a platform for Mrs. Winslow's offensive comments, and Pauline hadn't hesitated to let her feelings show.

"Brave."

"What?"

"That was brave of you, facing up to them all, especially a woman as powerful as Mrs. Winslow."

To her relief, Nate not only understood, he applauded her for her attempt to stand up for the often-taken-for-granted native Indian. Basking in his understanding, she began to open up. "My sister told me it was foolhardy, that I ruined my chances socially. And I realized that I didn't care, not one whit. Which probably says even more terrible things about me."

"I rather think you're like me." Taking her hand, he flattened her hand between his palms.

She lifted her eyes to his. She was like him? She would love to think so. He was quickly coming to represent everything she longed to be—brave, accomplished, respected. Unashamed of his passions and forthright in expressing them. And free, free to be whatever he wanted.

"Too bullheaded to listen to anyone else. Determined to make our own way. Refusing to be cowed by our so-called social betters. We're the same breed."

His lips turned up, causing his scar to crinkle. She adored his square-jawed face, scar included. After all, his scar marked him as a man who lived in the world, not above it.

"I hope I'm not making you feel worse, comparing you to me," he said.

"Not at all. I'm honored you can be so generous in your opinion of me." She spoke with unaccustomed diffidence. They were entering unexplored territory, an intimacy she had never approached with another man. "Especially after the trouble I've caused you."

"No trouble, mate."

She gave him an expression filled with disbelief.

"Well, not much."

"Since you recognized me from the first, I still don't understand. Why did you . . . take me on?"

He shifted on the log. Resting an elbow on one knee, he studied his palm. "You make it sound as if you're a chore."

"I usually am."

"Not to me."

Caught in his eyes, she didn't realize immediately that he had evaded her question. She almost asked, until the answer struck her, as clear as day. She saw it in his eyes, a warmth and longing she understood full well. She leaned toward him, a deep yearning filling her.

We're the same breed. We belong together. He felt this connection between us, this bright, glowing understanding, so he brought me with him and kept me close beside him.

So confident did she feel that she was right, she touched his face, tracing his scar with her fingertips. Though she knew he was sensitive about his scar, he allowed her the exploration. Her thumb teased his lower lip, and his lips parted. How she longed to taste his lips again! Cupping the back of his head, she nudged him closer, encouraging him to close the gulf that remained between them.

He didn't resist. He moved closer, his eyes burning like twin suns. His mouth was a hairbreadth from hers. Then he murmured, his warm breath teasing her face, "Your sister is paying me."

ELEVEN

Pauline surprised Nate yet again. One moment he was about to give her a passionate kiss. The next moment, she was grasping the short hair at the back of his head and yanking it. Then she was on her feet, glowering down at him like a warrior goddess.

"Hey, that hurt!" He rubbed the back of his head.

"Lily paid you? She gave you money to put up with me?"

"A little. She thought you ought to get a taste of adventure. Within reason."

"She wanted to get rid of me, you mean."

"At least you don't have to worry that she's worrying. No worries there, mate." He winced at the utter stupidity of his words.

He'd blurted out the last remaining secret between them in a desperate attempt to push her away. And it had worked like a charm.

She was storming about the camp, cramming the cook pot and tin cups into their packs, taking out her fury on an innocent bedroll by squeezing it into a tight, off-center spiral.

"Pauline," he said entreatingly.

"I never gave you permission to call me by my Christian name."

"You can't go back now, Pauline. You can't pretend any longer, not with me."

"That's right," she said bitterly. "You know I'm no lady."

"That's not what I mean. Keeping up with the social niceties seems bloody foolish out here. Miss Carrington and Mr. Savidge—"

"Yet you still call my sister Mrs. Drake, I'm sure."

"Well, yes, but she didn't follow me into the bush, now, did she? She didn't smear paint all over her face and try to pass as a man. She didn't . . ." He'd been about to remind her how she'd tried to seduce him the night before, but caught himself just in time. He was hardly making matters better. But comparing Pauline to her sister made no sense. They were entirely different creatures. He had no interest in well-spoken ladies. He found himself fascinated by a wild and audacious female named, simply, Pauline.

He tried again, instilling his voice with gentle coaxing such as he might use on a wild creature. "Pauline."

"Nate," she shot back.

Nate. He liked the sound of his name on her lips. *Nate.*

"You're despicable." She tied her bedroll to her pack with fierce, savage motions.

"I thought you didn't want to be like other ladies." Women! For the life of him, he couldn't please her, whatever he said.

"You don't know anything about me at all."

"I'm beginning to believe it." So much for being the same breed as she. Yet no matter what she said, he still believed she belonged out here, in an envi-

ronment such as this, rather than back home in petticoats, sitting in drawing rooms, fanning herself and
sipping tea. If that truth insulted her, well, so be it.

Picking up the tent, he finished folding it. "We're
wasting time, and we have a job to do, *Pauline*. A
bounty to collect."

She shrugged on her backpack. "I am well aware
of that, Nate." Her tight response showed that her
temper hadn't yet cooled. But it *had* lost its edge. It
wasn't much, but he'd take it.

They left the river and crossed sun-parched plains.
Several times Pauline caught sight of deer and bison
in the untamed grasslands. Above the plains loomed
the jagged Dantla Hills. Despite the serene surroundings, Nate remained watchful. At this time of
day, he explained, tigers would be relaxing in cam-
ouflaging brakes of bamboo or the tall elephant
grass lining the occasional watering hole.

After coming in sight of a distant village, they joined
a road leading along a cultivated field. Near the field's
edge, a boy no more than eight years old tended a
pair of gaunt cows yoked to a wooden wheel. Using a
long stick, the boy drove the beasts in a circle, causing
them to turn the wheel, which scooped water from a
deep well into an irrigation ditch.

Interested in anything to break the monotony of
his task, the boy smiled as they drew closer. *"Shikari?"*
he asked, his eyes on the rifle slung over Nate's
shoulder.

Nate responded in Hindi, and soon Pauline and
he were enjoying fresh—if slightly muddy—water

from the boy's well. Pauline smiled gratefully, and the boy's round face lit up with pleasure. "I wish I knew the language," she said wistfully. "I would thank him properly. I was just beginning to pick up some Punjabi when we left Simla."

"Wouldn't do you much good," Nate said, filling his canteen from one of the clay jugs emptying water into the ditch. "The boy speaks Hindustani."

Pauline passed him her own canteen to fill. "So many languages! I'll never sort them out."

Nate smiled and screwed the top back on his canteen. "You need a *munshi*."

"A what?"

"Expert in teaching languages. That is, you would need one if you weren't a white woman."

"What is that supposed to mean?"

Thanking the boy once more, he grasped her elbow and turned her away from the field. "You ladies. You expect your servants to speak your language. You wouldn't lower yourself to speak the heathen tongue."

Pauline bristled. Once again he was making assumptions about her. "I'm not like that."

He studied her. After a moment, his gaze softened. "Perhaps you're not. Still, you will always be pampered, Pauline. You have little need to rub shoulders with the locals."

"I have little need for men who want to tell me what to do," she shot back. She took a step away from him, wanting to vent her fury by striding forcefully away. After taking two steps, she slowed to a stop. She wasn't certain which direction they were headed.

Nate's eyes crinkled in amusement at her plight. "You can run from your life, Pauline, but you are who you are," he said softly. "You can never change that."

"Oh, be quiet."

He smiled, causing his scar to crinkle, reminding Pauline that, as strong as Nate was, even he could be vulnerable. She took satisfaction in that thought.

After checking his compass, he led her away from the road they had been traveling down. They entered a brake of trees along a deer track. The shadows gave only minimal relief from the midday heat. A trickle of perspiration wound between Pauline's shoulder blades. She wished she had been able to wash in the young boy's well water, too.

The forest grew denser, and she stepped carefully over the twisting undergrowth. Ahead, a tawny-colored rock appeared through the trees, sunlight flickering on its rough face. "We could rest by that big rock," she called out to Nate.

He glanced at her over his shoulder. "Or in it."

In it? After a few more minutes' walking, Pauline understood. It wasn't a rock at all but a temple. As they came near the cavelike entrance, her steps slowed. The structure defied the jungle's efforts to mask its presence, rising perhaps a hundred feet into the canopy of trees.

Where the sun broke through the branches, the temple's sandstone surface glowed pink. The roof resembled a mountain range, with several small hills leading to the highest peak.

"Hindu," Nate said. "There are dozens of temples scattered about here. Some bloke ran across them in the thirties. They're a thousand years old or there-abouts."

How could he sound so blasé? Pauline could scarcely contain her enthusiasm at this surprise opportunity to explore an ancient structure. Shedding her backpack, she ran up the steps to the lavishly carved archway and gazed into the murky interior.

That's when she realized how beautiful the temple really was. Meter-high statues and carvings in high relief covered every inch of the wall, both inside and out. The horizontal bands of sculpture seemed to grow out of the temple itself. Most were of people. She studied a statue of a young woman with slender limbs, a small waist, and very full, bare breasts. Her oval face, with arched eyebrows, carried just a suggestion of a smile. She wore very little clothing, only a cloth draped about her legs and tied to her rounded belly with a jeweled belt.

All too aware of her masculine companion, Pauline hoped he wouldn't notice the mostly naked woman.

As if he heard her thoughts, he was suddenly behind her, far too close for comfort. "That's an *aspara*, a heavenly nymph." Reaching out, he patted the statue's rounded bottom. "Nice bum. The Hindus know how to appreciate beautiful things."

Though she decided to ignore his remark, Pauline caught herself smiling at his audacity. She stood in the archway and gazed inside, catching glimpses of more statues and carvings, an abundance of them the like of which she'd never seen, not even in the cathedrals in Europe. "So many carvings, in such exquisite detail. The entire temple is a work of art."

Nate set his own pack down, removed his pith helmet, and pulled out the camp lantern. Lighting it, he joined her at the entrance.

"I take it you want to explore."

"Of course I do! Don't you?"

He gestured with the lantern. "Lead the way. I'll wager there are more naked ladies inside."

She shot him an annoyed look, but he only grinned.

She entered the interior. Under the sunlight that filtered inside, enhanced by the lantern flame, the strains of pink in the stone imbued the figures with flesh-like tones that made the people look almost alive. Elephant fights, mythical lions, even the strange Hindu gods and goddesses had been captured in stone.

But the carvings of the women stirred Pauline more than any others. The artists had captured women in so many everyday activities. She traced the fine relief of a woman writing a letter. Another depicted a woman brushing her hair. Yet others showed ladies dancing joyously and playing with their children.

"Look." Nate pointed to the ceiling, carved with geometric and floral designs. Despite his teasing, Pauline knew by his hushed tone that he too felt the magic of this place.

The temple spoke of a people and a culture foreign to her; still, the ancient and sacred place worked a unique magic upon her, making her feel closer than ever to the man who shared this experience with her. The man who made it possible.

"Thank you," she murmured, meeting his gaze. "Thank you for bringing me here."

His eyes widened slightly, and he took a small step toward her. Too aware of his nearness, she pulled her gaze from his and found her eyes on yet another sculpture. The bold relief stunned her. She tried to remain aloof, seeing only the fine carving as an art connoisseur might. But her skin began to prickle and the blood to pound in her ears.

The sculpture, unrestrained in its naturalness, depicted a man and a woman, neither wearing much more than belts around their waists. The man stood behind the woman, her back to his chest, her bare breasts high and full—one of them resting in the man's hand. The man's finger touched her distended nipple while the woman arched her neck, gazing at her lover in a rapture of ecstasy.

Pauline's eyes darted past that sculpture to the next one, and her mouth grew dry. This sculpture showed both man and woman naked, and his organ wasn't tiny or covered by a modest fig leaf as in Western art, but long and thick and thrusting upward, along the thigh of the woman he held.

And the next—*Oh, Lord.* Pauline slapped her hands over her eyes, but not quickly enough to keep from seeing the erotic position of the lovers. The man had been holding the woman high, one of her legs over his shoulder, his *organ* thrust between her legs.

"She reminds me of you."

Pauline started and yanked her hands from her face. Nate stood right beside her, studying the first erotic pose she'd noticed, the one with the *breasts.*

"How dare you—"

"Yours look a lot like that, Pauline."

He would never let her forget she'd revealed herself to him, the cad. If only he hadn't resisted. She imagined him touching her, holding her, his finger on her nipple like the couple in the sculpture. Beneath her tunic, her breasts felt full and heavy, darts of sensation tightening and lifting her nipples against the rough cloth. It was an agony of sensation, and he wasn't even touching her.

"These sculptures are horrid," she bit out, spinning away and heading toward the opposite wall.

"That's not what you said a few minutes ago. You must have been looking at . . . Yeah, okay." He began to chuckle, the deep sound resonating against the walls of the high-ceilinged stone chamber.

"Stop laughing."

"My, my, Miss Carrington. Your maidenly sense of propriety has finally kicked in. I never thought I'd see the day."

"That's not fair. It's just that I've never seen anything like these—these depictions. I never knew . . ." Her remarks faded as she caught sight of yet another erotic sculpture on this side of the temple interior. This one showed a reclining man being straddled by a woman, the man's organ—so huge!—barely penetrating that secret place between her thighs, his hands gripping the out-thrust globes of her bottom as she arched into him. Their faces bore ecstatic expressions. The exuberant passion of the scene made Pauline feel queerly exposed—and exquisitely aware of the man only a few feet from her. The temple walls exuded carnality, pulling her further and further under a tantalizing spell. Humanity's sexuality lay revealed to her, the core of passion secret no longer.

If Nate had taken her up on her naive offer the night before, would he have held her this way? Or touched her there, like that? Or done such with her? That was the word to use, *with*. Not *to* her, no. Both the men and the women in these scenes were enjoying the carnal act, their round faces wearing looks of exquisite pleasure.

"Maybe you shouldn't be seeing these," Nate said, his voice sounding strained. "They might give you nightmares."

"Why?" she shot back, determined not to show how rattled the sculptures made her. "Aren't these acts of love? What is there to fear?"

"Come, now. It's not like you've seen anything like these before."

"How would you know?"

Another dry chuckle. He gradually moved closer to her, until he was right beside her, his shoulder brushing hers. "You talk a good game. You even push the limits. But we both know you're a good little girl."

"Hah. I could do that. And that." She pointed at the first sculpture, then at another showing the man's tongue touching a woman *there*. Until now, she hadn't known such things were done. Maybe they weren't done by civilized people. Maybe—

"Oh, yeah, you could do that. Or let me do that to you. Most women love it." She couldn't tell if he was being facetious or suggesting he actually . . . Heat kindled deep in her abdomen and sizzled upward. She found herself swaying closer to him, despite her desire to appear unaffected.

She decided to play along, just for a moment. "If most women love it, then I'm quite sure I would love it." She swallowed hard, envisioning what she'd just claimed, imagining him touching her *there*, licking her there.

Despite her bravado, she couldn't bring herself to look at him—until he forced her. He grasped her chin and lifted her face to his. "Be careful, princess. I might take you up on your offer."

She yanked her face from his hold. "You had your chance. You walked out, remember?"

"Maybe that was a mistake," he growled.

Pauline found herself caught in his gaze. He was just as affected as she by the erotic art, she realized with blooming satisfaction. Despite the disparity in their experiences, he wasn't immune.

Her gaze flicked toward his hips, and she noticed a strain against his trousers that hadn't been there before. His organ must have grown long and stiff, like the men's in the sculptures. Stiff and ready. Any moment, he could take her, plunge himself inside her . . .

Pauline took a tiny step back.

"That's what I thought," he said, his tone cool. Turning, he headed back to the other side of the temple.

Be strong, she told herself. *The women—they like it, too. You know you want this man. Don't give him such an easy excuse.*

"Did you mean it?" she burst out. "When you said that my . . . that I looked like that woman? Without my shirt on, I mean." She pointed toward the first sensuous sculpture that had caught her eye: the woman with the full, round breasts and the man standing behind her.

At her question, he stared hard at her, his brows drawn tight. Despite the challenge in his eyes, she bravely met his gaze. His face began to soften, the passion in his eyes replacing his cavalier, worldly air.

He took a step toward her, then another. This time she held her ground and watched him, a calmness descending on her, an acceptance of whatever might come. Whatever might happen between them.

He moved around her, his pace as even and predatory as a cat's. When he was right behind her, he stopped. Though he wasn't touching her, he stood so close she felt the heat of his iron-hard body.

Then he touched her. His large palms caressed her waist, sending shocks up and down her entire body. His hands slid under her tunic to touch her bare skin. She sucked in a sharp breath and closed her eyes so she could concentrate on the amazing sensation.

Slowly he slid her tunic up her stomach, then over her breasts. The feel of the warm air on her skin gave her a glorious sense of freedom.

With a last tug, he slid the tunic over her head and arms, freeing her completely.

"Open your eyes," he commanded.

When she did, she realized they were facing the sculpture in question. Using the sculpture as a guide, he placed his hands on her body, one palm resting firmly on her stomach. His other hand . . . Oh, Lord, his other hand! Looking down, Pauline watched in fascination as he laid claim to her. His palm slid along the outer curve of her breast, slowly and surely moving toward the distended peak. He drew his finger toward her nipple with agonizing slowness. The anticipation of his touch was almost too painful to bear.

"You aren't going to tell me to stop, are you?" he rasped in her ear.

"Just . . ." she gasped out, barely coherent, "just touch me."

"Bloody hell." His fingertip finally hit its mark, sending a burst of pleasure through her. But unlike the sculpture before them, theirs was not a static pose. His fingers circled her nipple, flicked it, stroked it, gently pinched it. His magic fingers performed a delicious dance of seduction on her willing flesh. With his other hand, he anchored her tightly against his body, his palm splayed on her stomach. She felt that hardness between his legs on her bottom. Reaching up, she anchored her hand on his neck. Then, acting purely on instinct, she wriggled her bottom against what must be his seat of pleasure.

A deep groan issued from his throat, and satisfaction filled her at her victory. He may be experienced, but she was determined, willing, and oh, so ready.

Turning in his arms, she tightened both arms around his neck and pressed her lips to his.

Oh, yes. She had tried to forget how wonderful he tasted: tart tobacco, a hint of strong Indian tea, and something that was entirely him.

He pulled back, and something like terror throbbed through her. *Please, don't stop*, she silently begged. Rather than reject her, he merely showed her another way of kissing. Unlike their first passionate kiss, this time he took his time exploring her mouth with a thoroughness that amazed her and a reverence that surprised her. He reintroduced himself to her through their joined mouths in a way he hadn't before. His slow, painstaking attentions warmed her heart. This kiss wasn't meant to punish or taunt but to express a depth of feeling she hadn't expected of him. He was learning her, pleasuring her. Perhaps even—dare she hope—loving her?

He gently sucked on her lower lip, teasing the sensitive skin inside her mouth with his teeth. His tongue flicked along the edges of her lips, then lingered along the satiny skin inside before greeting her tongue, darting gently, slowly moving deeper, tasting her before taking her, slowly preparing her for more.

She clutched at him, feeling weaker yet more impassioned by the second. She was melting like candle wax in his arms, losing herself, leaving behind the sheltered girl she had once been.

This experience is too fantastic to be real. The muted shadows of this strange temple, so unlike any place she had ever imagined, cast a sense of unreality about her. Desperate to anchor herself with him for fear she would float away, she clung to his broad shoulders. That only satisfied her for a moment, for she wanted to touch him in turn, learn him as he was learning her. She pressed her palm to his beard-stubbled cheek, traced the scar that he had yet to explain.

She wasn't aware of how or when. She found herself cradled in Nate's lap on the temple floor. With his back supported by the temple wall, he was able to devote his caresses to exploring her body. His mouth drifted along her cheeks and jaw, lingered there, then began tracing her neck downward.

Her head fell back and her eyes landed on another erotic sculpture, this one displaying a man's mouth on a woman's breast. *I want that.* The need grew fierce and unquestioned inside her. Grasping his head, she urged him downward, toward her chest.

"Princess," he murmured.

His lips slid along her nipple, promising satisfaction to the growing need within her. "I want to feel that. I want to feel it all," she cried out.

TWELVE

Her cry struck him like a physical blow. She wanted sex. She wanted to explore her body, learn what it was capable of. And of course, she was under the influence of the erotic art that surrounded them.

Yes, she wanted his body. But she didn't want Nate Savidge. He was handy, that was all. And he had begun to fool himself into thinking it might mean more. He had been making love to her, not merely seducing her for pleasure. What a fool!

Her delicious nipple lay between his lips, begging to be suckled. *Don't do it, man. Pull back now, before it's too late.* Drawing on his deepest reserves of willpower, he withdrew his mouth and lifted his head. He gazed at her, his heart cracking. Aroused, she was more glorious than usual, her cheeks flushed, her lips parted in what might pass for orgasmic ecstasy. Yet they had barely even begun!

Bedding her fully was a pleasure he would never know. Carefully he lifted her from his lap to the floor, then reached for her tunic and began working it over her head.

Still in passion's thrall, she let him cover her, let him lift her arms and maneuver them into the loose sleeves. Her eyes were so dulled with passion, she seemed unaware that he was putting her clothes on instead of taking them off. He freed her long braid from the neckline of her tunic and stroked it into place down her back.

"Why? What are you doing?" she finally asked.

Rising to his feet, he grasped her hand and pulled her to stand beside him.

She looked around the temple, then at him, the confusion in her eyes giving way to annoyance. "We're done? That's it? You can't convince me there isn't more, not after all I've seen here."

"Of course there's more," he said, trying to sound as calm and uninvolved as possible. "Unlike you, princess, I know how to control myself." Part of his anatomy begged to disagree, but in a few moments, he'd have *that* under control, too. He hoped.

She crossed her arms defensively, right over those magnificent breasts of hers. "You're saying I'm out of control?"

"Aren't you?" he said. He adopted his familiar dry tone. It helped to keep her at a distance.

"Why were you—what about what you were doing to me? With me?"

He'd been making an utter fool of himself, of course. He wasn't about to confess that to her. "I was toying with you, princess. Seeing how far you would go."

"I don't believe you." But he could tell by her uncertain tone that she probably did.

"Believe whatever you want. A smart man learns about his adversary, finds out what he's up against. And I just found out."

"Meaning what?"

"Meaning you're damned desperate for a man, and I happen to be handy. Sorry, but I'm not in the mood to comply with your wishes, princess."

"You bastard!" Her eyes narrowed fiercely, making him feel like a man about to be pounced on by a ferocious tiger.

Instead of pouncing, which he almost looked forward to, she spun on her heel and marched toward the entrance to the temple. Where she intended to go, he had no idea. For better or worse, they were stuck with each other until they reached civilization. Not just a country village, either, but a city with a train station. Then he could send her straight back to her sister.

If he had intended to rid himself of her, he couldn't have done a better job. Then why didn't he feel at all pleased with his success?

Right outside the archway, she halted in her tracks.

Relief filled him. She was having second thoughts about running out on him. He knew she would come to her senses at some point, realize she had nowhere else to go. And he would have a chance to patch things up between them. Somehow.

She remained standing, still as one of the statues flanking the entrance, as he approached. "Pauline," he said softly.

She gave one sharp shake of her head, then, without looking, gestured for him to join her. Long years of experience in the bush taught him to read the smallest of signs. He took the hint and said no more. When he reached her side, he saw what had caused her to freeze.

His heart nearly stopped in his chest. Before him stood a myth, a fantasy, a dream. The aspiration of every hunter in India.

His namesake. The white tiger.

In all his years in India, he had never set eyes on such a remarkable beast. The debate still raged over whether such an animal even existed outside of folk-lore. Yet here she was, her chalky white coat a far cry from the orange-yellow he knew so well, its stripes a dark contrast. And her eyes: a shocking blue, the color of India's sky.

Keeping her eyes on them, she turned slightly, her paws treading softly on the underbrush not twenty feet from where they stood. She exuded grace and beauty. Lean muscles rippled beneath her coat. Nate quickly estimated her to be nine feet long from nose to tail, an excellent specimen in health and age. A collector would pay a fortune for such a pelt, if he could bring himself to part with it.

His rifle. It rested against his pack five feet away. Moving slowly, he crouched low and reached for it without taking his eyes from the white beast.

Rising, he slowly lifted the gun to his shoulder and took a bead on the animal. As if realizing the danger he presented, she crouched low and began to growl.

"Get behind me, Pauline."

He glanced at her out of the corner of his eye. She didn't move, damn her. Probably frozen in shock.

"Now!" he bit out under his breath. Couldn't she comprehend the danger they were in? If this female was hungry, they could die in an instant. He was far too used to being the victor in such confrontations to succumb because of a woman's stupidity. Centering his rifle scope on the animal's chest, he took careful aim and began to squeeze the trigger.

Before he could fire, the gun was snatched out of his hands from behind. *Pauline.* He turned and glared at his companion, but Pauline didn't react to his anger. She yanked on his arm, then pointed past the tiger toward the underbrush. He squinted against the midday glare, trying to figure out if she was seeing things. No, there was definitely movement. A second later, he made out the shape. There, between two shrubs, he caught sight of a small bundle of white fur. A moment later, it stepped into the clearing, joining its mother. Behind the white cub came two more, both the usual orange-yellow.

The mother looked once more at them, gave another soft growl, then turned and led her cubs into the shadowy forest. In a few minutes, they had vanished as if they had never existed.

Nate looked at Pauline, unable to hide his admiration. "Sharp eye. You'll make a hunter yet."

"I couldn't believe you intended to slaughter that beautiful creature," she said, her posture stiff with distaste.

"Her pelt would be worth a fortune."

"So some fellow can toss it on the floor or hang it on the wall for other fat sahibs to gawk at? Disgusting."

"Her pelt would be more than a trophy. A white tiger has never been bagged. This would prove they exist." He could tell by her dour expression that she wasn't convinced.

She crossed her arms. "Hmph. If they're so rare,

you shouldn't be killing them. Perhaps you don't deserve to be called the White Tiger."

"Ouch." He hated the thought that she might lose respect for him.

Her respect? He didn't *need* her respect. She was a rich girl who could never understand his life. "It's how I make my living. Not all of us were born with silver spoons jammed in our mouths."

"It's not as if I had a choice in the matter."

"Listen to you. Pretending it doesn't matter. You know bloody well it matters. You wouldn't be with me if you didn't have your wealthy family to fall back on. No matter what trouble you get yourself into, they'll be there to bail you out, to pay men like me to hold your hand and keep you from any real danger."

She flinched at his accusation. "I thought you understood," she said, her lips tight. "You spoke as if you did, as if you understood my need for adventure, because you feel it, too. Now you're categorizing me again, assuming you know me when you know nothing."

He knew he had caused her pain. Guilt nagged at him, but he couldn't resist throwing up a wall against her charms. His best defense—his only defense—was his experience. He needed to remind himself of Beatrice and the painful humiliation he'd suffered at her hands. Beatrice had used him, then thrown him aside when he was no longer useful to her.

He knew in his heart that Pauline lacked that predatory instinct. Still, the fear remained that, if push came to shove, she would make the same selfish choices as she'd been reared to do. And he would come out the loser.

"I know enough. I know rich women don't change. I know what they really want, what they're bred to want, and it isn't hardship and it isn't poverty, two things I'm very familiar with."

He braced himself for an explosion. It never came. Instead, she asked in a quiet voice, "What was her name?"

Her question stirred up old memories that seared inside him, and his stomach began to burn with long-forgotten pain. His voice turned cold. "I don't know what you're talking about."

She cocked her head, her hair golden in the sunlight. "Someone made you believe these horrible, unfair things about ladies like me. Who was it?"

Her astute question effectively sucked the wind out of his sails. "Never mind."

Shouldering his pack and placing his pith helmet on his head, he turned away from her. "Let's shove off, then. No more sightseeing, no more dawdling." His gaze skimmed the temple facade, where naked nymphs taunted him with their sensuous smiles. "We'll reach the prince's palace by nightfall. Good food, warm beds, palatial luxury. You'll feel right at home."

As he strode back onto the deer track through the forest, he could feel her glare burning into his back.

Nate had seen something that drew his interest. He checked his long, confident stride, and Pauline stopped behind him. She had been oblivious to her surroundings, mulling over their intimate encounter, mesmerized by their lengthening shadows on the grasslands through which they trudged.

As much as he annoyed her, she could never think less of his abilities, or deny how safe she felt with him. The man saw signs in everything. He knew a herd of buffalo had run across this plain not an hour before. And he had spotted the pug marks of a tiger in the soft ground by a waterhole, which had concerned him.

Pauline followed his gaze to a black, moving thing partially hidden by tall grass. Squinting in the afternoon sun, she saw that it was more than one thing. Two buzzards were pecking at something, their beaks red with blood.

They were feeding off carrion of some sort, a fresh kill. Where was the carnivore that had brought down the prey?

Nate glanced from the ground to scan the horizon on all sides, his head cocked for any unusual sounds. "Stay quiet and alert."

Their eyes met and Pauline nodded.

As they drew closer, the buzzards took flight. Now Pauline could see that the prey was covered in fresh blood and a mass of flies.

"Christ." Crouching, Nate swatted away the flies clustered on the fleshy remains, but only some of them relinquished their hold.

Yet it was enough. Pauline now recognized the thing for what it was. Her blood froze and her stomach shifted.

A human leg, severed above the knee.

A simple twine sandal, splashed with blood, still

adorned the foot. A remnant of silk, probably from a sari, trailed from a nearby shrub.

Such a small leg. A slender knee, a delicate ankle, the bones fine and sharp beneath taut, youthful skin.

"A girl, or—or a maiden," Pauline murmured. Amritha sprang to her mind, the young maiden Nate had purchased for his syce.

Her heart ached at the sheer horror the girl must have felt at being mauled to death. The terror of being stalked. The agony of sharp claws abrading her flesh. The hideous death as the tiger's teeth sank into her vital organs.

"Never stood a chance," Nate said, his scar prominent as his cheeks tightened. "The beast has brought down grown men twice this child's size."

Standing, he toed a haphazard pile of sticks nearby. "The girl was probably gathering wood for the family cooking fire when it struck. She must be from Ooberti." He expected to reach the village of Ooberti by dusk.

Pauline couldn't tear her gaze from the portion of humanity that remained after the tiger's bloodthirsty feast. She now saw more details. A simple yet fetching bead anklet decorated her ankle. Each small toe was stained red by ochre. The girl had spent time prettying her feet. And now . . .

Tears sprang to Pauline's eyes, and her stomach churned sickeningly. The maiden would never be able to primp or paint herself again. Instead, she was in an animal's stomach, being digested . . .

Pauline's stomach heaved. She leaned over just in time to avoid losing her lunch all over her boots.

Nate stroked her back, waiting patiently, staying by

her side. When she finished, he moistened his handkerchief and dabbed at her face. She accepted it from him and completed the task. He handed her his canteen, and she washed out her mouth, then took a refreshing swig. He continued to run his palm over her back in a soothing gesture, settling her nerves.

"I'm sorry," she murmured, returning his canteen. "You're so understanding, yet I'm so weak."

"Don't be daft. Grown men have lost their lunch over less grisly sights than this."

He screwed the cap back on his canteen and returned it to the hook on his pack. Pauline missed his reassuring touch.

"I hadn't expected it to travel this far west. We're miles from the villages the prince said have been terrorized. Damn thing's cutting a swath through the central provinces." He nodded in the direction they had been heading. "Ooberti is just over that rise. We'll stop there for the night. Regroup. Remember, we have to be even more careful than before."

He shrugged his rifle off of his shoulder and checked the chamber, then held it at the ready before him. "Never let your guard down. If you hear anything strange—anything at all—drop to a crouch and get my attention."

Though Nate gave her a strange look, Pauline nocked an arrow to her bow just in case something tried to jump out at her from the thick grass surrounding them on all sides. A slight breeze rustled the tips of the grass, but nothing else stirred the sultry afternoon air.

In this way, they walked the last half mile to Ooberti. Pauline breathed a sigh of relief when thatched rooftops appeared over a rise. She began to relax and returned her arrow to the quiver tied to her pack.

Nate didn't follow suit. Pauline wasn't sure what he noticed, but the closer they came to the village, the slower he walked. When they topped a rise, fifty feet from the first mud-walled cottage below, he stopped altogether.

He scanned the village from the rise. "It smells wrong."

"What do you mean?"

"No cook fires. And listen."

She didn't hear anything that alarmed her. She shook her head and gave him a questioning look.

"That's the problem. No noise. Where is everyone?"

Pauline's eyes widened. "You don't think . . ."

"No, the tiger didn't eat everyone in Ooberti. The people probably fled in terror."

They continued down the hill into town. As soon as they reached the hard-packed dirt track that served as the village's main street, Nate pointed to the ground. Even with her untrained eye, Pauline spotted a dozen pug marks within a few yards of where they stood.

"How long ago . . . ?"

"Can't tell. Its tracks are everywhere. It could still be here, in any one of these houses, looking out. Watching us."

A chill wended down her spine. She studied the darkened buildings on either side of the street. So many open doors, open windows. Square black eyes staring at them. It could be right there, inside the doorway, taking their measure. Gathering on its hind legs, preparing to hurl forth upon them.

"Don't let your fear take control, love," Nate said, speaking so softly she barely heard him. "The beast can smell fear as surely as sweet perfume. Walk in front of me. It's safer there. Keep your eyes open. And get your bow and arrow ready. It's not much, but it's better than nothing."

"We'll see about that." Pauline refused to let him dismiss her skills, despite the danger surrounding them.

He clenched her wrist so hard it hurt. His eyes burned with the intensity of the noonday sun. "Don't do anything foolish to prove a point. It's not worth your life."

Embarrassment coursed through her. She yanked her arm free of his grip and turned away. Preparing her bow and arrow, she took up a position in front of him while Nate turned to face whatever might come at them from behind.

In this way, back to back, they proceeded down the street. Step by careful step, looking for any sign of life. Pauline stepped over a broken bowl in the street. Leaking oil had congealed along a crack in its side.

The stench of rotting vegetables assaulted her nose. They were approaching an open market stall. Still no sign of life, or of the man-eating tiger.

When they crossed a blue slate courtyard common to a dozen houses, Nate stopped cold. He gestured for her to follow suit. He tapped his ear, indicating that he had heard something. On every side, the houses waited silently, their windows shuttered, their doorways yawning toward them, black with secrets.

Nate pointed toward a building on their right, what looked to be the largest house in the village. Shoving Pauline behind him, he pointed his rifle at the half-open door, then carefully nudged the door with the barrel of his rifle.

Pauline forgot to breathe. Nate believed something was in that house, and she didn't doubt him for a moment.

She stretched her arrow taut against the string, preparing to shoot whatever came through that door. Her fingers trembled so badly, she had to fight to keep the arrow nocked to the bowstring. Even if she aimed well, she didn't know if she had the force to wound an animal. Or the will. She had never shot anything but targets in her life.

All of her fantasies, her wild dreams about what she could do if given a chance—none of it meant anything if she crumbled when presented with an opportunity to prove herself. None of it—

She caught a flicker of movement in the shadows. Startled, she let her arrow fly.

THIRTEEN

A very human cry resounded from inside the house. Nate shoved open the door all the way, bringing them face to face with a pasty-faced Indian man cowering on the other side. Pauline noticed her arrow lodged in a pole in the center of the room.

Nate advanced into the room and yanked the arrow from the post. He turned to hand it to Pauline. "A tad trigger-happy, aren't we?"

"Oh, be quiet." She snatched her arrow back. "My aim was good."

He gave her an exasperated look from under his pith helmet, then turned to the quivering man by the door. The man had probably been peeking out the door at them as they came down the street. Nate spoke to him Hindi, and after a brief exchange, the man's countenance transformed from fear to outright joy.

He clapped his hands, then bowed repeatedly. *"Safed Sher!"* He said more than Nate's nickname, but Pauline only understood a word or two.

The Indian fellow closed the door, then turned and gestured for Nate to take a seat by the wall. Nate tugged Pauline's hand, directing her to sit beside him. "This is Gopesh, the village *malgoozar*. The headman," he explained at her questioning look. "He sent the villagers to the next town over just this afternoon, until the tiger moves on. Everyone in the neighboring villages has been terrorized the last few days. Stay shut up in their homes as much as possible. But eventually they have to go outside to collect food and firewood, even if it means taking their lives in their hands."

"Has the tiger moved on?" Pauline asked.

Nate sighed and said darkly, "The child was killed this afternoon."

"Ah, little Banhi, the tailor's daughter," the headman said in thickly accented English, wringing his hands. "She screamed, but we could not reach her in time." A desperate light entered his eyes. "The gods are punishing us. The beast has terrified the countryside with its thirst for human flesh! Every man in my village has lost a brother, or a wife, or a son. Many have suffered the tooth and claw marks of the evil *shaitan*. They will carry these marks to their graves."

"It's not a *shaitan*. It's a tiger, a male," Nate said, his tone matter-of-fact for the headman's benefit. "About five hundred pounds. It's limping in its left forepaw, and two toes are missing from its right, probably shot off by a rank amateur who failed to make a clean kill. It's also shedding mange wherever it goes."

Pauline couldn't hide her amazement. He had learned all this, simply from a handful of signs he had noticed on the way here.

"How far was the girl from the village when she was attacked?" Nate asked the headman.

"So near her home," he said in anguish. "In the western field."

Nate sighed and glanced about. "There's no telling whether it has moved on or is still lurking about." After a hesitant glance in Pauline's direction, he spoke in rapid Hindi to Gopesh. The headman looked her way, then nodded.

Pauline grasped Nate's arm. "What's going on?"

"We're staying here tonight."

Pauline glanced about the humble cottage. Though the headman's home was the largest in the village, it consisted of only three rooms. The main living area shared space with the kitchen and a nursery, apparent by the presence of a cradle in the corner. Two private rooms, probably bedrooms, took up the back half. The rooms were dark, the atmosphere fetid, and swarms of flies buzzed about the kitchen.

Still, sleeping here was better than sleeping outside, where the tiger might have an easy meal. Though, she admitted, she would sleep anywhere if Nate was by her side.

She smiled at the headman. "Thank you for your hospitality."

The headman's brown face split in a grin, his first since they had come upon him alone in the village. "I am honored to host *Safed Sher* and his woman."

His woman. A thrill shot through Pauline at the possession implied in such a phrase. She looked at Nate for his reaction, but he was occupied with unstrapping his bedroll from his pack.

Odd. Usually, he didn't pass up an opportunity to tease her. She studied him and noticed his tense, distant expression. His tight jaw and the harsh line of his mouth gave him an almost feral appearance, as if anything foolish enough to get in his way would pay a stiff price. No wonder he had received the name White Tiger.

As the headman retreated to the cottage's kitchen nook, Pauline began to wonder what was on Nate's mind. She sensed the men had discussed something more than sleeping arrangements.

"Nate?" she asked softly.

He didn't look up from unfurling his bedroll along one wall. "Take off your shoes, love," he said, sitting on his bedroll to unlace his boots. "It's good manners."

Pauline sat beside him and followed suit, but persisted in trying to learn their plans. "What about the tiger? When will we—"

"The sun is setting. It can't be tracked until morning. It could be miles away by now." His explanation sounded reasonable, but why wouldn't he meet her eyes? Rising, he set his shoes against the wall, then took hers and placed them beside his. The sight of their shoes so close together struck Pauline as deeply intimate.

The headman lit a fire under an iron pot in the crude stone hearth. Soon, the aroma of ghee, clarified butter used as cooking oil, filled the air of the cottage. Pauline's mouth began to water. She crossed to the small kitchen area, where Gopesh furiously chopped vegetables on a stone *adz*. "May I help?" she asked.

Gopesh frowned and waved her away. Pauline looked to Nate for help.

"He takes pride in hosting us," he said. He

crouched and unhooked her bedroll from her pack, then handed it to her.

Pauline looked about the small room for a place to make her bed, but already knew what she wanted to do. Her time with Nate was so short, she couldn't imagine any other choice. Besides, she had no reason to pretend a modesty she had long since given up where Nate was concerned.

Decided, she knelt and began unfurling her blankets right beside Nate's. Looking carefully at him, she braced for his reaction. He glanced up at her, but where she hoped for a wry comment on her brashly intimate move, she saw a hint of melancholy in his eyes that she couldn't begin to understand.

Gopesh carried over a bowl filled with a delicious-smelling mixture of vegetables and set it on a cloth on the floor. Pauline followed Nate's lead and sat down. She watched as Nate tore off a piece of the flat chapati bread, dipped it in the spicy dish, then popped it in his mouth. The food was delicious, though much spicier than she was used to. She was grateful for the lime water in a clay cup that Gopesh provided to accompany his simple meal.

She complimented the headman on his cooking, and he glowed with pride. Focusing again on Nate, Pauline asked him for details of how they would track and approach the tiger. To her consternation, he deflected her questions and appeared uninterested. Worse, he retreated into using Hindi with Gopesh, which cut her completely out of the conversation.

Annoyed, Pauline put her own bread in the bowl at the same time as he did, so that their fingers brushed. Still he didn't meet her eyes. He looked past her as if she didn't exist.

They were no longer alone, she reasoned. It made sense for him to forgo their usual brash familiarity.

Besides, they were closing in on their quarry. Naturally, he would focus on something other than her. He had a lot on his mind, with a potentially dangerous confrontation looming closer and closer. He had more important concerns than a spoiled rich girl, and she ought not to feel bereft merely to be without his attention for a single evening.

She almost managed to convince herself. Until his gaze met hers for one long second, his eyes filled with an almost palpable longing that sent her heartbeat fluttering.

A moment later, he looked away as if the moment hadn't happened.

As soon as Nate had taken his last bite of dinner, he slipped a pair of his hand-rolled cigarettes from his shirt pocket and offered one to the headman. Gopesh accepted gratefully.

Nate didn't even look her way when he quietly addressed her. "You're knackered. Why don't you turn in?"

It was on the tip of Pauline's tongue to protest her exclusion by the men, until she realized he was right. As if his words had made it so, fatigue hit her like a ton of bricks. Every muscle in her body ached from the past days' exertion. She still had not become accustomed to sleeping on the ground. The cottage's dry, even floor would be a welcome change.

Without waiting to see if she was settled, Nate joined the headman in the open doorway. His match flickered as he lit both cigarettes, then passed Gopesh one. With a sigh, Pauline rose unsteadily to her feet and crawled under her rough but sturdy blanket.

She sighed and lay back, listening to the low tones of the men's conversation floating on the warm evening air. She longed to know what they were saying, but they were stubbornly sticking to Hindi. They were probably discussing injuries the creature had inflicted on the people of this silent and desolate village. Or details of the coming hunt.

Pauline felt strangely edgy, her exhaustion not only physical but mental and emotional. She had tumbled headfirst into a new world filled with unusual experiences and unique landscapes, a world far removed from her pampered, easy life. Yet the greatest impact on her life had been knowing Nate. He had opened her eyes to new ways of living and thinking, made her feel things she had never imagined.

Memory of the passion they had shared in the temple caused her skin to prickle. She could hardly believe they had been so intimate, now that he had grown so distant. Her mind spinning from fatigue, she couldn't stifle a suspicion that Nate was planning something that excluded her.

She began to grow drowsy under the sound of the men's hushed voices. Gopesh's musical lilt contrasted with Nate's husky murmur. She could listen to his voice all night. She imagined him whispering in her ear, telling her sensual, secret things. Gradually, her eyes drifted closed.

When she next became aware of her surroundings, she found a deliciously warm body beside her.

Nate. He lay on his side facing her. If she maneuvered closer . . . She sidled toward him until her back was almost pressed against his front. Taking the hint, his bare arm slipped around her waist. She smiled in satisfaction. He was holding her again. Sleeping with him close beside her, there in the quiet night of an Indian hut, felt as intimate as their embraces in the temple. She had never imagined feeling so close to a man.

"I didn't mean to wake you," he whispered.

"Mmm. It's quite all right. I'm glad you're here." She sighed and settled deeper into his arms, against his firm yet giving body. Her fingers traced the corded muscles of his lightly furred forearms.

He pulled in a deep, shuddering breath. "Sweetheart," he whispered, then dropped a kiss on her earlobe.

Pauline felt as if a light glowed inside her. She'd been wrong, so wrong. He wasn't being distant, not at all. He still enjoyed her company. He still *wanted* her. As she wanted him. After they found the tiger, she would have to return home, alone. Tonight might be her only chance to be with this amazing man and experience fully the wild, feminine things he made her feel.

Desperate for his touch, she grasped his hand and pressed it flat against her belly. Fresh hunger coiled inside her, the same frighteningly real desire he had set flame to in the temple. How she wanted him! Even more than when he had cradled her nearly naked body in his arms, if that was possible. If she had learned anything being with Nate Savidge, it was to live in the moment, to take advantage of opportunities, to experience what life had to offer. And what life now offered, she did not have it in her to refuse. "Where is Gopesh?"

"In the back room. Asleep, I'll warrant. But we shouldn't make any noise. The walls are thin."

Pauline rolled over in the circle of his arms to face him. "Doing this doesn't make much noise." Twining her arms around his neck, she planted her mouth on his.

He grasped her lower back and pressed her hard against him, kissing her deeply and thoroughly, accepting her unquestioningly. He had expected this or, at least, wanted it as much as she. Not until her entire body had turned liquid, her heartbeat accelerated, and her toes were tingling did he break the kiss.

He said breathlessly, "You're incorrigible."

"I know. It's part of my charm."

His eyes reflected the starlight filtering through the gap between the wall and the roof. "Did you forget what I said in the temple?"

"That I'm using you? I haven't forgotten. Do you mind so much?" She slid her palm to his waist and found him wearing only undershorts. And she found something else—the hard, clear evidence of his desire for her. "I don't think you mind."

He sucked in a sharp breath. "Pauline . . ."

"A worldly man like you shouldn't be afraid to take what's offered. Isn't the hunt going to be dangerous? What if tonight is our last on earth? We shouldn't worry about what tomorrow may bring. About who we really are."

"You won't quit, will you?" Despite his words, she

sensed his resolve weakening by the way his palms played along her back.

"Are you going to satisfy my curiosity, or leave me hanging, always wondering what we may have missed? Force me to return to my dreary existence with those foolish boys and stuffy men courting me—"

"I'm bloody well not stealing your virtue. Not here in Gopesh's hut. Not anywhere."

". . . when you and I both know what we want." She began to press gentle kisses on his cheek, paying special attention to his scar. She loved his scar, even if he refused to tell her how he got it. She loved everything about him.

"We can't," he said, his voice rough. "When you marry, your husband will know. It will damage his trust in you."

"Not if I tell him before our wedding night. Besides, I'm never going to marry. I'm going to scare off all of my suitors until I become an old maid. Then I'll be free to travel wherever I want. I'm going to live like this forever. Day to day. Adventure to adventure. No more tea parties, thank God."

"You weren't born to this life."

"That doesn't matter."

"Of course it matters. You belong with your family, living the life of the idle rich. You—"

She cut him off with another thorough kiss. The last thing she wanted to do was discuss her family. She wanted no reminders of who she really was. Besides, he was wrong. She could be someone else. She could make her own life. Why couldn't he accept that about her? Why couldn't he forget, even for a moment, that she was an heiress? She wriggled even closer, pressing her hips against his swollen manhood.

With a growl, he rolled her onto her back. Lifting up on his arms, he stared hard at her. "Damn it, Pauline. I promised your sister . . ."

"If you mention my family one more time, I swear I'll shoot you while you sleep." Grasping him by his short blond hair, she yanked his mouth against hers.

He pulled away. To Pauline's shock, he grasped her in his powerful arms and flipped her onto her stomach. "There is something we can do," he growled, cupping her bottom.

"You're not going to spank me, are you?" she asked, mortification filling her. Did he mean to shame and punish her for her forward behavior? For tempting him?

His palm began moving in gentle circles. "Not quite. Unless you want me to."

Pauline could hardly breathe as she anticipated his next move. What was he going to do to her? Her own paltry experience seemed embarrassingly inadequate against the reality of his confidence, of his muscled strength. He could be planning anything. She was completely in his power, and she loved it.

His fingers darted between her thighs, sending jolts of pleasure through her. She jerked in surprise. "What . . . ?"

"You're interested in exploring, so I'm exploring," he said, his breath hot in her ear. "You."

"Oh."

"Lie still." Yanking open the ties at her waist, he thrust his hand beneath her cotton trousers and cupped the globe of her bare bottom. He squeezed it gently, then began to knead her. Pauline swallowed hard, her throat suddenly dry. Yet the area between her thighs was growing warm and moist. Her entire body began to relax into his touch.

Again his fingers slid between her thighs, this time skin against skin, touching her in alarmingly sensitive places she hadn't known her body possessed. A moan escaped her lips.

He yanked his hand away, ending the delicious torment. "Be quiet, or I'll stop."

"Yes," she said in a small, childlike voice, desperate to please him, desperate to continue. "Whatever you say. Just don't stop."

He resumed his delicious exploration of her most secret, feminine places, his fingers sliding between folds of skin, stroking her curls, sliding deeper into the recesses. "Open your thighs."

She instantly acquiesced under his command, spreading her legs apart. Her heartbeat pounded against the thin blankets beneath her.

His finger found an entrance, and he delved inside her, setting off a cascade of delicious feeling through her body. Pauline started to moan again, so she shoved her fist against her mouth. *Please, please, please* . . . She chanted silently, not knowing what she was longing for.

Before she was fully aware of it, she found herself on her back, gazing into Nate's eyes. His hand remained on her nether regions, again plumbing the mysterious passageway she knew existed down there. As she'd seen on the temple walls, during lovemaking, men thrust their organs inside this private place possessed by women. But he didn't need to do that to make her body tremble with feeling.

His thumb teased a different place, a nub where all her pleasure centered. She bit hard on her fist to keep from screaming in delight.

He smiled at her reaction, fine lines crinkling at the corners of his eyes. His touching intensified, became stroking, picking up a rhythm that seemed to echo the blood pounding in her ears. Hunger mingled with the pleasure he wrought in her, and she found herself thrusting her hips toward his hand, desperate for release from the tension building inside her.

"Yes, sweetheart, yes," he murmured, dropping tender kisses on her forehead and cheeks. "Let it go."

And then it happened. A burst of pleasure so intense, she thought for a moment she had died. Despite his admonition, a ragged groan escaped her lips. He stifled it with a punishing kiss that stole her breath.

Later . . . Was it hours or merely minutes? She lay in his arms and stared in amazement at her lover. "Is that . . . normal?" she asked, feeling incredibly naive.

He chuckled. "What do you think?"

"I think women should do this all the time. Every chance they get!" To think the married ladies she knew might be experiencing such passion with their husbands! That they hid such secrets under their corsets and petticoats, pretending to be serene and virtuous and ignorant of such things. She *knew* passion was special and important; she knew it all along! "I can't believe we never talk about it, that we pretend it doesn't exist. How utterly foolish."

"Sad, isn't it?" He scooped her into his arms and cradled her close. "You're one amazing woman, Pauline. If more ladies were like you, things might be different."

"What things?"

He grew silent, and she knew he wasn't going to elaborate.

"Nate?"

"Yes?"

"You didn't . . . That is, men feel it, too, right?"

"No, and of course." He stroked her scalp. "Tonight was for you, for the wild lady I'll never forget."

"Mmmm . . . " Pleased with his generous response, with the lingering glow of pleasure that weighted her limbs, Pauline settled deeper into his arms. "Is it proper to thank a man for . . . that?"

She felt his chest vibrate and knew he was laughing again. "I don't know the proper etiquette for ladies in the bedroom, sweetheart. But I accept your thanks."

Pauline's skin heated in embarrassment. She must sound so foolish to an experienced man like Nate. Worse, she had just reinforced his perception of her as a lady who had been drilled in etiquette since birth. Despite the intimacy they had shared, despite how he had explored her body and given her the greatest pleasure, they remained worlds apart, a fact he refused to forget.

I'm never going to wash away her scent. Nate's sentimentality surprised him. In the predawn light, he carefully removed his arms from around the sleeping woman beside him. He longed to stroke her, to feel her satiny skin under his callused hands, to make love to her properly. But he dared not. Instead, he pulled in a long, quiet breath, inhaling her scent and imprinting it on his memory as an animal of the forest might.

She gave a little moan as he pulled away, and adjusted her position. He sat quietly beside her, ready to lie back down if she woke. To his relief, she remained asleep.

So beautiful in sleep, so innocent. And completely naive. She still believed so-called adventure was a stroll through the park, a pleasurable pastime. She had so much to learn about life. But he could not be the one to show it to her. She belonged with her people, not with him.

He should never have allowed Pauline to travel this far with him. Her safe little adventure had grown far too dangerous—and not only from tigers. For he was the worst beast of them all. Lord, how he wanted to make love to her! But then what? Leave her to her shame?

He couldn't do that to her. No. There was no other way. Besides, this was easiest for both of them.

He should have sent her home much sooner, before this unquenchable longing had developed between them. If she hadn't been so eager for him . . . If he hadn't fancied her company so much . . . If he'd worked harder to make her adventure a chore . . .

Too late now. Nothing left for it but this.

His backpack and rifle waited by the door, ready for him. His worn boots rested against the wall beside her smaller, almost-new pair, a far cry from the satin and French-tooled leather that usually graced her feet. That *ought* to grace her feet.

As stealthy as a tiger, he put on his shoes, then slipped on his pack and shouldered his rife. Looking back at the sleeping lady, his heart tangled in a knot of pain. He knew he would never see her again.

Good-bye, sweetheart.

Turning, he forced himself to walk out the door.

FOURTEEN

Pauline stretched and opened her eyes. Morning light filled the small hut. Its door stood open and she could hear the sounds of villagers talking on the street outside. A delicious scent filled the room. A chubby Indian woman stood by the fire, stirring something in a pot. She must be Gopesh's wife.

Pauline pushed up on her elbows and glanced around. Where was Nate? Had he gone out during the night and hunted the tiger? From the sounds outside, it was apparent some of the villagers had returned to their homes.

"Good morning," Pauline said, drawing the woman's attention.

She smiled and shook her head, and Pauline realized she didn't understand. *"Safed sher?"*

A shadow filled the small doorway, and Pauline sat up in anticipation of seeing the man in question. Instead, it was Gopesh. He stepped inside his home. "This is my wife. She is cooking you a fine breakfast."

"Thank you, Gopesh." After making certain her clothing was in place, she threw off her blankets and stood. "But where is Nate?"

"You like *dahi*? She prepares it special," he said, referring to a yogurt dish.

"Yes, that's fine. But Nate. *Safed Sher.* Where has he gone?"

"To hunt the tiger, of course." He gestured toward the street outside, where villagers chatted with their neighbors. "We are no longer afraid, now that he has come."

"But where? Where did he go?"

"For the tiger, of course."

Gopesh was being frustratingly vague. She knew *that* much!

"When will he be back?"

Gopesh looked away from her. "I and three fellows are to escort you to the prince of Rawa's palace. It is only a half day from here. From there you are to take a train to Simla. Please, gather your things and we will set off immediately."

"Nate left me here?" He had abandoned her! She could hardly believe it.

At the same time, part of her felt absolutely no surprise. He had never really wanted her around. Never wanted *her*. Last night, he had pleasured her only to shut her up. He had taken no pleasure in return. *Because he felt nothing for her but a passing fondness.* What had he said the night before? That his "gift" was for "the wild lady I'll never forget." She hadn't understood he meant to leave this very morning!

And she would never see him again.

No. Her adventure would not end like this. She refused to allow him to abandon her just when they were about to reach their goal. She peered at Gopesh. Nate Savidge inspired deep loyalty in those who knew him, or even those who knew *of* him.

Gopesh was not going to be cooperative of his own free will.

But her will was stronger. So was her determination. Turning to her pack and supplies, she lifted her bow and nocked an arrow to it. Turning, she aimed the weapon right at Gopesh's chest. "Tell me where he went. Now," she said with quiet intensity.

Gopesh threw up his hands while his wife shrieked in terror. Pauline had no time to spare feeling guilty for her ruse. This time, the headman's cooperation was immediate and thorough. "He was heading to the field where the tiger was last seen," he blurted out.

"Thank you." She released the tension on the bowstring. Tying the weapon once more to her pack, she shouldered her burden and strode out of the house.

For hours Pauline half walked, half ran, determined to catch up to Nate before nightfall, praying she hadn't lost him altogether. She thought she was heading in the right direction.

After passing the spot where the girl had been killed, she found a fresh boot print, then another, heading southeast. It was enough to start with. But Nate charted his path by reading all sorts of signs on the ground, in the air, in the trees. He may have spotted pug marks she missed, or another sign indicating where the tiger had gone, and headed in a completely different direction.

The longer she was alone out here, the more worried she became. She had run off without so much as a hunting knife, much less a rifle to defend herself against a predatory tiger. Was the man-eater nearby? Warily, she studied the shadows between the trees. Was it watching her? Preparing to spring?

She had been a fool to run after him. The sun, painfully white in the sky, beat down mercilessly on her head. Still she straggled on, determined not to be left behind. Not to be lost. She passed buffaloes wallowing in shrunken mudholes, desperate to cool off, and pariah dogs panting under thirsty shrubs. She glanced around for shade trees or a creek, somewhere she could rest, but saw nothing of promise.

Far on the horizon, gray clouds clustered, but rain seemed an impossible dream.

Exhausted, her steps faltered as she scaled a rocky ridge. Sucking in a breath of the scorching air, she forced her legs to keep moving until she reached the crest. From her new vantage point, she looked down on a tree-filled valley—and spotted movement along a track halfway down the steep incline.

An animal? No. Nate's pith helmet. Relief surged through her, making her knees quiver. She had found him. Their time together wasn't over, after all.

For a moment longer she watched him stride along the path, away from her. With every step, he looked to each side, alert for any unfriendly creatures. He hadn't yet seen her.

She began to pick her way down the ridge.

She had almost reached the path when Nate yanked his rifle off his shoulder and spun on her, pointing his rifle straight at her chest.

Startled, Pauline threw up her hands. She lost her balance, skidded several yards, and landed right before him, slamming painfully onto her knees.

Straightening, she looked up. Twin rifle barrels filled her vision. She forced a smile to her face and struggled to her feet.

Nate lowered his rifle and removed his finger from the trigger. His face creased in a scowl, the scar dividing his left cheek turning a livid shade of red.

Without removing his stormy gaze from her, he clicked the safety catch in place and shouldered his rifle. "You were supposed to be at the palace by now."

A knot of anger tightened in her chest. "You didn't even say good-bye," she shot back.

He gritted his teeth so hard, a pulse throbbed in his jaw. "Good-bye." He turned his back on her and strode away along the rocky path.

Pauline stared after him in shock. He intended to leave her here, in this wilderness? She looked about. Should she try to find her way back to the village of Ooberti, or continue to follow Nate? After his cold rejection, she couldn't bring herself to take a single step in his direction. As the distance between them lengthened, she remained frozen, uncertain whether she was going or coming.

When Nate had taken thirty steps, he slowed and drew to a stop. He swung around to face her. She shifted her feet uncertainly, hope returning in a rush.

He stared at her for several tense seconds. Then his rigid posture broke. Swearing, he strode toward her in quick, even strides.

He stopped inches from her, his furious gaze pinning her where she stood. "Since you've come this far, I'm stuck with you. If I waste time taking you back, I'll lose the tiger's trail—not to mention, the beast may claim more victims."

"I won't be a burden."

His eyes narrowed. "Why stop now?"

She stiffened and met his gaze with a fiery glare of her own. "From what you told me, she is paying you well. I'm sure my sister didn't intend for you to abandon me in a tiny village in the middle of nowhere while a man-eating tiger is terrorizing the countryside."

If possible, he tensed even more. "I like money as much as the next bloke. But I'm not daft. I intended to leave you in a safe place before we came across the tiger. If you hadn't gotten this fool notion to traipse after me—"

"If you had told me your plans—"

"Would it have made a difference?"

"Not one bit," she readily shot back. She never would have allowed him to leave her behind, and they both knew it.

"Damn it, Pauline. If anything should happen to you . . ."

"What about you?" She grabbed his shirtfront. "Do you think I could leave you in danger? Not knowing whether you were safe? Do you think I care so little?" She gave him a shake.

He grasped her shoulders and dragged her hard against him. "Ripping my shirt won't solve anything. Maybe this will." His mouth descended on hers.

He grabbed her so suddenly, she lost her footing on the loose gravel of the narrow path. The ground shifted under her feet. She began to slide, bringing him with her. They tumbled down the incline and landed in a heap at the bottom.

Pauline landed atop Nate, nose to nose, her thigh

jammed between his. She struggled for breath, felt his chest heaving beneath her.

Their eyes locked. Pauline knew he felt as she did, that nothing else mattered but being in his arms. The rest of the world faded away.

Moving with mutual intent, their lips met in a searing kiss. This time Nate held nothing back. He devoured her like a hungry beast of the jungle. He kissed her cheeks, her neck, her jawline. "You were going to leave me," Pauline gasped between kisses, "without even saying good-bye."

"Bugger all. I was out of my mind." He lowered his mouth to the neckline of her tunic. "Out of my mind."

He growled so ferociously, it prickled the hair on the back of her neck.

His neck snapped up and his eyes widened. "Almighty God," he whispered, his face losing all color.

The growl hadn't come from Nate.

A tiger.

A second growl came, chilling Pauline to the bone. She arched her neck to the right. A fiery-orange-and-white apparition stood less than twenty feet away—a muscled, fierce creature with piercing yellow eyes and the longest, sharpest teeth she had ever seen. Caught off guard, they were completely at its mercy.

A shiver rippled through her, and her stomach churned in icy dread. *We're going to die.*

Nate's hands gripped her so hard, she knew he would leave bruises. "My rifle."

She followed his eyes up the hill. His pack had

made it halfway down, but his rifle lay discarded at the top. He had dropped it when she had fallen against him and sent him tumbling down the hill.

Her own pack remained on her back along with her small quiver of arrows. But her bow—where was her bow?

The tiger took a step closer to them, its nostrils flaring as it breathed in their scent. Her gaze flicked to its right foreleg, where two toes were missing. Its left leg showed a jaggedly healed wound, causing it to limp. *Just as Nate had described. The man-eater.*

This bold creature, used to killing weak humans, obviously thought the two of them made for easy prey, since it had allowed them to see it before it struck. The tiger skinned its lips back from its four-inch ivory fangs, then hissed a bloodcurdling sound that could mean only one thing: it was about to pounce. It gathered on its haunches, preparing to spring.

Nate threw her off of him and she landed four feet away. He sat up facing the tiger. "Run, Pauline. *Now!*"

She scrambled to find her footing on the rocky ground. Startled into action, the tiger pounced on Nate and sank its razor-sharp teeth into his thigh.

FIFTEEN

Nate screamed in agony. The horrific sound shattered Pauline's nerves, cutting her to the quick. He was being eaten alive right before her eyes.

"No!" Finally finding her feet, Pauline hurled herself at the tiger, unsure what she was doing, knowing only that she had to get it off of Nate.

Grabbing a rock from the ground, she hurled it at the back of the tiger's head. Startled, the tiger released Nate. Blood dripping from its jaws, it turned its attention to her and swiped at her with one claw-laden paw, scraping her torso enough to make her bleed. Pain sliced through her.

"Get out of here!" Nate cried out. Pauline didn't know if he was addressing her or the tiger. He had managed to rise to his knees when the tiger swung back around and insolently batted the big man off balance. He fell onto his back.

Do something. Anything. Find another weapon! She considered going for the rifle, but by the time she ran up the hill to reach it, Nate would be dead. She had to find something else to use against the tiger. *Please God, please God . . .*

As if in answer to her prayer, she spotted her bow

hung up in the branches of a shrub, just a few feet away. Wasting no time, she grabbed it. Arrow . . .

With one swift move, she reached over her shoulder for an arrow and nocked it to the bowstring. The horrible image of the tiger sinking its teeth into Nate's shoulder filled her vision, terrifying and sickening her. His expression of agony ripped her heart from her chest. This was no sporting event. *This one counts . . . no time to aim . . . have to aim, only one chance!* Moving faster than she ever had, she took aim and loosed the arrow, right at the tiger's exposed white undercoat.

The tiger yowled and released Nate. It jerked back and retreated into the bushes, the shaft of her arrow extending from its chest.

She'd done it. She'd scared it off, possibly even struck a fatal blow.

"Nate." She stumbled to his side on weakened knees.

He looked up at her through eyes bleary with pain. "Get out of here," he mouthed, still trying to tell her to save herself. As if she would ever leave him.

Yet she didn't know how much time they had, or how badly she may have wounded the beast. It could return at any time to finish them off. "Can you walk?"

His thigh was covered in blood, and a flap of skin had been torn loose from his shoulder. She had to stem the bleeding before he passed out.

Finishing the shredding of his shirt begun by the tiger, she tore off a strip of cloth, folded it, and pressed it to his shoulder. Taking his free hand, she pressed it into place. He flinched at the pressure on his fresh wound.

"Hold this in place. Keep the pressure on if you can." Tearing off a second strip, she bound the makeshift bandage in place, then began to repeat the process for the wound in his thigh. Here the tiger had got a better grip with its powerful jaws, leaving numerous puncture wounds on both sides of his leg. How could she possibly bind this? How could she get Nate the help he needed? Panic began to build within her. Valiantly she fought it down, determined not to fail Nate.

"Pauline." Nate grasped her arm. The weakness of his grip frightened Pauline more than she dared let on. "Where is it?"

"I shot it with an arrow. It ran off."

He swallowed hard. Perspiration moistened his brow. "It's not done with us."

"I'll be ready. Don't worry about anything, Nate." She hoped he took solace in the confidence that she struggled to project and didn't at all feel.

She nocked another arrow to her bow while she considered what to do. The rifle called to her from the top of the hill. If she ran as fast as she could, she could retrieve it in less than a minute. But the tiger might only need a minute to finish Nate off.

She spent a moment studying the bushes, listening carefully. No noises. No branches moving.

She had to risk it. She had no choice. Her arrows probably couldn't finish off a tiger of that size, not soon enough. She had to be sure it was dead before attempting to move Nate. And he needed help, now.

Pulling her legs under her, she moved into a crouch, ignoring the lancing pain from her own shallow wound. "Nate, can you shoot an arrow? I'm going for the rifle."

"Stupid weapon," he said, his words slurring from loss of blood. "Give it to me."

She helped him drag himself into a sitting position, leaning against a tree. Preparing the bow, she passed it to him. Despite his injured left arm, he had just enough strength to support the bow and draw back the bowstring with his right hand. A wave of trembles shook the arrow from the bowstring. He fumbled to slide it back in place. She bent to help him, until he bit out, "Hurry, damn it. This hurts like hell."

Spinning away, she sprinted up the hill as fast as she had ever run in her life, leaving him alone and vulnerable. Each step stretched into eternity, each pounding heartbeat propelling her forward in an endless, impossible quest for the rifle.

The hill couldn't be more than forty feet high, but years passed before she scrambled over the ridge to the top. Snatching up the rifle, she spun around.

A menacing snarl reverberating off the surrounding hillsides. Just as she feared, the tiger had sensed her departure and reappeared to finish off its kill. Its large oval head lowered to the ground as it prepared to spring on Nate. Her arrow still protruded from its bloodstained chest, but Pauline now saw how far right of his heart it had struck.

Nate was aiming an arrow at it but then his hands slipped, and the arrow became dislodged. Pauline jerked the rifle to her shoulder, threw off the safety catch, and fired into the air.

The noise startled the tiger and it darted once more into the bushes.

Pauline half ran, half slid back down the hill to Nate's side.

He smiled at her, but his expression looked more like a rictus of pain. Tossing aside her bow, he held out his hand for the rifle. "Good girl."

"You think you're going to fire this thing?"

"You think you are? I don't have the energy to argue."

"At least let me load it for you." Keeping it, she extracted a cartridge from his shirt pocket and shoved it home.

"Didn't know you knew how," he said. The wry tone returning to his voice gave her hope that he would pull through, if she could find him help.

Nate no longer struggled for the gun, and Pauline set up a vigil beside him. The rifle ready, she sat cross-legged beside him, the gun in her hands, her gaze on the bushes surrounding them. "Over there."

"You didn't bargain for this, did you?" he rasped.

"Neither did you."

"I was born to do this."

She gave him a sideways glance. "And I was born to eat from a silver spoon, is that it?"

"That's it." He coughed.

Pauline winced along with him as the reflex shook his injured frame. She leaned close and stroked his forehead. So clammy and cold.

"Now . . ."

While she was distracted with concern, he snatched his rifle from her grasp and settled it across his own lap. He smiled in victory.

Pauline decided to let him have his way for now, since it seemed to lift his spirits. If, however, the tiger returned . . .

Jerking the rifle to his shoulder, he fired off a round. The sound, so close, blew out her ears, but still she heard the telltale thump of something hitting the ground.

"That should do it." With that, he promptly fainted.

Pauline stared at the body of the tiger, lying half in and half out of the underbrush. It had reappeared, and she hadn't even heard it.

Thank God Nate had. If she had followed her first stubborn impulse and kept the rifle . . . She shuddered. She never could have aimed and fired with such deadly accuracy. Her entire body began to shake as reality crystallized into a sharp, frightening truth. She was out of her depth. Faced with the harsh life-or-death reality of the past half hour, her childish longing for adventure now seemed like the dreams of a fool.

How could she ever handle the challenges now thrust upon her? She had never felt so inadequate. She had caused this. If she hadn't pursued Nate, he would have remained alert and undistracted. He wouldn't now be dying.

Like hell, as Nate would say. She wouldn't let him die here.

But how could she possibly help him? Already a pair of long-billed vultures circled in the sky above, drawn by the promise of an easy feed on fresh carrion.

SIXTEEN

A dull throbbing pulsed through Nate. What was hurting, and why? The gray mists slowly began to release his mind, enabling him to think, to remember.

Tiger. Its powerful jaws piercing his flesh, trying to tear off a chunk of him. The sheer, blinding agony of being helpless in its grip, his impulses reduced to sheer desperation to survive. The certainty he would not.

At the painful memory, his thigh wound flared and sharpened, echoed by a lesser burning in his shoulder. He wasn't dead, or he wouldn't be hurting. Somehow, he had survived. But would the tiger be back?

Pauline. Had she escaped? Panic seized him and his body jerked, sending a bolt of pain through him.

His physical discomfort drew him past the last muddled mist and into full consciousness.

"He is rousing. The morphine is wearing off." The man's voice was one Nate didn't recognize.

Then a wonderfully familiar feminine voice spoke beside him. "He will recover?"

"In time. He has lost a lot of blood but is past the critical point. The wounds were deep, but I have treated the sepsis, and the stitches will hold."

"Thank God."

Joy filled him to know that Pauline was so near. Cracking his eyelids, he discovered he lay in an enormous four-poster bed of carved teak in a vast white marble room, with Pauline sitting beside him. Squinting against the light, he strained to focus on her face. "Pauline?" His voice sounded weak and scratchy, unlike his own.

She slid her hand into his. "I'm here. You still haven't managed to be rid of me."

"Where . . . ?" He licked his lips. His mouth felt stuffed with cotton.

Another feminine hand appeared in his line of sight, holding a water glass to his lips. The lady tilted the glass and he drank. It prickled along the roof of his mouth, and his stomach heaved momentarily from the shock. Turning his head, he saw an English nurse, complete with white apron and cap, replacing the glass on a nightstand beside the bed. Beside her stood the doctor, presumably, in a well-tailored suit.

A hospital, then? He shifted his attention back to Pauline. As he took her full measure, his sense of reality took another spin out of orbit.

She had Pauline's face and voice, but none of the hard edges he had grown so fond of. Instead of rough cotton men's clothing, a turquoise sari edged in the finest gold embroidery flowed against the curves of her lithe form. In place of a hastily knotted braid tossed carelessly down her back, her hair flowed in shining waves past her shoulders.

She looked as regal as a queen, the picture of elegant sensuality. She seemed at home in the native costume. He fingered her brocade-embroidered silk sleeve. "You're a rani," he murmured.

"Only while we're here in Rawa. The prince has been kind enough to help us."

"Safed Sher!" The man's booming voice yanked Nate's attention to the foot of the massive bed. He had met Prince Mahadeva only twice before, but—in the tradition of India's small community of princes and British rulers—had made a friend in the rotund, brown-skinned, and very European native. The prince wore a traditional Hindu saffron-colored satin robe and loose trousers befitting his station. Yet his hair had been neatly clipped and parted in the English style. With his Oxford education, he spoke English better than Nate, who had only attended small English-run country schools here in India. Nate tried not to hold that against him.

Grinning, the prince rubbed his plump hands together. "You are awake. It is good, it is very good."

Nate's voice worked better after his drink of water. "I don't understand. We were in the woods." He looked at Pauline's serene face. "How did we end up here?"

"Your lady friend is quite resourceful, and remarkably strong for a woman," the prince said.

Nate gave Pauline a thorough once-over. Yes, she was strong—for a slender young woman half his size. "You couldn't possibly have carried me."

"Don't be silly," she said. "You weigh twice as much as I do."

"One's problems are solved as much by the mind as the body," the prince said with an expansive smile.

Nate looked pointedly at Pauline, silently demanding an explanation and an end to his curiosity.

She smiled at his impatience. "It's truly not as amazing as it seems. My oldest sister, Hannah, dragged us all to the Natural History Museum more times than I cared to go. One room features displays on the Indians—American Indians, I mean. I put together a travois . . ."

"You built a travois? Out of what?"

"Well, yes. I couldn't think of any other way." Her fingers twisted the silk on her lap. "Your tent—I rather destroyed it, I'm afraid. And your hunting knife, the one you use to skin animals? I may have blunted it just a bit when I hacked down bamboo poles."

As if his equipment mattered! By God, if Pauline hadn't figured out how to use the few resources at her disposal, he'd be food for scavenging animals by now, his bones bleaching in the sun.

"I managed to rouse you just enough to move you onto it."

He nodded. "I recall you shoving and rolling me about."

"Some of that was the journey, I'm sure. The ground was hardly smooth."

His admiration for her threatened to bring tears to his eyes. "How far did you have to drag me? How did you even know where to go?"

"You have a compass. I headed east, toward Rawa. Well, I hoped I was going toward Rawa. Some travelers met us after a few miles and helped bring us here."

"You are tiring my patient," the doctor scolded,

shooting an annoyed look at Pauline. "You must leave the sick room now. Allow the patient to rest."

Before Nate could protest, the doctor leaned over him and inserted a needle into his arm. Once more, Nate began to slide into a blissful, dreamless sleep.

He had nearly died because of her. A lump formed in Pauline's throat. She gazed down at Nate, sleeping in the immense four-poster bed, a single bedside lantern highlighting the angles of his beard-stubbled face.

The doctor said his wounds were healing, and he would soon be out of bed. From there, it would only be a matter of time before he was back to full health. Of course, there would always be scars. Scars she had caused.

The lantern's glow gave his short blond hair an almost unearthly sheen. Her eyes played over the dramatic scar slicing across his cheek, its protruding ridge dividing his face into light and shadow. He had never told her what beast had wounded him so visibly.

Desire filled her to be close to him, to comfort him. Taking care not to disturb him, she slipped onto the bed. Though stretched alongside him, she remained outside the covers so that no one could accuse her of improprieties.

Oddly enough, she almost cared about that, not for herself but for Nate. She understood now how her family must have felt all those times she misbehaved, how her actions echoed to the people around her. Those she loved. *Thank goodness Lily learned of my*

*latest adventure, or she would have worried herself sick.
That would have been my fault, too.*

Nate was right. She was spoiled, thinking only of herself.

No more. Now that the tiger was dead and Nate was going to be all right, she would have to go back to being who she was, just as Nate had said all along. *And stop hurting those I love.*

Unless Nate wanted her, of course. Wanted to keep her with him. Hope filled her, and her chest felt as if it might burst with pleasure at the thought. To stay here in India, with Nate . . . What could possibly be more perfect?

She couldn't resist the urge to touch the man who meant so much to her. She stroked his forehead and ran a finger down the long scar that marred his rugged face. "Nate," she whispered. "I'm sorry."

His eyelids twitched, then opened. He focused on her. "Hello, love. Still on the deathwatch?"

She gave him a small slap on his uninjured shoulder. "Don't make light of it. You *could* have died because of my foolishness."

He seemed honestly mystified. "You? You saved me."

"I also distracted you. Without me trailing behind you and—and other things, you would have heard the tiger stalking you. You wouldn't have been hurt."

"Young ladies are good at weaving spells around men, making them forget their common sense." His eyes slid down her body, noting how close she lay to him.

Was he talking about someone other than her? He rarely spoke of his past outside of his hunting, and she burned to know everything about him. Perhaps tonight, with morphine relaxing his system, he would reveal his secrets. "If you weren't so pig-headed, you'd have the decency to tell me what you have against ladies like me," she said, knowing only a direct challenge would breach the walls he had built.

His eyes narrowed and he glared at her. Then he sighed and gazed at the ceiling. When he spoke, his voice was matter-of-fact. "Beatrice."

"Excuse me?"

"Her name."

"She could be named George, for all I care. What matters is what she did to you."

He didn't answer for a long while. The only sound in the room was the gentle night breeze through the latticed window screens, and their breathing. Pauline began to think he would never open up.

Finally, he began. "To my great folly, she made me believe I could actually be someone I wasn't. None of us ever can."

At eighteen, nothing in Nate's experience had prepared him for Beatrice. The product of perfect English breeding, she fulfilled his every fantasy of the sophisticated world beyond India.

He had met her aboard ship, on his way to England. His mother had decided he needed to meet his father, now that he was a man. Even before the ship left port, he knew he wouldn't fit in. He didn't know a soul in first class. He lacked the proper manners and stood out like a sore thumb. He hated the

vast, flat sea—until, three days into the voyage, he
met Beatrice.

She immediately encircled him with her bright
light of belonging. He basked in her warmth and
charm, and in short order he was in love.

When the ship reached England, he received her
promise that she would call on him at his father's
house.

Her visit was one of the few things that he could
look forward to. For two tedious months, he suffered
through dull, dreary days in his father's house, os-
tensibly becoming acquainted with his father and
brother. Rupert, the coolly diffident product of his
father's first marriage, resented the surprise appearance of a never-before-seen younger brother. His
father was no more enthusiastic to be dealing with a
lad from the countryside—and not even the English
countryside. Upon seeing Nate for the first time, his
father exclaimed, "By God, she bred me a peasant!"
And he treated Nate as such, making it clear his el-
dest was by far the favored son, the ideal of all he
held dear.

A thousand times a day, his brother and father
found fault with his manners and country-school education. The conclusion was obvious: he had been
wrong to come.

The only bright spot in his days was the frequent
visits of Beatrice, his lady love. To his relief, when she
was around, his father and Rupert treated him like a
gentleman. Only later did he learn why.

One evening, Rupert cornered him in their father's study, taunting him over his poor breeding.
Goaded to the breaking point, Nate threw caution to

the wind and took a swing at the thin, heartless creature called his brother. Rupert fell hard against a table holding a decanter of whiskey and two glasses, which shattered on the floor under his weight.

His blood fury high, Nate fell on his prey, determined to teach him a lesson with his fists that the namby-pamby city boy would never forget. He didn't count on Rupert playing dirty. Grasping a shard of broken glass, he swung it up and sliced through Nate's cheek.

The violent confrontation marked the end of all pretense. Rupert and Nate hated each other, and their father made his choice clear. As soon as his face was properly stitched, Nate made arrangements to return to his homeland, India.

Yet he could not leave his beloved Beatrice behind. His heart brimming with love, he finally gathered the courage to propose to her. They sat beside each other on a settee in his father's parlor. There, he told her how much he loved and needed her.

Her reply still echoed in his mind, still retained the power to hurt despite the distance and the years.

Her words came easily, as if she had rehearsed them. "I care for you, Nate. You know that. Yet you have taken my friendly manners to mean a depth of feeling I never intended. No doubt this is a result of your lack of experience with ladies of good breeding."

Her words seemed to come from a stranger. "Beatrice, we kissed. You led me to believe . . ."

Her fine-boned, aristocratic face turned stony, devoid of any warmth. "In truth, I am the wronged party. You have offended my feminine sensibilities with your forward behavior. You presume a cheapness of my affection when you have nothing of value to offer a lady. I hardly gave you leave for such familiarity. Truly, I am appalled. Besides, you cannot truly believe I would be pleased to live in your awful, savage *India.*"

"Beatrice . . ." Lacking proper parlor manners, he clasped her shoulders in a last, desperate attempt to keep her by his side. "You can't mean any of this."

"Stop pawing me!" Her expression filled with disgust, she shook him off and abruptly stood. She spoke down to him, like a goddess from on high. "You're little better than an animal, Nate. You must realize you're beneath me, despite your fortunate birth." She turned and strode from the room. He never saw her again.

The day he sailed for India, she announced her engagement—to his brother Rupert, the Earl of Avon, future Marquess of Bathurst.

Her response had devastated his young, naive heart. But he was a man now. He understood what had driven Beatrice to use him to meet his brother, to secure her place in society as a marchioness. He understood, but he could never sympathize.

Nate finished his abbreviated telling of his past without revealing his family's status. He couldn't bring himself to speak of it, their snobbery so disgusted him. Besides, his English heritage meant nothing to him.

Sliding her fingers along his forearm, Pauline gently turned over his hand and gave it a squeeze. Her touch pulled him back to the present, and he realized she had laid her head on his chest while he spoke.

Now she looked him squarely in the eyes. "I'm not Beatrice."

He smiled and stroked back a strand of her silky hair that lay against her cheek. "Thank God for that." Beatrice, with her refined manners and pampered life, could never have endured a fraction of what Pauline had.

As if hearing his thoughts, Pauline continued, "You can't believe I'm anything like her, not after everything I've done. Everything we've done together. I've run away with you."

He sighed. While her character was nothing like Beatrice's, her social position was much the same. "What have you really risked? Yes, you came with me. But your sister was protecting you the entire time. When you return to Simla, your family will put out a story that you returned from a visit to a relative or a friend. No one will ever know that you've been with me, unchaperoned. Intimate."

She clasped his hand and brought it to her mouth. Sliding her lips along the back of his hand, she tasted him, whetting his appetite for further explorations. "Then why not be intimate?" she murmured, invitation in her eyes.

Despite his recuperation, his body responded with fierce hunger. *Oh, God, give me strength!* He wanted to make love to her no less than she wanted to explore her carnality with him. Fighting down his growing desire, he tried to remember his rational objection to taking Pauline to bed.

I have no desire to be used, he reminded himself, *even for pleasure.* But his longing for the lithe, lovely woman pressed so close to him made it nearly impossible for him to keep to his best intentions. The pleasure she promised . . . He could hardly contain his need to feel close to her, to show her all her body was capable of. To remember what *he* was capable of, now that he had almost tasted death.

"I'm weary. Go to bed, Pauline." Firmly closing his eyes, he feigned sleep while fighting to bring his pulsing desire under control.

With an exasperated sigh, she climbed off his bed. He felt a soft kiss on his cheek, then heard her steps as she left his room.

"All of the villages in my district resound with celebration now that the tiger has been vanquished. The legend of the White Tiger grows throughout the land." Prince Mahadeva relaxed across from Nate in a thronelike settee covered in satin cushions the color of tangerines. His richly appointed office reflected the grandeur of his palace.

Pauline must feel at home here, Nate mused, glancing about. He hadn't visited Prince Mahadeva in years. The centuries-old palace hadn't changed, except for newly acquired fine art pieces in the prince's growing collection. Columns crowned with elephant heads carved from differently colored stones supported twenty-foot ceilings. Elaborately carved bay windows overlooked an enclosed garden snatched from Eden. The floor, decorated with intricate mosaics of plants and animals, reflected the heritage of the conquering Moghuls of centuries past, who had constructed this grand edifice.

"I am most impressed with your bravery, as always," the prince said.

"It's all in a day's work. Besides, Pauline is the real hero," Nate said, discomfited by the attention. Darts of pain shot up his leg as he shifted on an ornate rosewood chair. Noting his discomfort, the prince signaled one of a dozen servants standing silently nearby. Immediately, an ottoman was placed at Nate's feet, his ankles lifted gently to rest upon it. Another signal to a servant brought a hookah, which the prince offered to Nate. Nate shook his head, and the prince reclined and began gently puffing on the pipe.

"Ah, your woman. Lovely, and quite unique. My wife didn't know what to make of her, an English-woman dressed in peasant clothes. I trust you find the sari more flattering?"

Nate sighed. "Whatever makes her happy." Now that they had accomplished their task, he would have to say good-bye to her, and soon. With her "adventure" concluded, he had to return her to her sister, where she belonged. He had almost forgotten he would be collecting a generous fee from Mrs. Drake. Though being with Pauline had been trying—at least at first—he could hardly call it work. By God, the woman had saved his life!

"I notified the district commissioner in Simla that you were here," the prince said. "He forwarded a dispatch for you from the DC in Naintal. It is no longer timely; you are a difficult man to locate. I believe it is from England."

"England?" An ominous chill struck Nate. He

shoved it down, told himself not to jump to conclusions.

The prince signaled another servant, who carried over a gilt box. The prince opened it and extracted a folded buff paper. "I confess, I read it. It lacked an envelope, you see, as dispatches often do. I feared its news might cause you undue distress during your recuperation, so thought it best to wait to give it to you. I hope you will not find fault with my decision," he said, arrogantly assured of his rightness, as those born to royalty often are. At another signal, the servant delivered the creased and stained paper to Nate.

Nate had to force himself to accept the dispatch. Dread threatened to choke him. He had severed all ties with his supposed homeland. He wanted nothing to do with his father's side of the family. He hadn't heard from them in ten years. Why were they contacting him now?

The prince gave him a curious look. Nate knew he must appear odd, staring at the missive as if it might bite him. Pulling in a steadying breath, he flipped open the paper and began to read.

FROM: Lew Townley, Esq., Bristol, England
TO: NATHANIEL SAVIDGE, NAINTAL, INDIA
DATE: 9 April 1893
    TERRIBLE ACCIDENT STOP RUPERT DEAD STOP BEATRICE AND I COMING STOP ARRIVING BOMBAY MAY TEN ON HMS RANEE.

Rupert. Nate read the words again, their meaning finally sinking in. He ought to feel worse. That

was the civilized thing to do. Yet he couldn't con-
jure up the requisite mourning for this man he had
hardly known. A man who, in the short time he *had*
known him, had given him nothing but scalding
humiliation, followed in short order by heartache
and betrayal. Not to mention scars that would last
a lifetime.

The strongest emotion Nate managed to dredge
up was disappointment at what had never been, and
what never could be. He and Rupert would never
have another chance to try to build some kind of relationship from their only true tie, that of the blood.
He rubbed at the scar on his cheek, amazed that he
should feel at all maudlin toward Rupert. *Only because he's gone now.*

Blood ties meant nothing to Nate, at least those on
that side of the world. Rupert had been his only living relative, but ever since his mother's death, Nate
had felt alone.

I was never one of them, he reminded himself. *I never
could be. Now they're coming here. They're going to attempt
to change my life, take away all I hold dear and replace it
with a world I detest.*

Now that the news had been told, Nate realized
how many questions remained unanswered. The
brevity of the note, despite the weight of the news it
carried, annoyed Nate. His brother's solicitor, bearer
of the bad tidings, was still pinching pennies, even
after Rupert's death.

He tapped the paper against his palm. "What day
is it?"

The prince smiled knowingly. "The ninth of May."

"They arrive in India tomorrow!" With the delay

in receiving this message, he would have to face his brother's widow—the only woman he had ever loved—in a matter of days.

SEVENTEEN

Prince Mahadeva clarified Nate's dilemma. "Here, you are three days' travel from Bombay."

Nate thought rapidly. Although he could leave the pair to their own devices, he felt compelled to show them he could be a proper host in his own country—a courtesy he hadn't been shown when he visited England. Much as he had no desire to see either of them, he was no coward who would hide like a fox in a hole. Nor did he care to give them further proof that he was an unmannered bumpkin, an ill-bred country lad who ought not to associate with his "betters." Despite the passage of years, their mean-spirited words still stung his pride. Unconsciously, he rubbed at his cheek scar, the ugly proof of his rejection.

"I must send a wire to the P and O shipping office in Bombay, to be given them upon arrival," he said. "Instead of me traveling south, let them travel north if they are so determined to see me. I'll instruct them to join me at Beaumont's Hotel in Agra."

That would give him a few days' time to gather his thoughts and prepare to see these figures from his past. And a last few days alone with Pauline. She had wanted to see the Taj Mahal. This way, she would have time before departing for Simla.

"I need to send a second wire as well, to Pauline's sister in Simla. She can also meet us in Agra."

His plans sounded so logical. Pauline needed a proper escort home, and with his family business to attend to, unfortunately he wouldn't be available. Their adventure was finally nearing its end.

His heart pounded and his hands felt moist. He felt completely off balance, and not only from the news of Rupert's death and Beatrice's imminent arrival. Enjoying the prince's generous hospitality and Pauline's company these past weeks had lulled him into a sense of timeless pleasure, fostered the feeling that the world and its troubles were miles away. He had been injured, it was true. But his physical pains had easily healed under the care given by a surprisingly attentive Pauline. Now his idyll was ending.

Worse, his peace of mind had shattered. To his annoyance, he found that memories he had long repressed still had the power to sting.

"Nate." His name, as softly called as a lark's song, drew him from his reverie to a much more pleasant place. Standing before him was an image of sensuous femininity. Today Pauline wore a different sari, emerald with a golden flowered design. Her smile, just for him, warmed him, and he found himself unable to look away. "You're out of bed. How do you feel?"

Though his shoulder protested the effort, he used his arms to bear most of his weight as he pushed to his feet. He bit down against the throbbing in his thigh. The pain must have shown on his face, for Pauline rushed to his side, ready to offer assistance. He waved her away. He was quite through needing her and feeling utterly weak beside her. "Haven't you spent enough time playing nursemaid?" he bit out.

Her smile wavering, she hesitated, then stepped back. Her gaze flashed to his, and he knew he had hurt her. Why did this woman have the power to make him feel so horrible with a single look? It wasn't her fault he'd been injured. He owed her his life!

"If you will excuse me, Nate, I have business to attend to," the prince interrupted. On cue, a servant swung open the carved door, indicating Nate and Pauline should leave the prince's royal presence.

Nate took Pauline's hand and led her from the prince's office.

Once in the hall, she tried to slide her hand from his, but he tightened his grip and turned her to face him. "Looks like we're on our own. I hear there's a garden around here somewhere."

She glanced down, then to the left. "That way."

"Show me."

She did, though he sensed her reluctance. After the way he had barked at her, he couldn't blame her.

Passing through an open marble archway, she led him down a covered arcade stretching along a vast enclosed garden. In this patch of paradise, the blinding summer heat lost its sting. A rectangular ornamental pool stretched to the family mausoleum along the back wall, a marble structure flanked by minarets reflected in the shimmering water. More life-giving water flowed through narrow channels beside the pool, cascading over sculpted terraces and gurgling from ornate fountains. Bougainvillea vines softened the glaring outlines of the structures, geraniums and begonias spilled from hanging baskets, and turquoise-feathered peacocks strutted among the cultivated flowering plants and fruit trees.

"There it is." Pauline gestured toward the garden and began to turn away.

He threw out his arm and blocked her exit. "You look damned enticing in that getup," he murmured.

Her frown faded and her expression softened. She held out the sides of the form-fitting silk draped so seductively about her figure. "I don't know why it is, but I enjoy your compliments more than all the flowery words thrown my way by titled gentlemen."

If she knew who I was . . . Thank God she didn't. She liked the man who belonged not to England but to India.

So did he. In defiance of the unwelcome news from across the sea, he drew dangerously close and captured her gaze with his. "I'm no gentleman."

"That's been quite apparent from the day I met you." Smiling coyly, she pressed her palm to his shirt.

He captured her hand and gave it a familiar squeeze. "You like men who aren't gentlemen. If I *were* one—"

"Ha! Don't be ridiculous. If you were, you know I would have nothing to do with you." She lowered her voice. "Because, as you well know, I'm no lady."

He chuckled and stroked her shoulder. Sliding his hand under a loose fold of silk, he caressed her bare skin. In the bush, naturally they had been drawn to each other. The isolation and danger had practically guaranteed that.

But now . . . He ate her up with his eyes, longing to possess her. He had never desired a woman so deeply, with every part of his being. Indian women knew how to enhance their femininity, to use their natural allure to entice men. Under the care of the princess's personal servants, bathed and scented and set like a sparkling jewel in this glorious palace, Pauline was more irresistible than ever.

Yet he found himself touched by her character more than her beauty. If not for her bravery, he wouldn't be here now, enjoying her company. Enjoying anything.

With a gentle nudge, he led her toward an intimate corner of the verandah and drew her into the shadow of a jasmine-covered trellis. Yearning to express his appreciation, he settled his hands on her upper arms and gently drew her to him. Wonder filled him as he gazed down at her. Such a remarkable woman . . . "You saved me," he said, his voice reflecting the awe she made him feel. "Things are a little fuzzy around the edges, but I seem to recall you attacking the tiger when it attacked me."

She nodded. "A rock. I hit it with a rock."

He shook his head in amazement. "That deserves a kiss."

Leaning down, he briefly touched his lips to hers. Though the kiss was chaste, she inhaled sharply. He could feel her tremble under his palms, and her eyes took on a misty cast.

He continued, "Then you shot it with an arrow, am I right?"

She hesitated, then nodded. He had never seen her so bashful. For once, she had little to say.

"That's worth this." Holding her chin between his thumb and finger, he dropped reverent kisses on her face, tracing her cheeks, her forehead, and her temples with his lips. Her eyes fluttered closed and she swayed toward him, basking in his attentions.

Her trusting desire sparked his own passion. "Then what happened?" he rasped. "My memory is a little foggy, but somehow you retrieved my rifle. As I recall, I dropped it on the hill. You must have left me in order to get it."

She tensed and snapped open her eyes. "I couldn't think of any other way . . ."

"You never lost your head. You knew exactly what to do."

"I was desperate," she said, her voice quivering with emotion, a hint of moisture springing to her eyes. "I thought you were going to die, and it would be my fault."

"Yours?" Oh, yes. They had been . . . enjoying each other, completely distracted and not alert to danger when the tiger attacked. Yet, through sheer force of will, she had made things right.

His body vibrated with his need of her, with the need to celebrate being alive. Cupping her face, he drew her close. "I'm an experienced bushman—an experienced *man*. I knew better, love. But you—I could no more resist you that day than I can resist you now."

"Nate." Abandoning her bashfulness, she grasped his shirt in her fists and drew his mouth the last inch to meet hers.

EIGHTEEN

Joy filled Pauline as she succumbed to the delicious sensation of Nate's embrace. The sun glowed inside her. *He still wants me. He cares for me. He wants me to remain with him always.*

How she longed to stay by his side! Sometime in the candlelit nights, sitting vigil by his side, she had realized she could never leave him, never return to her old life. He had shown her what she was capable of. He had given her a glimpse of life's possibilities. He had accepted her in all her outrageous eccentricities. He had trusted her.

Perhaps he even loved her. Once again in his arms, conviction filled her that he harbored deep feeling for her. His love covered her like a soothing blanket, protective and warm. She couldn't imagine ever leaving these feelings—or him—behind to pursue a "normal" life with her family.

She could explain away their encounters in the bush. They had been thrown together into close, intimate circumstances. He may have been lonely, or tempted by an available woman.

Here in the palace, he could stay away from her, if he chose. But he didn't. Lily may have paid him to watch over her, but making love to her was his own choice. "Oh, Nate, I'm so glad—"

His kiss interrupted her. "Shh. No need to talk. Just let me . . ." He nibbled at her lower lip and her knees quivered.

Oh, yes . . . Just let him. She teased his ear with her fingers, encouraging him and letting him know how much she wanted him.

"Mr. Savidge? Are you out here?" The lilting voice interrupted from the direction of the archway. Nate pulled away from Pauline and stepped out from behind the trellis, and Pauline followed.

Spotting them, the prince's servant smiled and advanced. He bowed before Nate. "Your dispatch to the shipping office in Bombay has been sent."

"Thank you. And . . . the other?" He glanced at Pauline out of the corner of his eye.

The servant nodded. "Oh, yes! That one, too. To Mrs. Alexander Drake of Simla Hill Station."

Pauline counseled herself to be calm, but a tremor of foreboding slid through her. She waited for the servant to depart, then confronted him. "You sent a message to Lily. What did it say? Why didn't you tell me?"

"I was about to."

"When you stopped kissing me?"

"Relax, love," he said, looking less than relaxed himself as he stepped back and crossed his arms. "I notified your sister that we would be in Agra in five days, so that she can meet us there."

"And then I'm going home with her," Pauline said flatly, her stomach clenching as her world fell out from under her.

"Don't look disappointed," he said, casting her a cavalier smile. "You've had a good run of it. An adventure to tell your grandchildren someday."

A good run of it? What an inadequate way to describe an experience that had changed her life, with a man who meant everything to her.

He laid a hand on her shoulder, and she trembled at the familiar touch.

"I know how you wanted to see the Taj Mahal," he said, sounding unusually hesitant. "I've arranged for you to meet your sister in Agra so that you can visit it before returning home."

She tensed and turned away, pretending to study a nearby collection of planters. She ran her hand along the edge of an elephant-shaped pot, yet hardly noticed the fragrant waves of frangipani as she struggled to hide her pain.

As if echoing her devastation, the sun vanished behind a bank of storm clouds, casting a strange pewter-gray light over the earth. Long shadows filled the corners of the garden.

"The monsoon is coming," Nate said, looking toward the sky. "Should break any day now."

"That's interesting," was all she managed to reply.

He gave her shoulder a perfunctory pat, as if they had never been more than chums. "Come, now, don't pout. You knew you had to go home eventually. You didn't really think this would be your life."

He thought her disappointment was only about their adventure. The magic that surrounded and filled her heart didn't even exist for him.

After all they had been through, he would never see her as anything other than a spoiled rich girl, unsuited to a life with him. She had to accept that. But another truth stabbed her even deeper. He saw no future with her. He wanted to be rid of her, as if nothing had transpired between them. As if she hadn't given him her heart.

Thank God she hadn't confessed her feelings to him! She would never allow him to see how much she cared. Never. She would rather die than be that vulnerable to him.

She pulled away, breaking the contact between them, giving her room to breathe, to think. To accept. This had been her chance. There would never be another.

The truth settled in her chest like a rock. She could never break free, never live as anything other than an heiress. Nate had been right all along. A sense of despair filled her, but she fought it down. Years of breeding came to her defense, and she managed to subdue her feelings with a gracious, ladylike manner that was altogether foreign to her in any other circumstance.

She turned to him with a smile. "I do want to see the Taj Mahal. How thoughtful of you to remember that." On the train through the countryside, they hadn't taken the time.

Her deception worked. Her pain remained private, and he moved to a more respectable distance. "You're welcome." His gaze played up and down her body. "I'm sure this has been entertaining for you, playing at a different sort of life. But you'll no doubt be glad to return to the comforts of home you were raised in, with proper dresses and servants."

She boldly met his gaze. "No doubt."

"That's what I gathered." He stepped back and his gaze cooled. Already he was drawing away from her, putting distance between them. "Which reminds me: we have to talk about the man-eater and how you helped bring it down. I'm due a bounty—or rather, *we* are."

"I don't need the government's money, as you well know. Besides, you incurred all the expenses of the excursion."

"The district commissioner will ask questions, pet. When a man-eater is brought down, everyone wants to hear the tale. We weren't able to bring back the hide—"

"I was too busy bringing back *your* hide."

He smiled but continued, "Lacking that proof, I'll have to give a complete report on how we tracked it and killed it. My question is, where do you fit in?"

She nearly blurted out, *By your side.*

He stepped closer. Lifting a lock of her hair, he rubbed it between his thumb and finger. "Help me, Pauline. How do I explain you? I don't want to steal your thunder. But I can't think how to sing your praises without destroying your reputation."

In men's clubs across India, even in England and America, gentlemen would share the story of how a vicious man-eater had been tracked and killed. She had lived it. She had saved Nate. She had proven to everyone—to Nate, to her family, to herself—that she could stand on her own two feet, that she was brave, that she didn't need the traditional life of marriage and a husband. How she longed to revel in her success!

Yet . . . if the story got out that she had been alone

with Nate Savidge in the bush, no one would stand up and cheer her accomplishment. At best, people would think her a flighty, strange girl touched in the head. At worst, they would assume she was his mistress, a notorious female who brought disgrace upon her family.

Her mother's beloved face appeared before her mind's eye. So many times they had fought, but now all Pauline wanted was a hug and acceptance. From her father, too, who always looked on his middle daughter with weary resignation, as if he couldn't figure out what sin he had committed to cause God to saddle him with such a willful child.

And her sisters . . . Lily—My God, in all her gallivanting around the countryside, Pauline had hardly given Lily a single thought! Yes, her sister was happy with her husband and little Cecily, but Lily's heart was big and true, and she had probably spent sleepless nights worrying whether Pauline was safe.

Their two younger sisters, Clara and Meryl, had yet to forge their own identities. If the salons and drawing rooms in America and Europe rang with the story of the wild Carrington girl, respectable families would no longer want to associate with her family. She couldn't bring such a dastardly fate on those she loved.

I love them. I miss them.

"Pauline?"

Nate's soft query brought her back to the present. She lifted her chin, confident for once that she was making the right decision. "I don't care about my reputation. Surely, you've figured that out." He opened his mouth to protest, but she covered his lips with a gentle touch of her fingers. "I am, however, concerned about my family. Tell them Manu helped you, your trusty syce. Only you and I need know the truth."

He studied her silently for a long moment, and she wondered what he was thinking. "Manu it is." Grasping her arm, he gave it a squeeze. "I'm sorry." Releasing her, he took a step back. "We leave for the train station in four days." Turning, he strode back inside.

The sense of loss filling Pauline was so acute, it stole her breath and made her dizzy. She sought the closest bench and collapsed upon it. She clasped her hands in her lap, curled her shoulders, and squeezed her eyes shut. *No, don't be weak. Remain composed. You have to spend time with him or he'll suspect you harbor feelings for him. Never let him suspect!* She had to find an inner calm, something she couldn't begin to imagine in her pain.

Not like this. She couldn't let it end like this. Four days and he would be out of her life. Four days!

What else could she do but allow it? She had no power, no real choices.

No choices. Except one.

"Here you are. Hiding out again, I see."

At the sound of Pauline's voice, Nate tensed. Slowly, he lowered the Delhi newspaper he had been trying to read, and watched her enter the library.

"Hello, Pauline," he said, trying to sound nonchalant. He had a hunch he should discourage her from whatever she might be intending to say.

Tension brewed beneath the surface whenever they were within twenty feet of each other. Hell, fifty feet. A hundred. He tried to blame it on the weather. Even here in the luxury of the palace, the air hung heavy and torpid, and hotter than ever despite the punkah fan being pulled by a wallah in a far corner of the room. In the night sky, heavy storm clouds gathered, releasing bursts of thunder, an unfulfilled promise of relief from the searing heat. Prince, servant, and guests all waited in breathless anticipation of the annual monsoon, which seemed as if it would never come.

The summer heat of Central India would make anyone cranky, Nate reasoned. Yet deep down, he knew there was more to Pauline's attitude than the interminable wait for rain. Ever since she had learned she was going home, she had acted composed and sophisticated. Cold, even. In all ways making it impossible for him to forget she was a born heiress.

Or perhaps it was he who had changed. He could hardly look at her for wanting her. It had taken all his effort to remember that she was untouchable. In the bush, he had nearly forgotten exactly who she was, had almost given in to his animal passions. Each day stretched endlessly, being so near her and unable to touch her. Each moment lasted an eternity.

Finally, they had reached the last full day. Only this last night to go, and he would be free of the inexplicable power she held over him.

At least his physical strength had returned. No longer did she occupy the role of his nurse, which relieved and disappointed him at the same time.

He studied her as she crossed the room, her sari flowing elegantly behind her. He tried to read her as he would an animal in the bush—and failed.

She took the wing-back chair directly across from his. Toying with the folds of her sari, she sighed. "I can't wait to leave here. The palace is wonderful, of course. The prince has been quite gracious. This will be yet another marvelous story to tell my grandchildren."

He didn't miss the irony in her voice. For some reason, his comment about grandchildren had upset her, but he didn't understand why.

She gazed up at the twenty-foot-high molded ceilings edged in gilt. "Very nice indeed. But, as you don't hesitate to remind me, I'm used to Western elegance and Western food. And refined gentlemen."

Gentlemen. What a lie. Annoyed, he tossed the paper on a nearby table and glared at her. "You weren't acting like you preferred gentlemen a few days ago. You were all over *me.*"

She shrugged her shoulders, drawing his gaze to the mounds of her breasts under the silk, beckoning to him. He could almost feel their sensuous weight in his hands. "I was taking what was available."

For some reason she seemed determined to goad him. And it was working. His jaw spasmed. "You mean you were using me."

"Of course." She gazed coolly at him. "You don't think I meant anything by it, do you? You're part of my adventure."

"I'm so happy to oblige." All along, he knew she was using him. But to have her say it so bluntly hurt worse than he cared to admit. He could have been any man,

any man who wasn't a gentleman, and she would have
behaved with the same brash sensuousness.

She rose and strolled toward the shelves along one
wall, then drifted behind his chair. Her movements
reminded him of a tigress choosing her prey. Circling it, stalking it.

She stopped right behind his chair. He resisted the
urge to look up at her. His skin prickled from her
mere presence, even though she wasn't touching
him. Then her hand began drifting along his shoulder. When her fingertips danced along the back of
his neck, he sucked in a hard, silent breath, unable
to prevent his body from reacting in the basest way
to her teasing. Inwardly, he cursed his weakness for
the bold chit.

"If only my adventure were complete," she murmured.

"In what way *complete?*" he asked warily, deciding
he now confronted the most dangerous creature
God had ever placed on the earth.

She circled out from behind his chair, her posture
confident and one-hundred-percent female. "What
men and women do, of course. What we nearly did
in the temple. And before the tiger attacked us. And
that night in the village, you showed me . . . heaven."
She gave a bright laugh and resumed her seat.
"Goodness, we came close so many times, didn't we?"

He stared at her, astounded by her composure over
subjects other women would never dream of discussing. She sounded as if she were talking about the
state of her garden instead of the state of her virginity.

She frowned, her lips pulling into a gentle pout.
"You look confused. I'm talking about men and

women, you and me. . . ." She gestured to each of them.

As if he didn't already understand her meaning! He remembered all too well how close they had come. He spent his nighttime hours remembering. He hardly needed her to say it.

"Oh, well." She shrugged. Whether by accident or design, he didn't know, but her sari slipped to reveal a creamy shoulder to his hungry gaze. A few more inches and she would be naked. Deliciously, tantalizingly exposed to him. Again.

Christ Almighty, I want her more than ever. He hadn't given her any encouragement since their last kiss. He'd even tried to avoid her. But his best efforts could not douse the fire she ignited.

She continued matter-of-factly, oblivious to his torment. "Perhaps when I return to Simla I will find a man willing to behave like one."

How dare she! He jolted to his feet so fast, it caused a stab of pain in his freshly healed leg wound. Reaching down, he grasped her by the shoulders and jerked her to her feet. "That was a low blow, Pauline. I was being a gentleman."

Her brown eyes burned with defiance. "If I wanted a gentleman, I would have stayed in Simla," she bit out.

"You don't know what you're saying."

"How dare you assume I don't!"

The tension that had simmered between them boiled forth. He violently shoved her away. "Get to your room, Pauline. It's late, and I'm tired of your childish games."

She adjusted her sari around her. "No more tired than I. I'm sick of being here with you. Sick of you."

"Hah. You want to use me and you know it. You just don't want to call it what it is."

She jerked her chin up, her eyes fiery bright. "I thought I wanted to. Now I'm glad I'll be seeing the last of you. As soon as we reach Agra—"

"I'll hand you off to your sister, collect my money, and wash my hands of you."

"Fine."

"Fine."

Turning, she stormed from the room, her long, shiny hair cascading about her shoulders. He watched her exit, a storm of emotions roiling in his chest. He wanted to follow her. He wanted to grab her up against him and show her how much a man he could be. He wanted her beneath him, screaming with pleasure.

Instead, he spun in the opposite direction and strode out a side door into the hall. There he paused, uncertain where he was headed. The palace halls were muted and silent. Guttering wall sconces provided the only sound, and the only light. The prince was already abed, probably enjoying himself with his concubines.

He couldn't bring himself to return to his room. He couldn't sleep, not after Pauline had heated his blood to the boiling point and left him with nowhere to expend his energy—or his desire.

Instead, he headed into the courtyard garden. The full moon limned the garden in silver, while an evening breeze provided a touch of relief on his damp skin.

Damn the girl. Damn the *woman*, he corrected. The woman who wanted to explore her femininity. He couldn't help imagining such a brash, passionate female learning what her body was truly capable of. The erotic possibilities sent a shiver of desire through him so strong, he quaked with it. Too many times he had held her and kissed her and touched her. Too many times he had danced near the fire. Now he was paying the price.

Only one more night. One more night. One night. He repeated the words like a litany, desperate to settle his spirit and cool his overheated body.

Yet he couldn't help hearing her words over and over: "... *men and women, you and me ... taking what was available ... a man willing to behave like one.*"

I could so easily take her, he thought. *Show her exactly where her behavior and bold words led. Teach her a lesson she'll never forget!*

Hearing a squeak, he spun toward the sound. On the palace's second level, a pair of French doors swung open on a softly lit room. Standing between the doors on the balcony was a woman wearing only a thin night rail. The lantern light behind her highlighted the curves of her alluring figure.

Her arms, still holding the doors, dropped slowly to her sides. She stepped forward on slippered feet, into the moonlight. *Pauline.*

He stood rigidly below her, his eyes narrowing in fury. She looked so perfect, like an ethereal goddess. His Artemis, goddess of the hunt. Grasping the balustrade, she gazed down into the garden. Her eyes found him instantly. *Damn her. She knew I would be here, stalking her.*

Their eyes locked.

She didn't move, not a single inch. The moonlight enabled him to see the haughty challenge in her eyes, and tantalizing hints of her figure under the translucent cloth—the curve of her hips, her nipped-in waist, a suggestive shadow at the apex of her thighs. She allowed the light to reveal her, unconcerned that she appeared almost naked to him. Offering herself. Waiting for him to take her.

His heart pounded in his chest and his hands grew moist. He could give her exactly what she wanted, more than she ever dreamed of wanting. Like the predator he was named after, he only had to take what she offered. Mate with her.

Thunder rumbled so loud, he felt it in his bones. Electricity crackled along his skin. A heartbeat later, the skies broke and rain spilled forth. The parched ground pulled in the water like a sponge and began to give off a thick, rich scent, preparing for new growth that would spring up in a matter of days.

Acting on instinct, Nate stripped off his bush jacket, shirt, and undershirt to let Heaven's water wash over his hot, needy body. He sucked in a breath, reveling in the sensation of the fresh rain soothing his heated skin. The rain built into a glorious torrent, sluicing down his chest and back, plastering his hair to his head. Crouching down, he quickly unlaced his boots and pulled them off along with his socks so that he could dig his toes into the newly damp grass. As a boy, when the monsoon struck, he had danced naked in the streets with the Indian children. Now, as a grown man, he hungered to engage in a different sort of dance.

Above, Pauline waited, continuing to gaze at him, letting the rain soak her through as well. *Pauline!* his heart cried out with the need to be with her. *Dance with me.*

Through the monsoon, nature had released her tension, joyfully, unabashedly. Nate could no longer fight the tension coiled so tight and hot inside him. Giving in to his need, he charted a course to his goal. Three long strides brought him to the base of a tall planter. He leaped atop it, putting him right under her balcony. He grasped a carved waterspout, scaled the last five feet to the balustrade, and swung his legs over. He landed on his feet and stood before her, water puddling at his feet on the balcony.

She waited just inside her room, watching him draw near, luring him closer. Her body remained rigid, her hands fisted with fear or, more likely, anticipation. Behind her, her immense cedar bed beckoned.

Oh, yes. She knew exactly why he had come. She wanted this as badly as he did. If she changed her mind, she only had to scream.

She remained silent, rooted to the spot, her breasts as good as naked under her soaking wet night-rail. He could smell the desire on her. On himself.

His groin throbbed fiercely, pounding a primitive drumbeat throughout his body, his need so great it made him light-headed. He had to press her body against his, wet skin to wet skin. He had to possess her or die.

Taking a step toward her, he unbuckled his belt and stripped off his trousers, letting them fall to the marble floor. With his next step, he kicked them away. With his third step, he shed his undershorts, leaving him entirely naked, his manhood jutting prominently from between his thighs.

Pauline sucked in a breath at his naked state, but she remained unafraid, her eyes containing a challenge he could not resist.

A final step brought him so close to her that her taut nipples grazed his bare chest, and his manhood pressed into her abdomen.

She shuddered in response, her eyes briefly squeezing tight. Still she didn't move away, didn't protest. Lifting her eyes to his, she gave her silent assent.

In one decisive motion, he swung her into his arms and carried her to the bed.

NINETEEN

Pauline fell into the satin mattress. Nate crouched atop her, his arms and legs surrounding her, his eyes feral and intense as he gazed hungrily down at her in the light of the single lantern.

She tightened her fingers in his hair, and their mouths joined in a savage kiss. A sense of victory filled her, but she could hardly focus on how successful she had been in luring the hunter to her bed. He filled her senses, his commanding hands moving hungrily over her body, determined, sure, desperate to answer the longing pounding through them both.

When his fingers hooked around the neckline of her gown, he broke the kiss and reared back on his heels, his knees encompassing her hips. With one swift yank, he ripped the cloth in half, exposing her down to her waist. The harsh sound of rent fabric stunned her while setting flame to her own desire. Fascinated, she watched his massive arms flex to tear the cloth again, stripping away her last pretense of modesty. Leaning over her, his callused hands learned her, all of her. Reacquainting himself, he kneaded her breasts, shaped her ribcage, stroked her thighs.

She explored him in turn, stroking her palms

along the muscles rippling across his back, then sliding her palms downward to cup his buttocks. So hungry for him! She knew what ecstasy felt like. She wanted that now, with him, more than she had ever wanted anything in her life. Bending her knees, she drew him into the circle of her body, the prominent evidence of his arousal pressing against her stomach. She found him so beautiful, her chest ached. He was everything a man should be.

His fingers slid between her thighs, then into her, returning to that pleasure center he had taught her she possessed. She moaned and arched her back, bringing her hips against his. She was already so close to that pinnacle of ecstasy, the desire was almost painful. She clawed at his back in her effort to bring him closer, so close, to find completion.

Taking her cue, he reached under her knees and bent her legs so that they circled his waist. His manhood pressed against her center. He paused a moment, his cobalt eyes locking with hers. Pauline knew he was giving her a chance to back out. Instead, she dug her fingers into his back and rolled her hips toward his.

Squeezing his eyes shut, he thrust home.

Pauline gasped but felt no pain. A sense of wonder filled her. She had been made for this, with him. His body shook in her arms, and he again thrust into her, beginning a rhythm that took her to a new place of ecstasy. In mere moments, she tumbled over the edge into delicious oblivion.

This time, he didn't stifle her cry as her climax took command. His own cry mingled with hers, his thrusts slowly lessening as he spent himself inside her.

Nate sighed and kissed her cheek, then repositioned himself so he was lying beside her. A glow of satisfaction filled Pauline. She had done it. She had seduced him. She had lost her chastity and was now a fallen woman. Then why did she feel so wonderful?

"There you go," he said in her ear while his fingers plucked and tugged at her still-erect nipple. "Your adventure is complete."

"Yes, it seems so," she said, still breathless with passion. "Now, was that so awful?" she teased him. "So difficult? It didn't seem difficult."

"Stop that." Grasping her wrists, he pinned them above her head and hovered over her. His eyes sparkled with humor. "You won, love. Don't rub salt in my wounds."

Her eyes traced the pink U-shaped slash on his left shoulder. "You certainly don't seem wounded. Everything has healed nicely, and the White Tiger is roaring." Sliding her hand down his abdomen, she grasped his manhood and found him stiffening.

He chuckled. "I just took your virginity, and you're playing bed games like an experienced concubine."

"I tried to tell you I wasn't a lady, from the very first day we met."

A shadow crossed his eyes. "And someday you'll be playing with some other fellow, no doubt."

She swallowed hard but feigned nonchalance. "No doubt. Well, the so-called damage is done, as they say. Now that we've done it once, we might as well do it again, don't you think?"

"You're not sore?" He traced her hipbone.

She shook her head. "Not at all. That story about

pain on the wedding night must be an old wives' tale designed to keep girls terrified and chaste."

"You're so damned athletic, you probably tore it years ago."

"Tore what?"

"Never mind. As long as I'm the first." He frowned. "I am the first, aren't I?"

It warmed her heart that he cared, but she wouldn't allow him to see that. "Don't be rude. You know you are. If I had known what I was doing, it wouldn't have been so hard to get you into bed."

"You call this hard?" He scoffed. "All you had to do was goad me, and I was panting for you."

"Then it worked out nicely, didn't it? Now, are you worn out, or shall we do it again?" She tugged on his manhood, drawing a gasp from him and causing him to fully harden. "From what we saw in the temple, I know there's more than one way."

"You're incorrigible." His eyes glittered with heat. "You want an entire *Kama Sutra,* right now?"

"How many ways are there?"

"Infinite. Well, in the *Kama Sutra,* there are maybe thirty specific positions."

"Then lets try thirty."

He barked out a laugh and rolled to his back, his arms stretched above his head. "I'm damned virile, love, but even I can't manage that many times in a single night."

She pushed up to her elbow and looked down at him, tracing the planes of his chest. "How many times can you manage?"

"Only one way to find out." He rolled to face her. Grasping her waist, he drew her close and arranged her leg above his hip. A moment later he was once more inside her.

This time, he moved much slower, doting on her with caresses and kisses as he filled her with gentle strokes, taking her upward gradually yet thoroughly.

Under his loving caresses, Pauline's heart started to ache. She closed her eyes to keep him from seeing the moisture there. How she adored his attentions! He already thought her a spoiled lady who could never be anything else. Let him continue to think that about her. He could believe she was using him, if he preferred. If it made him more comfortable to take her chastity believing her heart wasn't involved. If he thought her only interest was exploring the multiple "ways," and not the need to be as close to him as it was physically possible for a man and woman to be.

No matter how many years passed, no matter where life took her, she would never be sorry she had slept with Nate Savidge.

Nate lay exhausted beside Pauline on the floor, shocked at what his body had been able to do with her. He had never in his life made love to a woman all night long, in so many positions and places. They had somehow ended up in a pile of bedding on the floor.

Outside, the rain continued to pour down as it had all night, thrumming on the roof of the palace. Now, however, soft slate-gray light traced the mosaic of water lilies that decorated the floor. Nate propped himself on his elbow and gazed down at Pauline, her lithe body stretched beside his. "It's dawn, hon. Time to leave."

She wiggled in response. "No, not yet," she murmured sleepily. The woman was a born lover. Hell, she was a born adventuress. There was nothing she wouldn't try. She had more than proved herself capable. She had fearlessly confronted death and drawn on her limited resources to save his life. And tonight, she had tossed away the safety of that virtue so prized in young ladies, without a moment of remorse. Simply put, she was amazing.

He had never met anyone like her, and knew he never would again. Later today, they would reach Agra, and he would hand her off to her sister. He ought to be glad to be rid of her, but after this night, how could he not miss her? If there was any way she could stay by his side . . . No, he couldn't ask that of her, not when his own future was so muddled.

One thing was certain. He couldn't accept payment from Mrs. Drake. He'd completely failed in his task. To begin with, he'd put Pauline in danger. Then, he'd had the audacity to take her to bed. He could hardly accept Mrs. Drake's two thousand pounds after how he'd enjoyed her sister.

And enjoy her he had. Hour upon erotic hour, in so many amazing ways . . . Ways he'd never even tried until now. Guilt teased at him, but he shoved it away. *She's using you, too,* he reminded himself fiercely. *She said as much. I'm her adventure.*

He fought down the dread that plagued him every time he recalled what had brought her to his bed. Never had he imagined allowing a lady to use him, not after Beatrice. But unlike Beatrice, Pauline had made her motives clear. He had no one to blame but himself. He had known exactly what he was doing, what *they* were doing.

So why did he feel a loneliness so acute, he struggled to keep from crying out in pain?

A knock on the door roused him. Pulling himself to his feet, he wrapped a sheet around his hips and answered it to a uniformed servant. "Miss Carring—excuse me, Sahib Savidge. Your ride to the train station awaits at your convenience. Of course, the train leaves in one hour."

Nate nodded. "We'll be right down."

He closed the door to find Pauline gazing up at him, a wide-eyed look on her face. Her waist-long hair lay in a tangle about her. "We have to leave, pet. We can't miss this train. How fast can you get ready?" He began gathering his clothing and started to dress.

Pauline stood up, shamelessly naked in the muted light spilling through the open balcony doors along with stray drops of rain. "How fast do you need me to be ready?"

"Half an hour?"

"I'll be ready in fifteen minutes."

He shook his head, again amazed. He had never known a lady who didn't take at least two hours to dress and primp.

Once dressed, he turned to the door. "Meet me at the palace entrance."

"Nate?"

He paused, then gathered his resolve and turned to face her. "Yes?"

"We may not have a chance to talk once we reach

Agra." She looked unusually solemn, and his heart soared with a hope he barely understood. What did she intend to say?

"You don't have to worry." She lifted her chin resolutely. "I won't misbehave anymore. I'm ready to return to being a proper lady. Well"—she smiled softly and glanced toward the unmade bed—"perhaps not proper. I know this is . . . everything there will be."

She almost sounded as if she were discussing their relationship, and longing for more. "Your adventure, you mean," he clarified, afraid to hope. "At least with me. You can continue to explore India with your sister."

She nodded. "I suppose so. The Taj Mahal and all." Knowing he was right about her feelings for him stung more than he expected.

She continued, "What I'm trying to say is, I know I can be difficult to get along with. It was good of you to put up with me. Thank you."

He opened his mouth to respond but couldn't utter a word. A wave of tenderness washed over him, and he longed to give her a hug and a good-bye kiss, at the very least. Yet her sudden display of maturity also disconcerted him. *She's all grown up. She doesn't need me any longer. Perhaps she never did.*

Finally, he resorted to a simple nod of acknowledgment, then let himself out of the room.

TWENTY

Nate hadn't mentioned how they would be arriving at the train station. Prince Mahadeva had provided them each with an elephant, garbed in brocade and decorated with silk. Pauline looked down from her elephant's howdah at the muddy ground and realized she was at least ten feet in the air. Her adventure hadn't quite concluded, it seemed.

Still, she thought, looking behind at Nate atop his own elephant so far away, she felt it had. Through the heavy rain streaming down beyond the howdah's curtains, he already seemed a world away. *He's through with you. You must accept it.*

The train ride also kept them apart. Dressed in a royal blue sari given her by the princess of Rawa, Pauline was made to ride in the purdah car with the other women. She slept most of the way and dreamed about making love with Nate.

She didn't see Nate again until the six-hour train ride ended at Agra Station. Immediately afterward, a short ride in separate rickshaws brought them to Beaumont's Hotel in Agra.

A pair of uniformed doormen held umbrellas over their heads to keep them dry the few steps from the rickshaw to the hotel entrance. No sooner had they entered the lobby than Pauline heard a familiar voice, at first hesitant, then ecstatic.

"Pauly? It is you!" Lily hurried over to them from the registration desk, her eyes glowing with excitement. She was elegant as always, in the finest French day dress of spring green, her hair done up elaborately under her jaunty hat with its delicate half veil.

Pauline hesitated, uncertain of her reception. "Lily. Hello."

"Oh, come now. Don't be so shy. It doesn't suit you." Lily pulled her into a warm embrace.

Tears sprang to Pauline's eyes, and she realized how much she had missed her sister. How could she have ever believed she could do without her family's love? "I'm crushing your beautiful dress," Pauline protested.

"It's merely fabric." Lily pulled back and clasped her shoulders with her gloved hands. "Oh, Pauly, I missed you so much. Worried about you, though I promised myself I wouldn't." She glanced at Nate, the man she had hired to watch out for her sister.

Pauline read her hesitance in her eyes. "You needn't dissemble, Lily. I know you hired him to put up with me."

Lily exhaled a relieved breath. She had probably been wondering how to explain her ready acceptance of Pauline's absence. She asked Nate, "Was she altogether too much trouble?"

Nate shook his head, a smile teasing the corners of his mouth. "No, ma'am. No trouble at all."

Hah. He was lying through his teeth. Pauline met his gaze, and her skin grew warm all over as memory of the previous night returned in a rush.

Lily gave him a contemplative look. "Indeed? Well, I'm glad you contacted me when you did. Pauline, Alex and I are leaving India. He's been called back to England, offered a high-level post in the Foreign Office. It's everything he ever wanted."

Trepidation filled Pauline at the news. "And . . . me?"

"You'll be going back home, to Mother and Father. They've missed you so."

Leaving India? She had so much left to see! "But—Mother and Father. They wanted to be rid of me. I'm trouble. Ask him." She cocked a thumb toward Nate, who looked exasperated. No doubt he was glad to be rid of her, too.

"Nonsense," Lily said in a soothing tone she had probably perfected over little Cecily's cradle.

"When—when are we going?"

"I've booked us on the afternoon train to Bombay. Our ship to London leaves in a few days. I've already arranged for an escort to take you the rest of the way to New York, though Mrs. Davenport won't be quite so colorful as Mr. Savidge here." She smiled at Nate. "Are you also staying here at the hotel?"

"Only tonight."

Lily nodded thoughtfully. "Very well. I—"

Her comment was cut off by a female voice crying out, "Nathaniel!"

Nathaniel? No one called the White Tiger by that name. Pauline spun around. A slender lady with black hair, trailed by a gaunt fellow in a severe suit, converged on them. Both wore black from head to toe, signaling that they were in mourning.

The woman threw herself at Nate, giving him an

embrace no less warm than the one Lily had given Pauline. Except, Pauline noted with satisfaction, Nate seemed too stunned to return it.

"Beatrice," he said. "You're here already? I thought you weren't arriving until tomorrow."

"We caught an earlier train. And this is . . . ?" Standing back, she gave Lily a cool appraisal.

Unflustered as usual, Lily gave her a gracious smile as Nate introduced them. He introduced Beatrice as Lady Bathurst.

Beatrice was a lady? But she had married Nate's brother, hadn't she? If his brother was a lord of some kind, what did that make Nate?

"I'm not a gentleman," he had said on more than one occasion. Perhaps he was an illegitimate son of a nobleman. Or perhaps his father had disowned him.

"I didn't think they allowed natives in this hotel," Beatrice said, her narrow eyes assessing Pauline. "And that one—why is she staring at us?"

Confused, Pauline had backed away a good ten feet from the reunion. Nate stepped over, grasped her arm, and pulled her before Beatrice. "This is Miss Pauline Carrington, Mrs. Drake's sister."

"Oh! I'm so sorry, I didn't realize . . ." Beatrice's eyes flicked up and down her sari-clad body. "Interesting costume. So quaint. Are you putting on a play or some kind of entertainment?" Without waiting for an answer, she turned back to Nate, obviously not interested in anyone else. "I hate to rush things, Nathaniel, but since we've traveled all this way to tell you about Rupert—may he rest in peace—we would prefer not to wait much longer."

"Yes," Lew Townley interjected, rubbing together his bony hands. "We have important matters to settle regarding the estate, milord." Smiling obsequiously, he bowed to Nate, then to Lily and Pauline. "If you lovely ladies would excuse us . . ."

"Of course," Lily said. "We must dress for dinner."

"And garb your sister in decently modest attire, I hope," Beatrice said under her breath.

Pauline hardly noticed the slight as she struggled to reconcile the word Mr. Townley had uttered with what she knew of Nathaniel Savidge. She stared hard at him, her chest tightening and her head spinning. "Did he call you *lord*?"

He looked ill-at-ease, but before he could explain, Beatrice planted herself between them and began chattering. Lily tugged at Pauline's arm, steering her away from them and toward the bank of elevators on the far side of the lobby.

"All your things are being forwarded to the port, except for a dozen sets of clothing to see you through the next few days," Lily said. "You'll want to put on something more suitable right away. Perhaps the lilac gown would be nice for dinner. You have a bit of a tan, but once you're wearing decent hats and gloves again, it should fade. Bala is in our suite with Cecily. She can help you dress."

Pauline listened with only half an ear. She continued gazing back at Nate and nearly ran into a gentleman exiting the elevator.

"Be careful, Pauline," Lily reprimanded. "Goodness, you're a thousand miles away."

Not yet, but soon enough she would be. She would probably never see Nate again. And she hadn't even gotten a chance to say good-bye. Not that he seemed to care.

For if he cared, nothing would stop a man like Nate from having what he wanted.

A man like Nate. What kind of man was he? Mr. Townley called him "lord," and his sister-in-law was a lady. "Do you understand what Mr. Townley was going on about to Nate—I mean Mr. Savidge? All that talk of estates and such?"

"He must have come into some property."

They stepped onto the elevator. "But Mr. Townley called him 'milord.'"

"Did he?"

"Yes!" Pauline sighed in exasperation. Ever since marrying and having a baby, her sister had been in another world. Thank goodness she was above such ridiculous sentimentality.

"Perhaps Townley was being particularly . . . deferential," Lily said.

"Well, what about Lady Bathurst? Have you ever heard of her?"

The lift operator stopped the elevator at their floor. Pulling a lever, he opened the iron mesh door, and the sisters stepped into a narrow, carpeted hallway leading to their suite.

A frown furrowed Lily's lovely brow. "Lady Bathurst . . . Lady Bathurst . . . She's a recent widow, obviously."

Pauline nodded. "That's right. She was married to Nate's brother, Rupert."

"Rupert Savidge? Rupert Savidge! The marquess! Of course. My goodness, if I'd known the White

Tiger was related to *that* particular fellow, I never would have allowed you to accompany him."

Lily tapped on the door, and her maid Bala swung it open, stepping aside for them to enter. Now that they were in private, Lily gave her sister an even less reserved embrace. "I'm so glad you're here with me again!"

Then she pulled back and gave Pauline a surprisingly hard shake, her dark eyes growing thunderous. "That awful note you left—do you really think even for one instant that we wouldn't have gone searching for you? That we would simply allow you to disappear into the Indian countryside and forget about you?" She tossed her hands in the air.

A marquess . . . What was a marquess? Pauline burned to know. Never interested in marriage or society, she hadn't bothered to learn about the various titles in the British peerage.

But Lily was too annoyed for Pauline to risk interrupting. She had probably stored up her irritation since Pauline disappeared. "We would have pursued you to the ends of the earth, if need be, to bring you back home. You're my sister, Pauline. I love you."

Pauline sighed. "I was causing trouble, Lily, like I always do. I made things terrible for you in Simla."

"Simla is not my concern. You are. Besides, you know Mother would never forgive me if anything happened to you under my care."

Pauline laughed dryly. "Mother adores you, Lily. She would know better than to fault you for my horrid behavior."

Lily gave her a thoughtful look. "She didn't adore

me when I was caught spending the night in Alex's room."

"Really?" Pauline gazed at Lily with new eyes. "You . . . you slept with him before you were married?" Her perfect sister had done such an outrageous thing?

Lily smiled and her posture relaxed. "I hope I have surprised you, Pauline. Most of us have our little secrets."

Heat warmed Pauline's face. Did Lily suspect that she had experienced a night of unforgettable passion in Nate Savidge's arms? Could she see it?

"Now, how are you, really?" Lily sat on the edge of the bed. Taking Pauline's hand, she pulled her to sit beside her. "Was your adventure everything you hoped it would be?"

"Why did you allow me to go?" Pauline asked.

"So that you would return to us," Lily said. She asked hesitantly, "Have you?"

"I . . . I'm not sure."

"Oh." Her eyes darkened with sadness as she studied Pauline.

"Oh, Lily, I'm disappointing you again. I'm so sorry. I'm sorry for everything. For worrying you, for frightening Mother with my antics. I've been a terribly selfish girl, I see that now. But part of me . . . part of me longs to continue as I have been, free to be the person I really am—even when I'm pretending to be a boy. I learned I'm strong, Lily. Stronger than I ever suspected."

Lily studied her thoughtfully. "You do seem different, as if you're more comfortable with yourself."

She frowned. "But the change isn't all good, I fear. There's more to it. Is something worrying you?"

Pauline bit her lip and nodded. Lily was far too perceptive. While Pauline couldn't bring herself to open up completely, she tried again to share at least one of her concerns. "You said most people have secrets. I think Nate has a secret. What, exactly, is a marquess?"

Lily gave her a curious look before she answered. "You're calling him Nate, I see."

Pauline shrugged, trying hard not to look embarrassed. "It's hard to keep up the formalities in the bush. That is one reason I loved it so."

"Loved it? Or loved him?"

Pauline gave a dismissive laugh that sounded horribly strained. Lily was dancing far too close to the truth. Pauline didn't know if she felt love, only that her heart ached to think she would never see him again. "What a silly question. Whatever good would loving him be? It's not as if he's the type to marry. Nor am I."

"Are you quite sure?"

"Goodness, Lily, you know I've never longed for marriage. I wouldn't want to be harnessed to a man who would expect me to act a certain way—"

"Would Mr. Savidge?"

She gave Lily a hard look, desperate to end her probing questions, which stirred up hope where none existed. "There's no reason to even ask, now, is there?"

Lily sighed. "I suppose it was silly of me to hope you had changed quite that much."

"You still haven't answered my question about Na—Mr. Savidge, I mean. If that's who he really is."

Lily continued to gaze at her a moment longer, making Pauline fidget. Finally, she explained, "A marquess is merely a step below a duke and one step above an earl. A very impressive title, as such things go."

Pauline grew faint at the revelation. A *marquess*. A step below a duke. Pauline began shaking her head, trying to reconcile the idea that her wild White Tiger belonged in England in a three-piece suit, strolling along Mayfair, tipping his top hat politely to the ladies. . . . No, it couldn't be. He belonged here, in this dangerous and beautiful land filled with contradictions. India was in his blood!

"Hannah's husband is an earl," Pauline murmured, her mind whirring as she struggled to put this information in perspective. When her oldest sister Hannah married Benjamin Ramsey, the Earl of Sheffield, their socially ambitious mother looked as if she had died and gone to heaven.

"Then Mr. Savidge would outrank him," Lily said.

"But—but he can't. He would have told me. He would have said something. He's keen on people living the lives they were born to, he believes a leopard can't change its spots—"

"Or an heiress be anything other than an heiress," Lily supplied.

"Yes!" A wave of anger engulfed Pauline. All of Nate's talk about people being born to their roles, about how she should be what she was meant to be, while he himself was living a life contrary to who *he* was! Never had she imagined he could be so false, so unwilling to trust her with his identity, so determined to keep her in her place!

Lily grasped her hand. "Pauline, are you sure there's nothing you want to tell me?"

Her perceptive question snapped Pauline from her inner turmoil. Determined to hide her deepest pain, she forced a smile to her face and abruptly stood up and changed the subject. "Aren't we supposed to be dressing for dinner?"

Lily looked at her in disbelief. "You *want* to dress? My, you certainly have changed!"

TWENTY-ONE

Nate gripped the sides of the chair in the hotel parlor and stared at the two people sitting opposite him, the two people responsible for turning his world upside down.

Lew Townley looked much as he remembered, when the solicitor had visited his father's house in Belgravia. Gaunt, hook-nosed, his hair thinner than before. Yet his expression, usually pinched in Nate's presence, now reeked of obsequiousness. Townley was still the sycophant he'd been while serving his father, but he had turned his groveling attentions to Nate.

He shifted his gaze to the well-dressed woman sitting primly beside Townley.

Beatrice . . . The years rolled back as he gazed at her. Her sculpted lips turned up in that lopsided smile which had stolen his heart as a youth. She had always been lovely. It had been easy to lose his inexperienced heart to her. Now, ten years later, her girlish prettiness had transformed into mature beauty. Always confident and well-dressed, she radiated sophistication. Even her black mourning attire bore the mark of the finest French craftsmanship.

"We're so sorry to be the bearers of bad news, milord," Townley said.

"Don't call me 'lord,'" Nate snapped.

"But, milord, with Lord Rupert's passing—"

"Lew, please," Beatrice interrupted. "Nathaniel is in deep mourning. Learning about his dear brother's untimely death has undoubtedly sent him into shock. It has shaken all of us." Snapping her purse open, she withdrew a black handkerchief made with lace matching that on her dress. She dabbed at her dry eyes, her fine mouth turned down in a tragic frown. "Goodness knows, his untimely passing has been difficult on all of us."

"Goodness knows," Nate said. "How did he die?" Probably too much strong drink. Or perhaps he offended a bad element while visiting one of his favorite East End brothels or gaming halls.

Studying Beatrice's carefully placed expression of grief, he refrained from voicing his speculations. She might actually have loved Rupert after ten years as his wife. Nate was in no position to assume otherwise.

She composed herself enough to explain. "It was dreadful. A hunting accident. One of the other fellows . . . The constable said his aim and eyesight were so poor, he mistook Rupert for a—a deer." Her voice broke and she dabbed at her eyes again.

Nate stared at her, trying to comprehend her story. His foppish idiot brother, who hated outdoor sports, had died in the out-of-doors? Someone shot him. Someone shot Rupert. From the little Beatrice said—and what she didn't say—it could very well have been murder.

He shouldn't be surprised. Even as a young man, he had known Rupert's violent temper and dissolute ways would be his downfall. Or so he had fancied, until Rupert had "won" Beatrice's hand, if not her heart.

"I'm sorry to hear it. For your sake, Beatrice," he said, unconsciously rubbing at his scar. Despite his better nature, his concern was less over Rupert's possibly deserved fate than over the situation in which he now found himself. "You needn't have traveled so far to bring me this news. The dispatch was sufficient."

"But Nathaniel, don't you see?" Beatrice crumpled her handkerchief and leaned forward, her large blue eyes intense. "Rupert and I . . . We never had children, I am sad to say." She sighed and pressed her hand to her chest, as if her heart ached. "I am merely the dowager now. But you, Nathaniel. You are the marquess."

Nate shifted uncomfortably in his chair. "I want nothing of my father's, as you well know."

"I am quite sorry, milord," Townley said, looking not at all sorry. "But you have no choice in the matter. Primogeniture is the law. You are your father's only remaining heir."

No. I refuse. I won't be anything of that man's! he longed to shout. "Damn it, Beatrice." He glared at her. "Why didn't you have the decency to give the fellow a son and leave me out of this?"

As he suspected, her grief was mostly show, for she glared right back.

Townley continued, "There is Henley House to manage, of course, not to mention the London home and the Paris residence. Then there are your duties in the House of Lords to consider. How soon will you be ready to return with us to England?"

Nate rubbed his face. "I hate England," he muttered to no one in particular. "With a bloody passion! I hate Henley House."

Beatrice rose from her seat and knelt at his feet, her black gown rustling. She patted his hand. "Dearest brother, don't fret," she said, her eyes wide with feigned concern. "Lew and I are both going to help you. You won't be alone."

Nate yanked his hand free. "The last thing I need is your help, Beatrice."

Her eyes narrowed and she rose to her feet. "Once a barbarian, always a barbarian, I see." She turned, flipped her full skirt back with one elegant motion, and resumed her seat beside Townley.

"You said it. I'm a barbarian. I have no desire to be anything else." Nate extracted a cigarette from the pocket of his bush jacket. Scratching a match on the sole of his boot, he lit the end and inhaled deeply, then blew out a satisfying stream of smoke in Beatrice's direction.

She grimaced. Then her features softened once more, as if she were straining to be patient. "Come, Nathaniel, it's a shock, I am sure. But you know you belong with us, in England."

She might as well have been offering him a ticket to hell. "Why are you so damned interested in what I do?"

She looked shocked. Fighting for words, she said, "You—you're my brother-in-law. Of course I care."

"That a fact?" He took another drag on his cigarette. "I haven't heard from you, or my *dear* brother," he said derisively, "in a decade."

"You're a difficult man to track down," Townley said.

"But you managed, without too much fuss." Leaning forward, he ground out his cigarette in an ashtray on the table. "How about if I book passage on the next ship to England?" he said, leaning back in the chair.

Beatrice started to smile, until he added, "For both of you. I stay here, you go play your roles back *home* in bloody old England, and I never need to hear from either of you again."

Townley began shaking his head, and Beatrice put a carefully placed pout on her face.

"If I may be so bold as to say so, milord, that won't suffice. There are formalities . . ." Townley began.

"There are things you simply must attend to in England," Beatrice said. "Becoming a marquess is one of them. The queen will want to meet you. Then there are your parliamentary duties—"

"Yes, Parliament will soon be in session," Townley said. "You must attend to your seat there."

He jerked to his feet, his stomach roiling. Say good-bye to India, his home? On top of leaving Pauline? His chest tightened in a painful squeeze. She was no longer part of the equation, or his life. He would be leaving her regardless. She was returning to her parents, where she belonged. Besides, she didn't really want him. She never had. He was her adventure, nothing more.

At that thought, the fight began to leave him. Still, he couldn't bring himself to admit defeat, not yet.

Unconcerned with his emotional upheaval, Beatrice rose and slipped in front of Nate to toy with his lapels. "We must dress you in proper attire. This bush outfit simply won't do."

He shoved her hands away. "Enough of this bloody business." Turning, he headed toward the archway leading back into the main lobby.

"Where are you going?" Beatrice called out, sounding near panic. "We have much more to discuss, arrangements to make."

"Supper," Townley burst out. "We have a table reserved here in the hotel restaurant for eight o'clock."

Nate paused in his escape. Squeezing his eyes shut, he took a deep breath. Much as he wanted to, he couldn't run away from this situation. Or from his fate. But he desperately needed time to think, to come to terms with everything he would be losing. "Very well," he said without turning around. "Until supper."

A soft tap on the door of Nate's hotel room pulled him from his reverie. He had spent the hours since dinner drinking whiskey, his thoughts muddled in the past. Beatrice's reappearance had rolled back the years, causing him to relive the few months he had spent in England, suffering embarrassment at the hands of his father and brother.

Now his tormenters were dead. If he returned to England, *he* would be the king of the castle. Why didn't that thought fill him with even the smallest flicker of satisfaction?

The knock came again. Nate pushed from his chair to answer it, praying it wasn't Beatrice. He couldn't take much more of her, not so soon.

Perhaps it was Pauline. He had seen her leaving

the hotel restaurant with her sister right before he entered, but she hadn't spotted him. Was she thinking about him at all? Somewhere in the hotel, she lived and breathed and dreamed and planned . . . and hoped. For him?

He grasped the cool door handle, anticipation thundering in his chest. With his shirt removed, he wasn't appropriately dressed—for anyone but Pauline. His lover.

He yanked open the door.

"Mr. Savidge."

Mrs. Drake, resplendent in a dinner gown, stood before him, holding an envelope in her gloved hands. Her eyes darted to his undershirt-clad chest. "If I might have a moment of your time?"

Suddenly conscious of his state of undress, Nate scrambled for the dressing gown lying on his bed and shrugged into it. He stepped back. "Come in."

She entered and he closed the door behind her. She turned to face him. "I appreciate that you were willing to take care of Pauline. You brought her back safe, if somewhat changed."

"Changed?" Did she know? He tightened his robe around himself. "It's not . . . that is . . ."

"She actually wants to come home. I don't know what you did, but I have a strong feeling she won't be causing our family heartbreak any longer." She held out the envelope to him. "Two thousand pounds, that's what we agreed on."

Nate stared at the thick envelope. Two thousand pounds. How important the money had once seemed to him. He began shaking his head before he spoke. "I can't take it. I don't need it."

Mrs. Drake studied him a moment, then gradually dropped her hand. "You're the new marquess."

"Don't remind me. But that's not the reason. It's Pauline. She—"

"Was that much trouble?" Her lips turned up in a smile.

His shoulders sagged in relief. "When you first proposed I take her along, I thought you were off your nut. But your sister . . . she surprised me at every turn. She's an amazingly resourceful woman."

"Which usually leads her into trouble."

His voice thickened. "She saved my life."

Her eyes widened. "My little sister saved you? I had no idea."

"I nearly became tiger food. If it wasn't for her . . ." A lump formed in his throat. He looked away, struggling to compose himself. He had never been so emotionally sensitive. Pauline had shaken his world. He stood by the small table and fingered his half-full whiskey tumbler.

Mrs. Drake crossed to the door and began to let herself out. "Well, thank you again. I doubt we'll be meeting again anytime soon."

"So, then, you're leaving for England right away?" he asked gruffly, wanting to keep her there a moment longer—this last tie to Pauline.

She faced him. "Since the rain is starting to let up, we're visiting the Taj Mahal in the morning. Immediately afterward, we're taking the afternoon train to Bombay." She hesitated and toyed with the envelope. "She wouldn't mind seeing you one last time. To say good-bye."

"That a fact?" Hope bloomed in his chest. Had

Pauline wanted her to tell him this? *Maybe she longs to see me again, as I long to see her.* He nodded to show he understood, and Mrs. Drake let herself out.

Pauline followed Lily to the street outside the hotel, where horse-drawn cabs and manpowered rickshaws lined up waiting to take guests to various locations around Agra, including the Taj Mahal. The weather had decided to cooperate, bringing a crowd of hotel guests outside to enjoy the sun and refreshing air cleansed of dust by the rain.

Pauline had longed to see the Taj, but this morning she found it difficult to dredge up enthusiasm for much of anything. She felt heavy and thick, as if she were wading through water. She tried to blame her feeling on her proper dress—her clothing had never felt so restrictive, her corset so binding. The whalebone stays, molding her flesh into unforgiving curves, cut into her with every breath she took.

Now back to being Miss Pauline Carrington, she had to dress the part—with a chemise, a corset, drawers, two petticoats, an underskirt, and a dress, not to mention gloves, a hat, and a fan. She felt altogether weighted down, stifled, unnatural. Still, she refused to complain. Lily had suffered enough at her hands. She didn't deserve to put up with a recalcitrant sister.

"Look, Pauline." Lily patted her arm. "It's Mr. Savidge and Lady Bathurst."

Pauline tensed. The two stood not ten feet away, beside the doorman, who was gesturing to a rickshaw *wallah.* Nate looked uncharacteristically dapper in a tweed suit, the same one he had worn that night at the club in Simla. His hair had been trimmed and his face was clean-shaven. Except for the ragged scar on his face, he looked the very picture of a gentleman.

Pain lanced through Pauline's chest. *I miss the bushman. I miss Nate.*

As for Lady Bathurst, she looked entirely too fashionable in her mourning attire, though the black did enhance her dark beauty. Pauline gradually straightened her spine, suddenly glad the corset lifted her breasts and tucked in her waist. She hoped her proper yellow dress with its flounces and lace would outshine Beatrice's black in Nate's eyes. He must like his women dressed as women, she reasoned. After all, Lady Bathurst hadn't been dressed as a man when he lost his heart to *her.*

Lily stepped forward. "Lady Bathurst, Mr. Savidge. Good morning."

"Good morning, Mrs. Drake. Paul—Miss Carrington." His eyes shone with new interest, as if he had never seen her before.

Pauline stopped breathing. Despite having been intimate with this man, she felt oddly shy under his perusal.

Nate cleared his throat. "We were about to leave for the Taj Mahal."

"What a coincidence," Lily said. "We were about to visit the Taj Mahal ourselves."

Nate gave Lily a charming smile, his eyes sparkling. A shaft of jealousy cut through Pauline at the secret understanding that seemed to pass between them. "Perhaps we could share a cab."

"*Nathaniel . . .*" Lady Bathurst looked as if she

would protest, but Nate ignored her and instructed the doorman to order a four-person hansom cab. The doorman waved off the rickshaw and signaled a carriage to advance.

Nate's gaze flicked up and down Pauline. The yards of fabric covering her failed to keep her body from reacting to the predatory gleam in his eye. She recognized, under his gentleman's suit, the passionate animal who had made love to her.

He took a small step closer, his voice dropping to a low murmur. "I almost didn't recognize you."

"I'm the same under all these layers of cloth," she whispered hotly.

His gaze heated significantly, and his lips twitched. Until she added, "Apparently, *you've* changed overnight, my *lord.*"

His eyes narrowed. The cab pulled up, drawing his attention. He helped Beatrice navigate the steps up to one of the two facing benches, then handed Lily in.

Pauline hung back, unsure whether she ought to be touching him again, here in front of other people. What if the others could see her feelings for him? What if they could see how familiar they had been?

"Miss Carrington." Nate extended his hand. Pauline realized the other women were already seated and waiting for her to join them.

Pauline reluctantly placed her gloved hand in his. For the first time, she saw the sense in wearing gloves, which kept skin from touching skin. "Mr. Savidge," she acknowledged, then whispered fiercely under her breath, "if that's even your name."

His eyes darkened and he gave her hand a fierce

squeeze before releasing it. "Pot calling the kettle black, Manu?"

His hand remained wrapped around hers, and Pauline didn't have the strength to yank it away. Until Beatrice's pouty voice broke their confrontation. "Nathaniel, what is the delay?"

Nate dropped her hand and took the empty seat beside Beatrice, right across from Pauline.

Pauline decided to take advantage of her position. The cab trundled toward the onion-domed edifice sparkling in the morning sun, but Pauline barely noticed where they were going. Sitting ramrod straight, her hands neatly in her lap, she kept her accusing gaze on Nate, silently challenging him. If she managed to get the man alone, she'd give him a piece of her mind! "Lord," indeed.

To her annoyance, he merely gazed back, as self-assured as a jungle cat leisurely studying its prey. Pauline could almost read his mind as his eyes traversed her bosom, now lifted by her corset. He was remembering seeing her naked, touching her breasts, kissing them. Well, let him! He would never see her body naked again. If she had known he was lying through his teeth the entire time, she never would have allowed him so close.

His insolent gaze began to make her feel hot inside her corset. Snapping open her fan, she whipped up the air around her face. Finally forced to give in, she turned her attention to the dome topped by a golden spire rising beyond the trees at the highway's edge.

"Who lives here?" Lady Bathurst asked. She sat ridiculously close to Nate on the carriage bench.

"It's a tomb, Beatrice, as I explained," Nate said. "It

was built by Shah Jahan as a tomb for his wife. His pecunious son placed the shah's body there, too, rather than build a twin black Taj as his father planned."

"The shah must have loved his wife dearly to build her such a gorgeous creation," Lily said, a dreamy smile on her face. No doubt she was again thinking of her own husband, who was tying up his affairs in Delhi before joining them in Bombay.

"A tomb! You mean a grave? How utterly morbid." Snapping open her fan, Beatrice waved it before her face.

Nate ignored her, and continued, "It's hard to believe, but the Taj was very nearly stripped into pieces earlier in the century."

"No!" Lily said, aghast.

Pauline felt as sick at the idea as Lily looked, but couldn't bring herself to respond to Nate's comment.

"By a British nobleman, no less." He gave Beatrice a cool look, and she frowned.

Nate explained, "Lord William Bentinck, in the sheer arrogance of his noble kind, intended to strip off the marble facades and ship them to London. He meant to sell them piecemeal to his friends, to decorate their precious estates. He had already stripped facades from the Red Fort in Delhi. The demolition crew was about to start on the Taj. Just in time, word reached him from London that the auction of the Red Fort pieces had been a failure, so he decided stripping the Taj wasn't worth the money."

"Thank goodness," Lily said.

"Typical of noblemen, who think they own the world and everything in it."

Pauline stared at him in confusion. *He* was a nobleman, wasn't he?

"As it is, people keep chipping out pieces of agate and carnelian from the walls."

Beatrice interrupted the discussion of the Taj, frantically beating her fan to stir the torpid midmorning air. "If these flies would stop pestering me, I might be able to tolerate this filthy country. I cannot fathom how you can bear living here, Nathaniel."

Despite being furious with Nate, Pauline couldn't stifle a surge of sympathy at his former love's disgust for his beloved India. His gaze caught hers, seeing her sympathy before she could hide it. Without words, he acknowledged her support.

Despite herself, she responded to his appreciative gaze with an even warmer look. The secret intimacy drew them together, despite their being with others. Nate understood that she, too, had come to love this land. He understood her better than anyone she had ever met. As she understood him . . .

Until she had learned he was a nobleman! Pauline jerked her gaze from his, fury rising anew.

Beatrice patted Nate's hand where it rested on his thigh. "When you return home where you belong, you'll understand my distaste."

"I haven't agreed to anything, Beatrice." His voice carried a definite chill.

"You will," Beatrice gave him a confident smile. "Trust me, Nathaniel. You will."

TWENTY-TWO

Pauline paused just inside the arched marble gateway entrance to the grounds of the Taj Mahal. For a moment, she forgot to breathe. Beyond a thousand feet of unkempt gardens rose a Persian fantasy in stone, a creation sprung from her childhood dreams of distant places and times.

The Taj itself was separated from the entrance gate by a thousand feet of gardens laid out in geometric precision. Puddles of rain dotted paved paths that divided patches of overgrown grass. Little fountains gurgled in the sun. A brass band played on one square. A pair of British soldiers, their uniform coats unbuttoned, lolled in the shade of an overgrown cypress, guzzling liquor from amber bottles. Beyond all this, the celebrated mausoleum and its four slender minarets rested on a platform overlooking the Jumna River, now swollen from the rains.

Pauline turned her attention to the intricately carved and shaped archway above her. "The ivory gate through which all good dreams pass," she murmured.

"What is that?" Nate asked.

"Something Rudyard Kipling wrote about this place."

Appreciation filled Nate's eyes, and Pauline had the curious sensation that he wanted to kiss her.

Beatrice laid a possessive hand on his arm, ending the moment and stealing his attention. "Walk with me."

Looping her arm through his, she steered him away from Pauline.

"Don't fret, Pauline," Lily said beside her. "They've known each other for years and probably have a lot of catching up to do."

"That's perfectly fine with me," Pauline said. "You don't think I care, do you?"

She stared after them as they strolled down the path on the right side of the garden, Nate carefully leading her around the few puddles still drying out under the summer sun. Beatrice kept her arm in his, showing far more attention to her companion than to the towering monument nearby.

Her behavior grated on Pauline in the worst way. Pauline took pride in always being straightforward with people, men included. She had never acted like a coquettish kitten begging for scraps of attention. Yet most ladies did. Most ladies knew no other way to get what they wanted. And Beatrice clearly wanted Nate.

What would that woman think if she knew how Pauline had seduced Nate, boldly and confidently appealing to his animal passions and her own? If only she could tell her. Beatrice's silly pretense toward sophistication would melt under the heat of the passion she and Nate had shared!

As if it mattered. Their tryst had ended, with no thought on his part to repeating the experience. Perhaps she was wrong, and Beatrice knew what she was about, dangling promises in front of Nate. Perhaps Pauline had ruined her chance by being so bold. Her mother's warnings rang in her head, and she finally began to see the truth in them.

Beatrice and Nate paused by a gurgling fountain. The woman took Nate's hands in hers and pressed them close. And Nate allowed her the familiar touch.

Pauline's hands tightened so hard on her fan, she nearly snapped it in two. "She's set her cap for him."

Lily protested, "She's still in widow's weeds."

"Then why are her hands all over Nate?" She jabbed toward the couple with her fan. "That woman threw Nate over to marry his brother, years ago. And now I know why. His brother was the favored one, with the house, the lands, the fortune. And the title! She wanted to be a marquessa, or marquis, or whatever."

"Marchioness. Is that what happened?"

Pauline nodded, struggling against a firestorm of competing emotions. She longed to face Nate, to demand answers. At the same time she felt increasing sympathy for him, being pursued by that predatory spider.

"Well, I should think Mr. Savidge is capable of taking care of himself," Lily said mildly.

"Hah! He wouldn't be standing here now if I hadn't—" She stopped midsentence. No, she didn't want to brag. She didn't want anyone to know he had once been as weak as a kitten and needed a woman's help to stay alive. She felt strangely protective of him despite her anger and didn't want his reputation to lose any of its luster.

"Hadn't what?" Lily asked.

"Never mind."

Lily returned her attention to the couple in question, who had now begun strolling toward the mausoleum. "I must say, you have a point."

"What do you mean?"

"Lady Bathurst seems the sort to pursue a man for gain. I've met dozens of ladies like her. Station and class mean everything to a woman like her."

Knowing how she had hurt Nate, Pauline already hated her. Seeing how beautiful she was had made her loathe her. "I knew she was a bad sort," she said, filled with vindication.

"Oh, don't misunderstand me. She's probably not wicked or anything of that nature. She merely has a different set of priorities from us. Englishwomen often do. Marriage is a means to an end. They live by their heads, not their hearts. They may not be as happy, but they never risk bringing shame on their families."

Her own outrageous actions struck Pauline in a new, uncomfortable light. She couldn't begin to match Beatrice's suitability. She would be poison to any titled gentleman. Her own mother had long given up on marrying her to one. Nate had once loved Beatrice. Who was to say he wouldn't fall in love with her again? If he preferred refined ladies like Beatrice, he would never consider a future with Pauline.

What was she thinking? She didn't expect Nate to *marry* her; she never had. She never wanted to marry in the first place! *Besides,* she reminded herself fiercely, *I'm too furious with him to marry him, even if he asked me.*

Which, she felt with deep sadness, he had made perfectly clear would never happen.

A moment later, Nate and his lady friend disappeared from sight around the far corner of the mausoleum. "We can't stand here all day. Let's walk," Pauline said, moving into a quick stride in the direction where they had vanished.

Lily hurried to catch up. "I didn't expect to be running, Pauly," she said.

Pauline barely heard her. Rounding the corner, she saw Nate and Beatrice disappear toward the temple entrance. Lifting her skirts, she sprinted toward the entrance, leaving Lily behind.

"Pauly, please!" Lily called out.

Pauline continued the pursuit. She didn't slow her stride until just outside the massive portal. Here, the visiting Indians had removed their shoes before entering the sanctity of the tomb itself. Only one pair of Western boots rested by the door—Nate's. The British saw the Taj Mahal as nothing but a curiosity, not a sacred place. Disgusted by the lack of respect shown by other Westerners, Pauline stooped and untied her laces as fast as she could. Leaving her French handmade ivory shoes beside his, she padded into the shadowy interior in stocking feet.

She found herself in an enormous marble room, the octagonal burial chamber of the royal couple. Pauline waited for her eyes to adjust to the interior, illuminated only by sunlight filtered indirectly through marble screens. Ignoring the chattering of British visitors around her, she approached an octagonal screen carved in filigree so fine, it looked like lace. The screen surrounded two caskets inlaid with mosaics of precious stones.

Beatrice's high English voice reached her right before she spotted Nate. He stood a few feet away, a head taller than the half-dozen visitors surrounding him, marveling at the tomb. Like a bird sensing its prey, he glanced up and looked right at her.

He'll think I'm pursuing him! Pauline felt like melting into the shadows, until she reminded herself she had every right to be there. She felt so naked and alone, standing there in her stocking feet. She shouldn't have left Lily behind!

With a heavy sigh, she crossed the floor to one of the walls and pretended to be fascinated by the bas relief carvings. When Lily caught up with her, she would encourage her to leave. She would plead a headache, though she had never used such a silly ploy in her life. She would beg Lily to take her to Bombay immediately, even if they had to wait three hours at the train station.

Here in the dreamlike Taj Mahal, a strange unreality filled Pauline. Nate preyed on her mind, making it impossible for her to think straight. She couldn't begin to sort out how she felt about him; she only knew that as long as she was near him, she would never stop yearning to be with him. She had to leave him for good, before she completely lost her sense. This outing was sheer torture, being so close to him yet so distant. Pretending they were different people, not secret lovers. Becoming who they were supposed to be.

"So, you're going back to America." His quiet,

husky voice startled her and she whirled to face him. He had stalked her as efficiently as a hunter after his prey, his stocking feet silent on the mosaic flooring.

She braced her spine and stared boldly at him, despite the tumble of excitement in her stomach. "Our plans haven't changed, if that's what you mean, *milord.*"

He stiffened. "Don't call me that. Not you. *Ever.*"

She cocked her head, determined to push her advantage, to make him answer for his deception. "Funny how one can think she knows a person, only to discover he has been entirely false from the very beginning."

His eyes sparked fire. "That's a strange accusation coming from *you.*"

She crossed her arms defensively. "You *are* a marquess, aren't you?"

"It seems so," he said, his eyes darkening. "I had no intention of being false, Pauline. It's not the sort of thing one has a choice about."

"You had the choice of telling me."

"I saw no reason to," he shot back.

"You were a *lord* all this time! As silver-spoon as they come. Yet you've been playing the part of the simple country fellow. Well, not simple, but certainly a far cry from a nobleman!"

"Why in bloody hell does it matter?" The dome above magnified his words, and they bounced back to her above the muted conversations of the other visitors. *Matter, matter, matter* . . . Conscious that their argument was drawing the attention of other tourists, Nate lowered his voice and whispered fiercely, "You're never going to see me again anyway. Why does it matter whether I'm here or in England?"

Because you belong here! And so do I! "I don't like being made a fool of!" she whispered back. Snapping open her fan, she waved it briskly before her face, desperate to cool her heated cheeks.

"Like you tried to fool me by dressing as a *boy?*"

Pauline's fury boiled over. She didn't care if she made a scene. After all, that's what she was best at. "So I tried to be something I wasn't. Isn't that what you've been doing your entire life? You kept telling me people should be who they are, that you can't change. I can't begin to count the number of times you told me that! All these weeks you've insisted I belong with my family." Closing her fan, she jabbed it at his chest. "Well, by your own logic you belong in bloody old England, not here!"

Not here, not here, not here . . . By the time she finished her tirade, her words echoed throughout the chamber, causing every other conversation to still. Brits and Indians alike stared at them, some in annoyance, others with smiles on their faces at the free show they were being offered.

"A *boy?*" Without warning, Beatrice appeared by Nate's side. She stared at Pauline in utter amazement. "Did you say she dressed up as a *boy?*"

Nate ignored her, his eyes locked on Pauline's. "I would hardly compare our situations. This has been nothing but a lark, a game, to you," he said, his harsh words flaying her. "All of it. It's time to grow up, Pauline. The game is over."

Over, over, over, over, over . . . Pauline's heart trembled, threatening to crumble into pieces, killing her right there. He was wrong, so wrong. She had never felt more strongly about anything than she felt for this man and this country. But she would never, ever tell him so. Not when he didn't need her. Not when he was so willing to let her go.

He barreled on, unconcerned how his words dug into her heart and soul, savaging her the way his namesake savaged its prey. "You said it yourself. You're happy to return home to your family. To where you belong. Just look at you, all prim and proper like a regular lady, flicking your fan about, your hat sitting just so. You would think we had never—that nothing had changed. Nothing *has* changed." He sucked in a breath and his face took on a determined cast. "And while it kills me to do it, I'll go where I belong. To England."

"Oh, Nate, I knew you'd see sense!" Beatrice clapped her gloved hands, her eyes bright with pleasure under her netted veil.

His declaration destroyed Pauline's last hope. She had been a fool to imagine he would want her, a fool to believe he was different from other men. When society came calling, he eagerly swung open the door. Beatrice would have him groomed and brushed and behaving like a regular gentleman in under six months, destroying forever the noble White Tiger.

The thought sickened her. "Yes, Nate," Pauline said, her voice filled with derision. "Go home to England where you belong, with your land and your title and your money. And your lies."

Lies, lies, lies, lies . . . The dome threw the charge back at Nate again and again.

"Impertinent colonial girl!" Beatrice said, her eyes shooting daggers at Pauline, her possessive hands tight on Nate's arm. "What gives her the right—"

Pauline turned her fury on Beatrice. "Oh, be quiet, you witch. I know why you traveled all this way to drag Nate home. You want to keep being Mrs. Marquess, or Lady Marquis, or whatever—"

"Marchioness," Lily supplied, quietly appearing to stand by her sister.

"Marchioness. You expect to drag Nate to the altar. I know how you threw him over because he wasn't good enough for you. Not then. But now that he's the marquess—"

"How dare you accuse me of such a thing, with my dear departed Rupert barely in the ground! I'm in deep mourning."

"Then why are your hands all over Nate?"

Beatrice jerked her hands off of his arm as if he were on fire, but Pauline's point had been made.

"You'll fail, too. I know something about Nate that you don't. He's not the marrying kind. He would never let a woman tie him down, even if—" Just in time, she stopped herself from blurting out, *"even if she loved him."*

Or would he? With a sick feeling, she realized she didn't know Nate at all. "That is, he used to feel that way, before he decided to be a nobleman. Who knows who he really is anymore?"

"Damn it, Pauline!" Nate grasped her arms and swung her around. "Stop speaking for me! You don't have the faintest idea—Christ Almighty." Releasing her, he dug his fingers into his hair, gripping it as if he longed to pull it out.

"Are you—you were intimate with that girl, weren't you?" Beatrice said, looking utterly appalled. "What a little tart! She's not fit to be in polite company."

Determined to keep her pride to the last, Pauline lifted her chin and glared at the man she loved, the man who wanted to send her across the sea, far away from him. How she hated him at that moment! Hated him, desired him, was enraged by him! "Yes, I slept with him," she said to Beatrice, her eyes locked on Nate's. "If you knew what we did together, you would faint dead away. And I wish to God I hadn't!"

He flinched, but before he could respond, Lily confronted him, her color high. "Mr. Savidge! I thought you a gentleman! You gave me your word—"

"I hardly took advantage of her," he said roughly. "Your sister, Mrs. Drake, is the most determined female I have ever had the misfortune of knowing." He shot a hard look at Pauline, and she glared right back.

"As if you needed that much convincing," Pauline countered.

"Pauly! You seduced him?" Lily looked so stunned, Pauline couldn't tell if her sister was about to burst into tears or laughter.

"And that surprises you? You know what kind of girl I am, Lily. What kind I've always been. But it's over now, and it's going to stay that way!"

"Damned right, it is!" Nate shot back.

Pauline knew she had to leave, *now*. Before she burst into tears and thoroughly humiliated herself. "Come, Lily. Let's leave them to each other." Grasping Lily's arm, she dragged her sister away.

Pauline's legs shook so hard, she nearly collapsed before reaching the entrance. There, her pretty shoes waited beside Nate's dusty boots.

TWENTY-THREE

The ride to the train station passed in a blur.
Pauline felt as if her very spirit had been extin-
guished, leaving only a dead shell behind.

She barely noticed her surroundings as Lily led
her to a carriage, then onto the platform at the
train station and into a private railway car. Her sister's calm guidance enabled Pauline to put one
foot before the other, to pull air into her lungs and
release it, to pretend she wasn't crumbling to
pieces.

Hours later—or was it merely minutes?—the train
to Bombay pulled from the station, taking Pauline
away from India and away from Nate Savidge. Lily,
who had been trying to comfort her with gentle plat-
itudes and reassurance, locked the door of their
private rail car and took the bench beside her sister.

For a long while, Pauline felt the rhythm of the
train tracks clicking softly beneath her. Finally, the
motion broke free her words.

"I caused a scene, in the middle of a holy place,"
she whispered, aghast by her actions in the Taj.

"Don't be hard on yourself, Pauline," Lily said.
"None of the visitors were giving the queen's tomb
the respect it's due. They think nothing of turning it

into a pleasure ground, used by Brits and Indians alike for all manner of entertainments. I've heard dances are held there, and concerts, right inside the dome itself."

Pauline shook her head, dismayed by her sister's story. "But I'm not like them. I was supposed to be different. I was supposed to understand, like—like . . ." She couldn't form his name and maintain any semblance of composure. "I've failed." The dam burst, and tears began flowing down her cheeks.

Lily pressed a linen handkerchief into her hand. "I think more is bothering you than that."

"But that's the crux of it, Lily. I've failed myself." Pressing the handkerchief to her eyes, she blotted away her tears, only to find fresh ones springing forth. "I never wanted to marry, to become tied down to a—a *man*. I promised myself I never would. But now my heart feels like it's been crushed under the wheels of this train."

"You're in love with him."

In love with him. Lily's calm statement anchored the truth in Pauline's heart. Oh, yes, she loved him, desperately and undeniably. She lifted her tear-filled gaze to Lily. "I'm so confused. I wasn't looking—I didn't expect . . . When I imagined being tied to a husband, I never pictured a man like him. Being with him . . . it was . . . everything."

Lily smiled in understanding. "I know."

"Everything for me. But not for him." She gripped Lily's hand. "He doesn't love me, Lily. He never said anything of the sort."

"Did you tell him how you feel about him?" she asked softly, her eyes searching Pauline's.

"I . . . no." Pauline swallowed hard in a swollen throat. "No, of course not. He's not the sort to—to want that. That's what I liked about him, at first. He was daring, and different. Not like the gentlemen Mother always pushed at me."

"You found yourself in love with a man who has no use for love."

Pauline nodded, acknowledging the miserable situation she had got herself into.

She had thrown away her relationship with Nate out of fear that she was falling victim to a desire for love and marriage. Terrified of her own feelings, she had refused to tell him how much she loved him. Instead, as their time together had neared an end, she had buried her pain under anger. She had hung her feelings on his new status, nursed her fury to a fever pitch, caused a confrontation sure to make the leaving all hers, and none of his.

As a result, she had lost him.

In a matter of days, she would be home again, in New York. And he would be leaving India for his own new life.

With a deep, unshakable certainty, she knew their paths would never again cross.

New York, six months later

"What's wrong with her?" Meryl crossed her arms and cocked her blond head. Joe Hammond, the son of her father's business partner, came up behind her. They had just been arguing about how he was learning nothing at the university that would help him run Atlantic-Southern Railroads someday—a job she fully intended to have for herself.

"All Carrington women are touched in the head," Joe said.

Meryl spun around and gave him the coldest glare she was capable of. "Go bother someone else, Joe. Just because you're going to Columbia doesn't give you the right to insult me or my sisters."

Joe tugged her long braid, an annoying habit of his since they were children. "You're jealous, Meryl, and you know it. If you could attend university, you would jump at the chance. Unfortunately, you were born a *girl.*"

"I *am* going to university next year! Just wait and see. And I'll be a much better student than you could ever dream of being."

"Meryl, Joe." Clara's gentle words broke into their argument. "If you could please think of Pauline now. We have to do something to help her."

"What's wrong?" Joe's smile faded. At least he had the grace to show concern, Meryl thought. After all, the Carringtons had been an extended family to him for years.

Clara clasped her hands before her. "Pauline is so different now. She used to love being outside. Now she spends all her time in her room, scribbling at her desk."

"Why?" he asked.

"If we knew that, we wouldn't have to discuss it," Meryl shot back.

"Even mother is growing concerned," Clara said. "At first she was glad that Pauline had settled down, as she put it. But she's so *changed!* I'm worried the melancholy has taken such a firm hold, it will never release her."

"We simply have to get her out of her room," Meryl said, determination filling her.

"I suppose you know how to do that?" Joe asked.

"As a matter of fact, I do. Joe, go sit in the parlor. Or better yet, go back to school. I don't need you."

"As bratty as ever, I see." He didn't seem too concerned by her dismissal, unfortunately. He never took her seriously. Meryl sighed as she watched his tall figure stride down the hall to the sweeping staircase. It simply wasn't fair. Every year he grew better-looking, and she, at age seventeen, she still had a figure fit for a girl. Not that she ever wanted to impress *him*. At least he no longer pined for Lily, now that she lived across the sea in England, married and a mother. Then again, she would love to see him suffer for love. Or just suffer, period.

"So, what is your plan, Meryl?" Clara asked, a teasing smile giving her delicate face the visage of a mischievous angel.

"I'm thinking . . ." Meryl thought fast. "Let's go inside. I'll come up with something."

She knocked softly on Pauline's door. "Oh, Pauline! May Clara and I come in? We need desperately to talk to you."

After a moment, Pauline's distracted voice answered. "Yes."

Meryl swung open the door and entered. As usual, Pauline sat at her writing desk, the sheet of paper atop it still wet with ink.

"Pauline!" Meryl said with theatrical alarm. "You have to help me." Dropping to her knees by Pauline's chair, she threw her head in her sister's lap and gave a fair imitation of a sob. "Oh, please, help me! I don't know what to do."

"Meryl? Sweetheart, what is it?" Pauline returned her pen to its well and placed her hands on Meryl's head. She looked up at Clara, who found herself struggling not to laugh. "Clara?"

Clara found it difficult to lie, but knew she ought to make a decent effort to support whatever wild tale Meryl concocted. "I think it has to do with Joe," she said as inspiration struck. "She's upset because he's being mean to her. Again."

Pauline sighed. "That never bothered you before, Meryl. You merely put him in his place."

Meryl raised her face, which was remarkably dry of tears. "This time it's different. You have to come with me, Pauline." Jumping to her feet, she grabbed Pauline's hand and tugged her from her chair.

"I'm in the middle of writing," she said.

"All you do is write," Meryl complained. "And always about India."

"Writing helps calm my nerves."

Clara frowned, concern filling her. In the past, her steely-spined sister had mocked ladies who complained of weak nerves. She had been right to worry. Kneeling by Pauline's chair, she took her sister's hands in hers. "You've never been the nervous sort. What happened in India?" she asked softly. "Was it truly awful?"

Pauline's eyes took on a distant cast. "Not at all. If I could return . . ."

Clara began to understand. Pauline hadn't experienced some unspeakable trauma during her foray into the wilds. She suffered from a sickness of spirit, rather like homesickness. Her home used to be here in New York, but India had somehow captured her heart. "You're going back there every day, aren't you? In your mind, I mean. You're writing your memoirs to relive your experiences."

A hint of a smile traced Pauline's lips. "Not quite. I'm improving on what actually happened. It's the only way . . ." Her voice fell off, and she picked up her pen as if she meant to shut out her sisters once more.

Meryl took up a position right by her desk, making her presence impossible to ignore. "When will your story be done? You could sell it to the papers."

"I don't care about that."

"But you could become famous!" Meryl said.

Clara settled her hand on Pauline's shoulder. "May I read it, Pauline? You know how I love a good story."

Pauline looked as if she would object; then, with a sigh, she passed the sheaf of paper to Clara. "I don't suppose reading this part would hurt. It's about the Indian . . . wildlife."

Clara gripped the papers, praying some indication of her sister's troubles would be apparent in her words. "Thank you. Now, you need some fresh air. Perhaps you'd like to join me in a walk?"

"No, thank you."

"But I need your help!" Meryl said. "I challenged Joe to an archery contest. I don't know what got into me. He's just so arrogant. And you know how awful I am with bows and arrows."

Clara looked at her little sister in admiration. Meryl's fibs came almost too easily.

"You merely lack patience," Pauline advised, but Clara could tell she wasn't that interested. "Put greater tension on the string and keep your arm steady before you loose the arrow."

Meryl appeared on the verge of panic. "I'll never remember all that. You have to come with me, talk me through it. I can't allow him to win!"

Pauline sat back and returned her pen to the inkwell with a sigh. "You aren't going to let up, are you? Very well." Pushing up from the desk, she allowed Meryl to take her by the hand and lead her from the room, then down the massive curved staircase. On the way, Meryl chattered loudly about the pretend archery competition so that Joe would overhear and catch on to her plan.

Following more slowly, Clara glanced over the papers Pauline had given her. Soon, she found herself engrossed in the story her sister told. If only others could read Pauline's tale. Her work was too good not to be shared. If, as Meryl suggested, the newspaper published her stories, Pauline would have to consider them finished.

And, Clara thought with rising hope, this chapter in Pauline's life could also end. Perhaps then her sister could leave India behind.

If only he could leave India behind.

Leaning by the window, Nate stared into his brandy glass. The gaslights from the misty street outside flickered in the amber liquid. The color of a woman's eyes. Pauline's eyes.

God, it's stuffy in here. Shoving a finger into the collar of his shirt, he unclasped the button and unhooked the collar so that he could breathe. He hated parties. He hated London. Ignoring Beatrice's vociferous protests, he had spent most of the past few months at his country estate. He had left Henley House to her, here in London, as her allowance. And avoided her and the city ever since.

Within one week of arriving in London, he had put Beatrice in her place, making it clear he wanted as little to do with her as possible. She had actually cried. She had flattered him shamelessly. She had debased herself, attempting to seduce him and failing miserably. He had taken no satisfaction in the embarrassing scene that had once been a hurt young man's fantasy.

Now all his fantasies were in India, with Pauline.

A single hope drew him back into the city this night. He was attending tonight's party only because the invitation had been sent by the Drakes. Pauline's family.

He had carried a slim, albeit ridiculous, hope that she might be here, visiting her sister. An hour since arriving, he had seen no sign of her and had finally retreated from the crowded drawing room to the deserted gaming room, where a billiard table and well-stocked bar had kept his mind off his disappointment—for about ten minutes.

"Lord Bathurst, you're alone."

He turned from the window. "Mrs. Drake, good evening."

"I'm so glad you decided to accept our invitation. I know you don't attend many functions."

"You're right about that." Reaching into his pocket, he extracted the same beat-up cigarette case he had always used. It clashed with his neat black suit, but he refused to part with it. He popped it open and extended it to Mrs. Drake. "Smoke?"

She shook her head, so he extracted a lone cigarette and repocketed the case. Lighting up, he restrained himself from asking about Pauline too quickly, despite his desperate hunger to know. Had she married? Was she still in New York? *Does she ever think about me?*

Instead, he fell back on the time-honored tradition of discussing the weather. He gestured to the rain-streaked window. "Blasted rain. Does it ever stop?" He flicked ash from the end of his cigarette onto the carpet, causing his hostess to frown in dismay. "Uh, sorry about that. Bush habits are hard to break."

Her shoulders relaxed and she smiled softly. "You miss India."

"That obvious, is it? I'm not cut out for this."

"Life in England doesn't suit you. It never could."

"It was a bloody stupid idea, me coming here. Matter of fact, I'm going back home, now that I've got my affairs in order. England can get along just fine without me."

"When are you leaving?" She actually appeared interested, though he couldn't imagine why she would care. The polite interest of a well-bred lady, no doubt.

"A few weeks."

"I see."

Why was he telling her this? From some ridiculous hope she would tell Pauline? Even if she did, what difference could it possibly make? Still, he longed to know about her, about her life. Any news at all. Gathering his resolve, he finally asked after her. "Your sister. Is she about? I thought she might be here."

She shook her head. "No. I'm sorry, she's not."

He gave a self-deprecating laugh, hoping to cover his burning disappointment. "Of course not. She's still in America." He studied Mrs. Drake. "That is right, isn't it? New York? With her mum and dad?"

Mrs. Drake glanced at the floor, then back at him, her eyes sparkling. "She's not married yet. If that's what you're asking."

Yet. Did that mean she was engaged? Being courted by some namby-pamby bloke? Why in the bloody hell couldn't he stop wondering about her, thinking about her? Longing to see her again?

"Yeah, well," he said, trying hard to sound uninterested. "I was about to go. Thanks for having me." He dropped his lit cigarette into his brandy glass, then set the glass on the billiard table.

He took a step toward the door, but Mrs. Drake slipped in front of him, on her way to remove the glass from the furniture, no doubt. Instead, she looked up at him. "I received something from my family which might interest you. It has to do with Pauline. Only if you're interested, of course."

Nate struggled to restrain his curiosity and sound decently casual. "Well, sure."

"Then come with me."

Nate allowed her to lead him to another room

down the hall, to a morning room decorated in feminine pastels and white gilt furniture. Crossing to her desk, she slid open a drawer and extracted a folded piece of newspaper.

It had to be an engagement announcement. Well-bred ladies rarely made the newspaper except for social notices. Pauline had found herself some dandy just a few months after leaving him. The distressing thought gnawed at him, sparking a primal fury he hadn't expected to feel. *She's mine, no one else's. Whether she likes it or not. If I ever see her again . . .*

Who was he fooling? She had made her feelings toward him perfectly clear.

Returning to his side, Mrs. Drake held out the paper to him. "Would you like to see it?"

He had to force himself not to snatch the paper from her hand. He nodded, and Mrs. Drake gave it to him. His stomach in knots, he unfolded the newspaper clipping to find a story titled, "The White Tiger of India."

In the heart of the jungle, the late afternoon shadows parted to reveal a glorious sight. Every living thing rejoiced, as did I, that we stood in the presence of a miracle. Stepping into the sunlight came a magnificent beast of grace and strength, the white tiger. Nothing in my experience prepared me for his feral beauty, his savage yet noble demeanor, his muscles rippling with grace and power unmatched by another of his kind. Never had I imagined sharing the earth with such a beautiful creature. Never had such a one touched not only my heart, but the very essence of my being. A scar marred the perfection of his countenance, but where others saw imperfection, I saw the mark of a true survivor. Our eyes locked in silent understanding, mine brown, his the blue of an Indian sky. At that moment, I forever lost my heart to India.

The raw lyricism of Pauline's words brought tears to Nate's eyes. He found himself back there, that day outside the temple when, standing beside her, they had seen the elusive white tiger.

He read the piece again, and yet again, trying to relive that day through her words and finding it increasingly difficult. The tiger's coat had been free of scars, as far as he could recall. Which is why its pelt would have been worth a fortune.

Another, even more obvious contradiction struck him. He began shaking his head. "She's got a gift for words, I'll say that," he murmured. "But I don't know . . ."

"What's wrong?" Mrs. Drake asked.

"Well, I was with her that day. The tiger we saw . . . It was female." He glanced at her. "Her account makes no sense."

"I think it does." Mrs. Drake's eyes met his, warm with secret knowledge.

Nate's heart flipped over as understanding dawned. Hope burst inside him, making him lightheaded. The day she had seen the White Tiger, a male, wasn't in the jungle but at the Kalka railway station.

Pauline was writing about *him*.

TWENTY-FOUR

"Pauline, come quickly!"

Pauline looked up from removing arrows from the straw archery target her father had placed on the back lawn. Meryl was running toward her, skirts held high, her face filled with excitement.

Reaching Pauline, she panted, "There's a man at the door, asking for you. And he's *huge.*" She held out her hands as far as they could stretch.

Huge? Only one man in her experience could be described that way. Pauline's heart hitched as she contemplated such a possibility and instantly rejected it. No. It couldn't be him. "What is his name?"

"Lord something or other, I can't remember. Though he's not dressed like a lord. More like an explorer. He's wearing a tweed suit and a pith helmet! Come on. He wants to see you." Meryl grasped her hand and began dragging her toward the house. "He's English, I know that much. And very handsome, even though he has an awful scar on his face."

It had to be him. "Nate." Pauline slowed to a stop.

"Pauly, what is it?" Meryl asked over her shoulder, still trying to tug her toward the house.

Pauline extracted her hand from Meryl's. "I can't see him. Not now." Or ever. She turned away.

"Too late. He's coming out here."

Meryl's warning froze Pauline in her tracks. Slowly she turned around. He was striding toward her across the lawn, his steps confident, his carriage and presence even more impressive than in her most treasured memories. No memory could compete with the sheer joy she felt upon seeing him in the flesh. *God, how I love him.*

Panic filled her. Despite the passage of months, she was still vulnerable to him, in body and soul. Her heart wouldn't be able to survive another meeting, another leaving. Yet what could she do but face him? In seconds, he had closed the distance. His steps began to slow as he stepped up to her.

She would have to make the best of it. Calling on every ounce of her etiquette training, she straightened her spine, pasted a pleasant smile on her face, and extended her hands in greeting. "Mr. Savidge. Why, hello."

Ignoring her outstretched hands, he yanked off his pith helmet and propped his hands on his hips. He stared down at her, his eyes exploring hers as if he hadn't seen her in years. Despite herself, she found herself eating up his countenance in the same hungry manner. Those eyes, bluer than she remembered, that face more dear.

"My, aren't you the polite one?" he said, the trace of a smile on his lips. "I had a different sort of greeting in mind. Excuse us," he said, shooting a glance at Meryl.

Meryl began to back away but continued to stare at them in fascination.

"Go back to the house, Meryl," Pauline commanded, finally getting her to obey. In a few moments, they were blessedly, terrifyingly alone.

Much as she longed for Nate's potent touch, Pauline wasn't about to give him the opportunity to kiss her. She took a step away and lifted her chin, determined not to let him see how his sudden appearance had rattled her.

"My, this is quite a surprise," she said, trying to sound as she would greeting any old friend. "What brings you to New York? The last thing I remember, you were going to London."

"I'm heading back to India," he said. He glanced down at the grass, then back at her. He seemed uncharacteristically uncertain, as if he were searching for the right words. To what? Tell her good-bye again? Or quite the opposite, something she hardly dared imagine? *Don't be a fool,* she chastised herself. *He left you before; he'll leave you again.*

"I found myself in your neck of the woods and thought I'd drop in for a short visit," he explained.

"Indeed? New York's quite a detour, considering India is in the other direction," she said dryly.

His eyes narrowed briefly at her parry; then his strangely awkward demeanor returned. "The thing is, I could use you. That is, if you'd like to come back to India with me."

He could use her? She stared at him in shock. The nerve of him! "You want me for your *servant?*"

He grimaced. "That isn't exactly what I meant."

She propped her hands on her hips. "Oh. You mean as your mistress. I've done that already, and I don't care to repeat the experience."

He closed the distance between them to a few

inches. Gazing down at her, his eyes lost their uncertain cast and glowed with intensity. "I know that's a lie."

Tossing his pith helmet on the grass, he reached inside his jacket and pulled out a folded piece of newspaper. Spreading it open, he pressed it to the straw target, yanked an arrow out of the straw, and pinned it in place. He turned back to her, his eyes hot with challenge.

Pauline stared at the article Clara and Meryl had sent to the newspaper without her permission. She had been angry at first but had since discovered that the newspaper's readers were interested in what she had to say. How had Nate come across that particular account, all the way over in England?

"You wrote about the white tiger," he said.

Tingles wove up her spine. She had written about him so many times, but never once imagined him reading a word of her private meanderings. Lord, let him not realize the truth! She cocked her head. "Yes, I did. So?"

He grinned victoriously. "It's about me."

"Well, I . . . That is, not really. It's . . . I . . ." Her heartbeat thundering in her ears, she forced herself to meet his challenging gaze.

"You lied to me, pet. How long have you been in love with me?"

His blatant question stunned and alarmed her. "How dare you!"

She yanked the paper from the target, crumpled it up, and tossed it right in his face. Spinning on her heel, she began striding toward the house.

He caught up with her in two strides. Wrapping his

arms around her from behind, he lifted her, kicking and protesting, into the air. "Cut it out, Pauline." Turning her around, he dropped her yet kept her in his embrace. The deliciously familiar heat of his body destroyed her resistance and she allowed him this victory.

Anchoring his hands on her shoulders, he pinned her in place as surely as he had the newspaper. In the space of a heartbeat, they were once again as they had been in India, as if the months hadn't passed, as if the miles had never separated them. Their rising tempers had banished his awkwardness and her denials. Her love lay open to him; in every word she had written, words burned into both their hearts.

"I just need to know if you still love me," he said. "That's all. Just tell me one way or the other."

She stared up at him, desperate to keep some shred of dignity. "Why does it matter?"

"You were angry because I lied to you. I'm sorry. The thing is, I never thought of myself as a nobleman, so at least I was being true to myself in not mentioning it. But you . . ." He gripped her chin and tilted her face to his. "You lied, too," he said softly. "You loved me, and you led me to believe I was nothing but your adventure."

Her heartbeat thundered in her ears. Why did it matter to him, after all this time? Why did he persist in rubbing her face in her folly?

"If you still love me . . ." he began.

"You'll what?" she asked defiantly. "Drag me back to India with you to be your mistress?"

"Don't be daft." He dropped his hands from her. "Show a little mercy, Pauline. I've never done this before."

"Done what, exactly? Insulted a woman?"

His scar turned a livid shade of red. "Damn it, Pauline! Isn't it obvious? I'm asking you to marry me."

"Oh." Pauline stared at him, stunned, the anger draining from her like water from a sieve. He wanted her. Joy filled her. With supreme effort, she kept a tight rein on her feelings, terrified of how vulnerable he made her feel. "Why?"

"Because it makes sense." He rubbed at his scar. "You like India, don't you?"

"Yes."

"And you love me."

Swallowing hard, she admitted it to him for the first time. "Yes."

He sighed in satisfaction. "I know I'll never find another woman like you. It amazes me I found you at all. I figure we can marry straightaway, without any fuss, and take our honeymoon on our way back to India. We can even visit the Taj Mahal again, if you like, though I'd prefer it if you didn't make a scene this time." He gave her a teasing smile.

Much as she had dreamed of this day, she resisted the sweet seduction of the man before her. She couldn't imagine marrying him if he didn't love her in return. It would destroy her. She mouthed the word, but no sound came out, forcing her to try again. "No."

Her whispered word stunned him. He stared at her, his smile fading. "What?"

She cleared her throat and tried again. "No," she said more firmly. "I can't marry you, Nate. Not if . . ."

forcing herself to meet his gaze, she finished, "you don't love me."

"Are you blind as well as foolish? Bloody hell." He raked his hand through his hair. "I thought you could read the signs. You're a woman, after all. You ought to know when you've snagged your prey."

Was that his way of professing his love? For Pauline, it wasn't enough. She had given him her whole heart. She needed his in return. "So, I trapped you?"

"Well, yeah! Why do you think I traveled all the way here to claim you? If I wanted a mistress, I could have found one in India."

"I'm sure." That, she didn't doubt. Still, he hadn't said what she needed to hear.

His eyes widened. "You don't think I want your money . . ."

"What money?" she lied. "My parents have disowned me for consorting with a man like you."

His expression turned bleak, and for one awful moment, she thought he no longer wanted her, that his desire *had* been for her money, not herself. "I'm sorry to hear that. But I can take care of us both. You don't have to worry. I was left with a hefty bank account and land holdings, along with that blasted title."

"That's nice." Relieved her dowry wasn't the attraction, she gladly confessed. "I was lying, Nate. My parents haven't disowned me."

His eyes narrowed. "You were testing me."

She wrapped her arms around herself, still afraid to believe he returned her love. "I used to think my wealth was all a man would want of me."

"You thought wrong." His voice was thick with emotion. A glimmer of moisture shone in his eyes. "I haven't had a decent night's sleep since I left you. You're all I bloody think about. Dream about. Every day I was in London, you were with me. Then your sister showed me what you wrote, and if that was about me . . ."

She nodded. It felt good to share her feelings with the man she loved. "Every word."

He grinned, his warmth of expression rivaling India's summer sun. "Come here, love." Grasping her hand, he reeled her to him and locked her against him. He kissed her forehead, then her cheeks and nose. "Marry me, and make me the happiest fellow in the world."

Pulling back, she looked in his eyes, searching for that admission she longed to hear. "Tell me, Nate," she murmured, stroking the blond hair from his forehead. "Tell me. Why I should marry you?"

He eyes filled with yearning. "Because—" His voice broke. "Because, Pauline, I love you."

So much joy and passion filled her, she feared she would burst. She twined her arms around his neck and gave him a fierce kiss. "Yes, I will marry you, Nathaniel Savidge, or Lord Bathurst. Whoever you are. Wherever you live. Whatever you do. I love you, too."

Laughing joyfully, he lifted her into his arms and began striding toward the house.

"You're not going to carry me inside, are you?" she asked, thinking how her mother would panic to see her being manhandled by a giant like Nate.

"I'm not about to let you go again."

* * *

A short time later, Pauline's mother and sisters were seated in the parlor. Pauline and Nate stood before the fireplace, holding hands. Mrs. Olympia Carrington stared warily at the fellow being so possessive toward her daughter.

"Mother," Pauline said, "This is Nathanial Savidge, the Marquess of Bathurst."

"Marquess!" Her mother's expression turned from wary to awestruck.

"And I'm going to marry him," Pauline finished.

"With your permission," Nate added needlessly.

Meryl shrieked in glee. Clara hurried over to give Pauline an affectionate hug. And Mrs. Carrington promptly fainted.